CURSE OF BLACK HAWK'S TREASURE

MARVIN MASON

B. LOVE PUBLICATIONS

Copyright © 2020 by Marvin Mason

All rights reserved.

No part of this book may be reproduced in any form or by any electronic or mechanical means, including information storage and retrieval systems, without written permission from the author, except for the use of brief quotations in a book review.

As this is my first novel, I have to take a moment to thank all the incredible people who helped make this dream possible:
Megan Joseph, you are truly my horse whisperer. I will always follow your voice.
B. Love, thank you for taking a chance on a novice writer such as myself. I love your vision and am proud to be a part of the BLP family. To my BLP fam, thank you for being so inviting and willing to help mold me as a writer.
To The Family (Marquis, Barry, Chris, Clifton, Weimar, LeRoy, Johnny, Stephan, Marvin W., C. Nick), thank you for all the years of being my brothers and family.
To Bellwood School District 88, thank you for rocking with me no matter what classroom you place me in. Especially, to my running partners – Tanya, Sarah and Janeen.
To my brothers, Mark and Earl, I will always love you.
To my father, Marvin, Sr., you have always allowed me to pursue my dreams no matter how outrageous and stood there waiting to collect me no matter the outcome, you are my guiding light.
To my wife, Diane, who vigilantly stood by protecting me from all harm as I regained my footing to find my way to the release of this book, I love you dearly.
Most of all, to my mother who I know has been guiding me through this journey even after death. You will always be in my heart, mind,

and soul. I love you Gertrude Carroll Mason aka Gertrude Gaylord Carroll aka mom.

To all my readers: thank you for taking the time and energy to join in on this endeavor. I hope to take you on many rides.

You can follow me on Twitter at: SED5489; Facebook at: Marvin.Mason

BALTIMORE COUNTY PUBLIC LIBRARY

Reisterstown Branch
410-887-1165
www.bcpl.info

Customer ID: **********5246

Items that you checked out

Title: Curse of Black Hawk's treasure
ID: 31183200520028
Due: Thursday, February 15, 2024

Title: The awakening
ID: 31183201260830
Due: Thursday, February 15, 2024

Title: Willa of the wood
ID: 31183192236153
Due: Thursday, February 15, 2024

Total items: 3
Account balance: $0.00
Checked out: 3
Messages:
Patron status is ok.
1/25/2024 3:18 PM

Free to Be All In
Late fees no longer assessed for overdue items
Ask for details or visit bcpl.info

Shelf Help 410-494-9063
www.bcpl.info

ID: 31183200620024

ID: 31183207260830

PROLOGUE

MOLICA PHILLIPS She agreed to meet her grandfather at a grill along Clark Street less than a mile north of Wrigley.

Molica Phillips believed she would arrive early, but the blocks were filled with cars securing parking places for residents in the area.

It was an overcast day and she had not thought to bring an umbrella. It was too late to listen to the radio for a forecast. She was going to rue the day if she got soaked, having just spent a fortune getting her hair done. She just couldn't find good hair dressers to address the natural, curly hair in Phoenix.

Parking nearly five blocks away, she risked it after spending twenty-plus minutes trying to find an open spot, to park her rental car.

She walked briskly to the corner restaurant arriving five minutes late. He sat at a table next to a window waving at her as she approached.

He had the biggest smile as he rose to greet her. She stopped dead in her tracks as she spotted that stupid coin from a short distance.

As they sat down, he complimented her on how great she looked.

He also congratulated her on how well she was doing in school from the reports he had received from Veronica and her mother. He asked her what plans she'd made after she graduated.

She had been presented an opportunity to attend Arizona State on a partial scholarship. She jumped at the chance even though it meant leaving Veronica in the old man's clutches. She prayed Chad Beecher would step up and be the father that Molica herself had never had the possibility to encounter.

She wound up spending summers working in the office at the resort that had been gained off her back, *so to speak,* and whatever else Mr. Holland had accomplished with her in the wee hours almost six years ago.

She set her sights on Business Management as a degree, having successfully reached the dean's list, she tendered the scholarship resources that made finishing school less of a hurdle.

She had every intention of not coming back that summer to work at all. She had been offered an opportunity to spend the few months interning at an up and coming brokerage house in the area.

She even decided for Veronica, or Roni as she used to call her younger sister, to spend the summer with her.

Then she received the call to meet with the old man.

Knowing that her plans had changed, a phone call was placed by her mother to come visit for the week she decided to take off before starting the internship.

A plane ticket was en route; first class.

"Round trip?" she recalled asking.

She acquiesced but decided to stay at lodging in Rosemont just in case she decided to return to the campus. Traffic was brutal around the airport as President Carter was in town attending the 1978 Cook County Democratic Dinner on May 25th.

She was most anxious to see Roni but elected to let this presage out of the way loathsome of a family reunion.

The doctor had a practice in a suite of offices near the Andersonville Historic area.

He appeared bloated and somewhat anxious as he fumbled with that foolish old coin.

"Hey, Pumpkin, how's school?" he nervously asked.

Her patience was thin. She needed to get this over with.

"What can I do for you?" she asked cutting to the chase.

He sputtered a small laugh.

"Business as usual," he perceived.

"Absolutely," she said coldly. "Time is money."

"I think I have found the location," he said smiling a toothy grin.

She nearly fell out of her chair. His pursuit of some bogus legend of a treasure had made him a wealthy landowner, but somehow, he was still incomplete.

"It's our legacy," he said. "But I need your help."

She could only imagine.

More important, she could envision what he would have planned for Roni. Even if he looked at her as trade bait because of her mixed heritage, his quest for these phantom riches could impair anything he may have felt for his "pure" granddaughter.

She listened as he laid out how she would merely have to stifle the son of the treasurer to a group of potential buyers of his next target.

The club's portfolio was large enough to counter the offer he had made for the land, but he saw an opportunity - Danny Alexander.

The actual task didn't sound that complicated. However, the target was closer in age to Roni. There could be statutory ramifications if she went too far. She could easily manage his request and keep her sister from harm's way.

He gave her a time and day to arrive at Dodgers Lake Resort. She would only need a weekend, thus not interfering with her internship. Provided she receive another first-class round-trip ticket.

The old man gasped, choking on a chardonnay, but he agreed.

Done.

HURT

~~~~

The Catalina edged close to the curb as it slowed to a crawl before finally stopping. Danny knew the area well even though he had never been to this exact location on Vincennes and 75th Street. He stared forward, looking out the passenger's side as his father shifted into park. The car idled briefly before cutting off.

For an early Sunday evening, the street appeared quiet. With his father's deference to the air conditioning unit's use even at Chicago's hottest Summer temperatures, the windows were rolled down allowing Danny to take in the late summer smells from the neighborhood barbeque joint one block down. His father pulled the keys out of the ignition and lightly placed his hand on Danny's thigh.

"I'll be right back," he said to his boy softly. "You all right?"

Danny nervously nodded without ever glancing at him.

The car door closed harshly, startling Danny for a moment, but he kept his eyes forward as his father slowly walked toward the silver Mercedes parked in front of them.

Uncle Mac, a tall, gaunt man emerged from the driver's side and leaned on the door as he offered his hand to Danny's father. They shook briefly as Uncle Lou, a smaller, stout man with a silver natural hairstyle greeted the two somberly. All three men turned towards Danny with solemn looks in their eyes. Uncle Mac moved away from the car door as Uncle Lou closed it from the side.

Danny's father walked to the passenger's door and opened it as the other two men advanced toward the brick ranch house to Danny's immediate right.

"C'mon, son," he said. "Let's get this over with."

Danny unfastened his seatbelt, letting it fly as he crawled out the door. His short pants hugged his thick legs that were made even tighter by the Ace bandage wrapped around his right thigh.

The tall man stopped and reached out for Danny, grabbing him by the back of the head. His long fingers gingerly gripped Danny's skull.

"How's the leg?" he asked.

"The hospital ran some tests," Danny winced as he said hoarsely. "I have to go back for x-rays later."

All four of them approached the concrete steps slowly. Uncle Lou grabbed the iron rail and pulled himself up the five steps. Uncle Mac aided Danny to the porch as Danny's father took two at a time to hit the landing.

The wooden door was wide open, only the screen door kept them out. Danny's father hesitated before placing one of his grossly large fingers on the doorbell.

The chime was loud. Danny was sure the entire neighborhood could hear it. He glanced around quickly, but no one jumped out of the bushes.

Danny tempted to suggest they leave became heart broken when voice faintly reached the door.

"Coming," it said an old, female voice morosely.

All four men lowered their heads.

A small gray-haired woman with luminous caramel skin appeared at the door. She wore a black cotton dress with white rose prints scattered all over it that draped to her knees.

"Hello," she said as she quickly glanced over all four men.

Danny's father walked toward the door.

"I'm Dan Alexander," he said. "I'm here to see Bonnie, um, Mrs. Hamilton about her son."

"Oh," she said cocking her head in an owl-like fashion as she unlatched the screen door and pushed it open for the men to enter.

"I'm Bonnie's cousin, Cynthia Hightower," she said. "Is she expecting you?"

Mr. Alexander puffed his face. "I'm afraid so," he said as he turned to catch the door.

"These men are family friends, Mr. Lou Thomas and Mr. Mac Watley." Respectively, the short man nodded followed by the taller one. He reached for Danny and pulled him inside. "This is my son, Danny. He was friends with Lamont."

Her eyes widened as she took in Danny's presence. She frowned but stretched out her arms to embrace him. She wrapped her arms around him and squeezed him tightly, as the men entered the house.

She finally released him, then scrambled ahead.

"Bonnie," she said, "Mr. Alexander is here to see you."

The living room was filled with a variety of potted flowers and a sea of cards scattered upright on a cocktail table.

Walking around in black open-toed house shoes and shear stockings, the heavyset woman lithely turned toward the men.

"Can I get any of you something to drink?"

Mr. Watley stood in front of one of two matching upholstered aqua-blue dining chairs opposite Mr. Thomas.

"What do you have?" Watley politely asked.

"Iced tea, lemonade, or beer," she said.

As he took a seat in one of the chairs, Watley said, "I've got a long ride back. I better have iced tea, please."

Thomas took the chair on the other side of a small lamp table.

"Same here, if you don't mind," Thomas blurted out.

"Not at all," the woman said. She turned to the elder Alexander, who shook his head.

"Nothing for me," he said softly.

Mrs. Hightower faced Danny like a hostess. "How about you? Iced tea or lemonade? You don't seem old enough for a beer. How old are you?"

Sheepishly, Danny's stared at her feet.

"Seventeen," he said. "No ma'am. I don't want to trouble you."

"No trouble at all. Would you like some tea? I just made it an hour ago."

Awkwardly, Danny said, "That would be nice, ma'am."

She smiled at him. Lowering her head to get his eyes trained on her.

"Have a seat, please," she said, pleading with the boy.

A white couch wrapped in plastic was set against a wall adjacent to a piano. Framed pictures of Lamont surrounded the top of the instrument.

Danny was transfixed on the photos as he plopped down. The cushion enveloped his legs. He grimaced and grabbed his right thigh above the bandage.

Mr. Alexander lowered himself next to his son. His golf shirt rode his body snuggly, as an anchor tattoo peeked from the right sleeve as it rode his right bicep.

All four men took the room in quietly when Mrs. Hightower left. The living room was almost a shrine to the young Lamont Rhimes. Graduation photos, science fair pictures, math board work collages. All the accomplishments of the young man adorned the room. His own personal mausoleum.

In a sprightly fashion, Mrs. Hightower carried a tray with large glasses spilling frothy beverages onto it.

She pushed some of the sympathy cards out of the way to make room for the metal carrier. She quickly served each man a glass. With one lemonade left untouched, she nodded to the elder Alexander, "Just in case you change your mind."

Mr. Alexander smiled and graciously thanked her. Uncle Lou and Uncle Mac nearly downed their beverages before she could exit the room, not allowing their perspiring goblets onto the table top.

"How silly of me," the woman said. She quickly retrieved place holders for the glasses which the men promptly utilized. She looked to Uncle Mac and Uncle Lou. "Looks like you two could use a refill." They both shook their heads refusing another helping and thanked her.

She turned to Danny who held his glass. Ice chunks floated atop the beverage, but it was otherwise untouched.

"Would you care for something else?" she asked.

"No, ma'am," he said. He immediately took a sip that became one long gulp until half the glass was empty.

She stood satisfied.

From the shotgun hallway, Mrs. Hamilton slowly emerged. All four men rose from their seats to pay respects.

Mr. Alexander promptly rushed toward the demure woman. He offered his hand that became an awkward embrace.

With her head buried in his chest, came a small sob.

Watley turned away with embarrassment as Thomas moved forward to lend assistance.

Danny froze in his place. The glass nearly slipped through his fingers as condensation dripped from the ice.

"Mrs. Hamilton," Thomas said, "please sit down."

Helping the fragile woman to the couch next to Danny, the two men leaned on bended knees to console her. Watley waddled to their aid, as the trio offered comfort.

"Please, Mrs. Hamilton," said Thomas. "We just want you to know if there is anything—"

"Anything," Watley said, echoing him.

"That you need, please don't hesitate to ask," Thomas said.

Mr. Alexander took the lead, holding her hand solemnly.

"These are my associates," he said. "We are here to let you know we are going to take care of all the financial arrangements for the services."

"We are having the body brought back immediately after an autopsy has been conducted," Thomas said.

"You can have all the information forwarded to us and our organization will be more than hap-," Thomas said, then paused noticing tears streaked down the woman's cheek as she looked up at the men.

"What happened to my baby?" Mrs. Hamilton asked as tears streaked down her bony cheeks as she glanced at the men. "That's all I want to know. What happened to my boy?"

Blank stares shot back at her. Slowly, she turned to Danny. His hand trembling as the ice rattled, clunking from side to side.

"Were you with him when it happened?" she asked.

Danny's eyes shot straight to his father's begging for direction.

"Go on, son, you can tell her," he said.

Danny's eyes welled up by the betrayal. He should not have come. He should not have taken this ride. He didn't falsely promise Lamont's safety; he merely cosigned the value of the opportunity to break free from his mother's apron strings and enjoy himself.

A wave of guilt and remorse washed over him, and he was trapped as all eyes were on him.

"Tell her, son," his father repeated.

Danny cleared his throat. He placed the glass on a coaster on the table. Looking at her reflection on the cylindrical holder as beads of sweat dripped from it, he said, "I wasn't with him when it happened. I got there when they pulled him from the pool. There was a man trying to pump water from him, but..."

He turned to her. She was studying him intently, hanging onto every word about the last moments of her only son's life.

"It was too late," he said.

Danny felt a wetness under his arms and his back, as perspiration began to flow.

"Why was he in the pool?" she asked pressing for details Danny didn't want to offer.

"I taught him...I was teaching him to swim during the trip," Danny said.

Now he couldn't turn it off.

"He wanted to impress this girl, so he asked me to teach him."

"What girl?" she asked.

Mr. Alexander couldn't shut Danny down, but he knew as did his friends, Danny gave too much information.

"She was a girl he met earlier at the lodge," Danny said straining with his recall.

"Where was she?"

"They went swimming together that night. She was with him," he betrayed Lamont out of fear as he looked at the carpeted floor never once allowing himself to address Mrs. Hamilton eye to eye.

"So, she let him drown?" her voice curdled as she shrieked out the words.

Watley took her hands and clasped them together.

"That's not what the boy is saying," he said.

A new stream of tears rolled down her cheeks. She nodded. She understood. She gave a weak smile, closed her eyes, and rocked herself for a moment.

Danny noticed Mrs. Hightower standing by the kitchen entrance. Her eyes were glued on him. He reached for the glass but stopped as his hands trembled profusely.

Mrs. Hamilton reversed the grasp and now held Watley's long fingered hands, then released him. She turned back toward Danny, briefly wiping away her tears.

"Go on," she said.

Danny hesitated; overwhelmed.

"Go ahead," his father said.

"Anyway," he said. "When I got to the pool, they were trying to resuscitate him."

"Where were you at the time?" she asked.

Danny gingerly patted his knee as he said, "I was at the inside pool. It has a jacuzzi. I injured my leg earlier teaching Lamont to swim."

"Danny's a very good swimmer," Mr. Alexander boasted. "He taught himself years ago."

Another flood of tears filled with gratitude flowed from her.

"So, you were teaching him to swim?" Mrs. Hamilton asked.

Danny nodded, "Yes, ma'am."

"I'm sure he appreciated that."

Her hand grazed Danny's cheek. Danny didn't move as she softly stroked it.

"He looked up to you, you know," she said.

Her hand fell on his cheek with a thud. Then again. It jolted him, as it landed harder.

"Where were you?" she asked. "You promised to not leave him alone. Where were you?"

The strokes became strikes. She was pulled off Danny by the three men who dove in on her as she began to swing wildly at him.

"Where were you?" she screamed as the men dragged her back.

RANDALL RHIMES

The casket slowly lowered into the ground on the overcast day.

It was early afternoon by the time the church service ended. A small procession of cars followed the black hearse to Longfellow Cemetery.

Lamont nor his mother belonged to a church nor had a denomination. A family member asked her church to handle the services and since that party sat on the church board, the pastor was more than happy to comply, especially after the generous donation that Dan Alexander's golf club made to the church.

As Mrs. Hamilton watched the casket descend to the earth surrounded by her sister and two distant cousins, along with Mrs. Hightower all attired in long black dresses.

The First Tee Golf Club members and their wives made up the bulk of the constituency in attendance.

Also standing on the opposite side of the casket was Randall Rhimes, and two other offspring of Luther Rhimes, her deceased ex-husband, who were seventeen total years older than Lamont. She dropped his name after she remarried, taking on the name Hamilton from her late husband, Gerald.

Danny stood next to his father in a sport coat and slacks his mother had him purchase at Wieboldts just days earlier.

Swallowed by the grief of cajoling Lamont's mother into relinquishing her only son, her beautiful gift, Mrs. Alexander was noticeably missing. Unable to bring herself to attend the funeral, she regretted taking away the only thing worthwhile that Luther Rhimes had given to Bonnie Hamilton in the two and a half years that she put up with that philandering fool.

Mrs. Alexander was not able to forgive herself for trekking to Mrs. Hamilton's home after three years and pitching the tremendous time her pride and joy was going to have that week hanging out with his new found cousin. Promising her it would be the best week of his life and guaranteeing "no harm will come to him." Those were the most salacious six words she had ever spoken. How unprophetic those words were. Not that she ever would take them back, but how on earth could that have been so off the mark?

She believed she could handle it better if Lamont had broken his leg while with them at the resort, or if Danny had perished, than the misery she carried in her heart taking this woman's only love, her son; snatching it from her.

No, she told her husband, she couldn't face this woman just yet. So, she sat in her house, alone with a vodka martini to settle her guilt. More like three or four of them, as her two men bravely consoled each other and Lamont's mother.

Mr. Alexander made sure that he was as close to Lamont's mother as possible but was grateful that she had a group to insulate her. He kept an arm around his son's shoulder, thankful that no harm had come to him. Many details of that night alluded him, but he and his family were still standing. They would heal together.

His buddies had also made the journey to the burial even though many were unaware that Lamont had even been at the lodge during their annual golf tournament event.

While nine couples in all were in attendance, many were there to make sure the funds were properly allocated for the burial. Members made sure the resources weren't absconded for some nefarious event as the former treasurer had done when the group attempted to purchase their very own resort.

Professional men representing the medical field, the hotbed of Chicago politics, even a Captain on Chicago's police force was present. Most important were Dan Alexander's best friends; Lou Thomas and Mac Watley. It was the two of them that not only recommended that the expenses be paid for by the organization, they coerced the votes that secured the eight thousand dollars which brought Lamont's body back to Chicago from Wisconsin and the church donation as well as the burial services in the private lot. It was money that may have served the group better, but they were able to tithe this offering to account for a mishap they could never have foreseen in the eleven years they had attended the resort.

As one of the members' wives sat on the Board of Education for Chicago Public Schools, the two men also offered an endowment to Lamont's tear-streaked mother on behalf of the group. There was also the promise of a scholarship fund to Lamont's school on behalf of the family for years to come.

As patrons made their way to senior and junior Alexander, Randall began to trek over toward them as well.

His gait was lumbering as he walked on two prosthetic legs without the use of a cane, crutches, or walker. The knoll was a hearth of grass that was day's off from trimming which made it tough for Randall to navigate as his stumps pushed his metal heels into the ground even deeper because of the muddiness of the dirt beneath him.

Mac Watley shook hands with Randall and offered condolence, "Your brother, Lamont was a tremendous young man."

Having barely had a real relationship with his baby brother, Randall still took the compliment in stride as if he did have a hand in raising him.

"We're heading out," Lou Thomas informed the senior Alexander. He, too, shook hands with Randall, firmly, then saluted him saying, "Stay strong, soldier."

"Let us know if you need anything," Mac Watley said. He gave the younger Alexander a hug, then walked off with his compadre. They reached their wives and headed to their cars.

Many of the golf members moved on after paying respects to the family they didn't know, then drove off.

Mrs. Hightower wrapped her grieving cousin in her arms and with assistance began to move the mourning mother to the hearse.

But Bonnie Hamilton seemed to have something else on her mind as she moved toward the Alexander men.

Mr. Alexander immediately took her hands into his and pulled her into him for a final embrace.

"I'm so sorry for your loss," he said. "If there is anything I can do, please don't hesitate to ask." It ate him up to have to offer those very words, but he struggled whenever he imagined that anyone could possibly have been saying that to him instead.

The mother, bereft of any energy, lifted her head. "Thank you," she said. She rested her weary eyes on Danny and shifted her weight, leaning on his father. Randall stood by as if he were a hand-picked bodyguard. There was no real love lost between the two.

She held her arms out to Danny. Befuddled, his eyes wandered to his father who nodded assuredly. He moved into her fold as her heaving bosom consumed him. She held him momentarily as if he were her own.

Her hands pressed against his cheeks and another torrent of tears slid down her cheeks. This time she meant no harm and had no questions to ask.

"He loved you like you were his big brother," said Mrs. Hamilton as she sniffled. "He so looked up to you. He thought the world of you."

She held his cheeks so lightly. He wanted to look away as his eyes watered, consumed by shame.

She brought his head down and kissed his forehead. "Thank you for all you did."

They both cried as Danny wrapped his arms around her. He still felt trepidation of what she might be capable of doing to him, but he wanted this pain to end and surrendered himself to her.

Mrs. Hightower embraced her cousin and separated the two. She cradled the woman as Randall looked on.

Mr. Alexander reached out once more and briefly clasped her hands.

"Goodbye," she said softly with finality.

The three men watched her disappear into the long black car, then walked to their cars on the side of the road of the cemetery – the Catalina for the Alexanders, a metallic-gray '77 Corvette for Randall Rhimes.

Once again, Randall placed his arm over Danny's shoulder and began to swing him toward the drop top.

"Do you mind if I talk to him for a minute, Uncle Dan?" he asked the elder Alexander.

Mr. Alexander glanced at his son. He shook his head and became Catalina-bound. As he entered the driver's side, Randall guided Danny to the passenger's side of his car.

"What happened to the Spyder?" Danny nervously asked.

Randall smiled.

"I traded that bitch in two years ago along with my second wife," he cackled. "They didn't move with me in the way they should." He winked at Danny.

Danny nodded with nary a clue to what he was talking about.

"Climb in," he said.

Danny opened the door and immediately fell into the leather bucket seat. While there was a seat behind him, the car was a two-seater for all he cared.

There was a teeter-tatter cadence to Randall's walk as he went to the driver's side of the car.

He slammed the door shut, then turned to Danny. "What do ya think?"

"About what?" Danny asked.

Randall frowned, barely recognizing this older Danny. This Danny had become more closed off than the younger, toothy-smiling kid he remembered. This version of Danny seemed far too defensive.

"The car, what do you think about the car?"

Danny stared at the panel, the dashboard, then the stick. He noticed there was a clutch pedal as well as a brake and accelerator.

"I thought you controlled everything in the steering wheel," Danny pondered.

"Hell no, I can't stand the feel of those things," Randall said. "I've got to be able to feel all the movement."

Randall grabbed the steering wheel, stroking it. He leaned to Danny.

"Plus, those things are for cripples," he laughed heartily with a cackle. "Ain't no cripples here, right?"

Danny smiled as he glanced at his kin's prosthetic legs, then stared him in the eyes.

"Look," Randall said, "I haven't had a chance to talk to you, but I need you to tell me what happened that night."

Danny closed his eyes, "Aw, man!"

He reached for the door handle, but Randall grabbed him by the arm. His grip vise-like.

"No, no, I know it wasn't your fault, little man. I just need you to give me a little detail about this electric shock shit that happened in the pool."

Danny was jolted.

"How'd you hear about that?" Danny asked.

"Was he shocked in the water?" Randall softly interrogated.

Danny shook his head. "No, Daphne, the girl Lamont was with said that's why she couldn't save him. Some force wouldn't let her into the pool."

"So, how'd he get out?"

Danny looked far off before answering.

"Some older guy dove in and pulled him out. When he got there, he was trying to resuscitate him." Danny fell quiet before continuing by saying, "That's when I got there. But it was too late. He was dead."

Randall reached for a pair of sunglasses from his ashtray. He flicked them open and placed them on his head.

"I've got one more question, then you need to go."

Danny turned and cautiously looked Randall in his eyes. He didn't see pain, hurt, nor loss. He saw rage.

CARROLL ALEXANDER

The drive home was long, but quiet as neither Alexander had much to say to one another.

The weight they both carried, while different, still burrowed through them.

For the senior, he not only had to deal with ways to generate funds to replenish what the golf club paid in Lamont's expenses, but now he faced insurmountable scrutiny in the responsibility of losing someone's child on his watch.

As a man who had served in two wars, he had lost many friends in battle, but this tragedy hit closest to his time in Germany. The time when his buddies on a weekend furlough were slaughtered in a German whorehouse while he served kitchen patrol duty because he talked back to the Captain.

Never sure how he would have made out if he had attended, it was his connection that took his fellow soldiers to the pub with the backrooms set up for visiting "allies." His best friend, Al Thompson, had his throat slashed from ear to ear. Someone held him from behind breaking his ribs while holding him in place and letting a razor do the work.

He always regretted even mentioning the place, never dreaming Al, Jojo, Harris, and Bunk would go without him. They were dead now but lived on in his memory. Haunting him for what seemed an eternity.

For the junior, this event had torn him apart. Not only did he lose his best friend and cousin, but he shouldered the burden of not watching over him. Letting a female or the lure of that companionship take him away from his duties.

How confident was he really before he had his hands on that girl to not let Lamont cock block him? While his closest friend was a bundle of nerves, Danny's confidence drove him to coerce his cousin into a plan. Danny talked him into splitting up their prospective conquests with Lamont going poolside under the watchful eyes of the girls' family barbeque. Danny would whisk the other sister away to the inside pool where he could access the Jacuzzi for his stupid leg injury.

Lamont knew he was the wingman and was more than willing to comply. Danny was more a brother to him, than his own three had ever been. Whenever they socialized, they treated him like an outcast, like he was different. They never understood him and labeled him a "mama's boy." Danny wasn't that much different from him only he navigated his sensibilities and allowed himself the opportunity to be an egghead when it benefitted him, but he took his street knowledge and applied it when necessary.

Danny thought it was time to apply some Chicago loving to this girl with the promise to make it up to Lamont if he would just block as he made his escape from her family's gathering with this girl. Lamont was on his team.

This is what being on his team got Lamont. Drowned. He had only a few lessons, but for some reason he tried to impress this girl, who exclaimed earlier in the day what an excellent swimmer she was. So how did she let Lamont drown?

He should have just kept Lamont with him or maybe they could have snuck away with both girls for some other activity. Whatever he should have done, he didn't do it.

Lamont now lay buried because of him.

DANNY USED his key to open the back door of the brick house as he waited for his father to lock the door to the detached garage.

Danny took the five steps that led to the kitchen and dining room area which his father had recently opened to make open concept. His bedroom was directly off the kitchen. He tossed his sport coat onto his bed then trailed behind his father into the living room.

Carroll Alexander sat in a love seat staring out the giant window pane. Holding a martini in one hand and the sheer tan curtain in the other, she appeared fixated on activity taking place on the playground across the street.

"Hey, mom," Danny said.

A twenty-four-inch RCA color television screen emitted a Cubs baseball game nearing the seventh inning stretch.

Danny's mother was no sports fan, especially the Cubs. If anything, she supported the White Sox since she was born and raised on the South Side.

She also wasn't a drinker, not to Danny's knowledge. She sat in her seat with her glass raised in her hand. A lipstick smudge at the base getting smeared as she glanced at her son while she took another sip.

"How long have you been back?" she asked innocently.

"We just walked in," Danny said.

"Oh." She glanced at her only son and took another sip.

The senior Alexander's footsteps echoed through the hallway as he made his way into the living room.

"You been sitting there all day?" the older man asked.

"I got up," she said as she turned her back toward the window.

"What's to eat?" Dan asked.

"There's lunch meat in the 'frigerator," she said matter-of-factly.

"Shit," was his final remark as he walked out of the room as quickly as he came in.

Danny stood, flummoxed. *What's happening to mom and dad?*

Danny jumped as the refrigerator door slamming cracked into the living room. His mother was undeterred.

For the first time, that youthful look she always carried was gone. Carroll Alexander had aged significantly in the last seven days as wrinkle lines permanently appeared on her forehead.

Her shiny black hair was half gray and there were worry lines on her once smooth-as-a- baby's-bottom forehead she had never had before.

Not one to talk, Danny himself had acquired a gray patch in the middle of his scalp, but Aunt Marian told him it was hereditary. Even though it came in the last week as well.

The kitchen phone rang as the elder Dan rummaged through the refrigerator once again cursing lightly to himself. How long was this bullshit going to go on? Everyone needed to move on with their lives, just like he had when news hit the barracks about Al.

He slammed the door shut with a pack of bologna in his hand. He laid it on the counter and picked up the receiver, ringing on the wall unit.

"Hello," he answered gruffly.

Danny softly walked toward his mother. He glanced out the window over her shoulder and saw the usual crowd playing basketball in the park.

"Game any good?" he joked.

She didn't respond. She just held the curtain open, then turned to take a sip of her martini.

His father walked into the living room's entrance and called out, "What did Randee talk to you about in the car?"

Startled, Danny whirled around in his father's direction.

He shrugged his shoulders and said, "Nothing much. He asked me about the accident. That's all."

"What did you tell him?" his father interrogated.

"Just what I saw. I told him I didn't see what happened to Lamont. He was dead when I got to the pool."

"What's wrong?" Mrs. Alexander asked.

"My sister called," he said. "Martha says Randee drove off after the funeral heading to the resort."

"Maybe he should let it go," Mrs. Alexander spewed out as if she read her husband's mind.

Dan held his tongue before replying, "He took his armory bag with him."

Danny's jaw dropped. Randee came back from Vietnam with a bag of firearms he'd "acquired" overseas.

He called it his "shopping bag." The last time he used his shopping bag was to shoot up a local pool room he claimed ripped him out of five hundred dollars.

Randee was going shopping.

BOOK 1 — LAMONICA HAYNES

That summer of 1978, the embers of love were growing inside Danny as they would with any teenage male experiencing the throes of young lust.

Knowing he had less than thirteen hours to address the ache he was feeling for LaMonica Haynes, he quickly made his way toward the outer pool.

She held his hand as her feet flapped in the rubber soled shoes, trying to match his steps even as he hobbled on his right leg.

As they passed the picnic grounds, a small group gathered around the open pit. A large carcass of pig twirled on the spit. Danny recognized the cook who almost immediately made his way toward him once his eyes found Danny.

LaMonica's stepfather, Mr. Beecher, pulled off the chef apron he wore over his golf shirt and khakis.

Danny smiled as LaMonica gripped his hand tightly. Maybe in an act of defiance against this white man her mother had married to create a blended family.

Briefly, Danny's eyes averted to a crowd of people on the other side of the picnic grounds. A chain link fence divided the property from the swimming pool.

"Danny," Beecher called out.

"Uh-oh," LaMonica sighed softly.

"What?" Danny asked as his attention reverted to the lanky gaunt man of 6'2".

"Don't tell him where we were, okay?" she asked.

"Danny, you need to hurry," Beecher said as he finally approached the couple. "It's not good, son."

"*Son?*" Danny scoffed as he wondered what the hell the man was talking about. *Gee, pops, your 'son' is about to bust a nut inside your stepdaughter. How 'bout dat?*

Danny gripped LaMonica's hand and pulled her toward him. He tensed up as Beecher stood before him.

"You need to find your parents, son," Beecher pleaded. "It doesn't look too good."

"What doesn't look good, sir?" Danny stood firm as his fingers interlocked with LaMonica's.

"Good?" the word came at Danny like a Bullet Train. Just the sentence. What the hell? How racist could he be? Plus, his step daughter was black. The thought just screamed at him. *What don't look good?*

From a distance he heard, "Oh my God, Mo!" and his head whipped back to the crowd gathered at the swimming pool.

A rottweiler chained to a post by the grill looked up and growled. As Daphne made her way toward the couple, the dog also tried to circumvent the grounds to find its way to LaMonica. Before the dog could leap to aid her, the collar snapped it back. In recoil, the dog growled as it choked on its chain.

Beecher turned to the pooch, "Stay down, Ace, it's okay."

Emerging from a crouched pack, came Daphne, LaMonica's half-sister, and Beecher's daughter, running around the fence at breakneck speed in her two-piece polka-dotted bikini.

LaMonica released her grip on Danny's hand and began to sprint toward her sister. Confused, as her sibling wrapped her arms around her and began to sob uncontrollably.

Danny could hear her yelling, "What's wrong? What's wrong?"

Suddenly, an internal shot rang out in Danny's senses. His eyes darted to the swimming pool, then to the two girls embracing. Mr. Beecher's mouth moved, but Danny couldn't fathom the words. He turned his attention back to LaMonica who turned her head toward Danny and said, "Oh no, Danny."

LaMonica held Daphne as she twisted to break free.

Danny's view of the party on the pool side of the chain link fence glimpsed a balding pate giving CPR. Danny could see the first responder's arms pump up then down.

Danny approached the fence as he tried to spot Lamont.

Where the hell was Lamont?

If Daphne was all frantic and that connected to what was now happening with LaMonica, it must have been family related.

Still about fifty yards out, Danny got a better glance at the man performing some type of rescue. There were roughly ten people surrounding him as he pumped, then pinched, and dropped his head for mouth to mouth.

Once again, Danny turned his head trying to find Lamont. Was he in the crowd of ten or so? Had he run off to find more competent help?

LaMonica reached out for his hand, lightly grazing it as Danny breezed past her.

An EMT unit came running from the opposite side of the fence. Danny's eyes bucked at the urgency that they pushed forth as the chain link gate opened for them.

The pain in Danny's leg persisted as it slowed him down when he approached the picnic area. He could hear the sizzle of the spit as it charred the pig on the rotisserie. The man who had taken over the cooking duty from Beecher, kept rotating the pig. He lifted his head in Danny's direction and released the crank. Heading in Danny's direction, he stopped just before making impact as Beecher waved him off.

The man performing CPR rose off his knees, save for a pair of shorts, he was shirtless and shoeless. A rotund, portly man with a crown of grayish-red hair surrounding his dome, turned to one of the medical technicians and gave credentials Danny could faintly hear.

"I'm a doctor," the man told one of the first responders. "I have tried compressions, but to no avail."

Danny made it to the fence. Beecher's voice rang passed him as the balding man looked up. Gloom in his eyes, he moved away from the first responder and dropped to his knees to apply pressure to the still body lying on the concrete slab.

The doctor walked slowly to Danny as the crowd turned in his direction. It was Danny's first opportunity to gander at the person in need of care with his short and curly afro.

Another shock hit Danny, as the beefy man approached him guiding him to the other gate in the fence.

"What's your name, son?" the husky man asked Danny almost in a neighborly way.

"Danny," fell from his lips as he felt an explosion in his head as he tried to answer, "Danny Alexander. What's wrong? Why is my cousin on the ground?"

"Your cousin has had an accident," he calmly informed Danny.

It was nearly impossible for the man to exert any pliable pressure to Danny to hold him back. Accepting this fact, he allowed Danny to wrestle himself loose from his grip and rush to the limp body of Lamont.

The EMT team was still applying service on Lamont's pale frame. Danny showed respectful restraint in hopes that like a miracle of all miracles, Lamont would rise like Lazarus and be born anew.

"Call it," a muscled responder called out to one of his cohorts.

Danny stood frozen in his space not willing to believe what he had heard.

"Time of death, 21:02," replied the other responder.

Danny wailed, falling to his knees. He reached out for Lamont but felt the hands of many pull him back.

"God, no!" he screamed. "No, please God, no!"

LaMonica drew Danny near her to shield him as he lay his head on the concrete. He sobbed as Daphne wrapped him and LaMonica, contributing to the caterwaul.

"Hey, Danny," a voice called out.

Danny shook free and sprang upward to find the voice. He wasn't sure if he wanted to run toward the voice or away from it.

It was hard to miss the bow-legged gait of Uncle Lou Thomas. The stride of his steps almost appeared as if he were climbing down a flight of stairs.

"Danny," came again, this time from Uncle Mac Watley, a tall, gangly man who as he approached his fifties was acknowledged by the pot belly that proceeded the former semi-pro tennis champ.

Danny lifted himself up waiting for the two men to approach as they picked up their pace toward him.

"Are you all right?" Mac Watley asked before the two men froze.

Their eyes fell to the concrete floor as the EMTs placed Lamont on the mobile transport stretcher and hoisted on the adjustable frame. The pediatric trolley buckled under Lamont's weight, then steadied itself.

Lou Thomas suddenly turned away in horror at the realization as Mac Watley continued toward the EMT staff.

"I'm a medical doctor," Mac said. "Can you tell me what's going on? I'm with the family."

An older white male in his late thirties, shook Mac's hand and gave a brief assessment, "It appears the young man's lungs took in an excessive amount of water. He drowned from an accidental submersion in the pool there."

The first responder pointed toward the portly bare-chested man who gave CPR and said, "I'm sure that gentleman can provide you with more information."

"Really?" was Mac's response.

"Yes, sir," the EMT leader said. "He actually is a doctor himself. He tried to provide resuscitation after pulling the young man from the pool."

Danny stood in shock as the trolley was rolled out. He watched as Lamont's body, now strapped in with a white sheet covering it, bounced around over the cracks in the pavement.

Mac Watley walked over to an open-mouthed Danny. He embraced him and held him from the pool grounds.

Lou Thomas followed when Mac turned toward him with Danny flush against him.

"See if you can find Dan real quick," he directed his friend. "We'll be in my suite."

Lou Thomas gathered himself and moved towards the lodge building.

"Lou," Mac called out. The shorter man turned around while still in motion.

"Yeah?" he said.

"Just Dan. No one else."

Lou nodded then continued to walk in one direction as the other two departed for the other entrance to the building.

Stretching himself into a t-shirt, Lamont's rescuer stepped in front of Danny and offered a warm gesture with his outstretched hand.

"Danny, that's your name, son?" the old man asked.

Mac halted along with Danny and took the man's hand in his offering. "I'm his uncle. Mac Watley."

The man retrieved a pair of wire framed glasses from his back pocket.

"My name is Gil Gillette," he said. "I tried to rescue the boy. He was swimming with my granddaughter when the accident occurred."

Mac glanced through the crowd and saw the faces of the young ladies.

"Which one is your granddaughter?" Mac asked.

Awkwardly, the man pointed at Daphne.

"I'm a retired doctor. I tried to administer CPR," he said, "but it was too late."

He bowed his head solemnly as he said softly, "He was already gone by the time I pulled him out the water."

Mac narrowed the man, gazing at him up and down. "You say that's your granddaughter?"

Mac released Danny and walked toward Daphne. Gillette followed behind trying to explain the complications that ensued in the rescue attempt.

Mac turned and shook the man's hand again, then said, "I appreciate all you've done." He turned directly to Daphne whose face was flush, redder than a strawberry.

"Can you tell me what happened, young lady?" Mac asked aware of the sensitive matter at hand.

LaMonica held onto her sister as both had heaving shoulders trying to calm the other.

Gillette nodded for the girl to proceed when Beecher interrupted, "I'm sorry," he blurted, "now who are you?"

Mac stretched his hand out to Beecher.

"I'm the boy's uncle," he addressed to the younger man. "I'm a doctor as well. I just want a word with the young lady as to the events that took place."

Gillette, once again, nodded approval toward Beecher.

In a whisper-like voice, Daphne said, "We were swimming in the deep end, when Lamont dove deep down."

Her eyes floated from Gillette's to Mac Watley's. Danny still off in the distance, began to approach.

"He was swimming in the deep end?" he asked. "Why for God's sake? He could barely swim. Why would he swim in the deep end?"

Daphne moved back to the safety of LaMonica's arms as Mac grabbed Danny's forearm and pulled him close.

"Now, let the young lady continue," he begged hoping to peel this very mystery apart.

"I tried to help him, honest," Daphne shot back, "but an electric-like current stopped me from getting back in the water."

"What?" Mac asked, snapping unintentionally.

"It was like the devil was holding me back," she said softly. As she whimpered, her body convulsed impulsively again as her half-sister pulled her away.

Gillette turned toward Mac and said, "We will do everything we can to get you answers on this tragedy."

He waved the family to assist the girls.

"Right now, may not be the right time. Can we exchange information and meet in the hotel restaurant later?" Gillette asked.

Mac felt pressed. His concern for Danny and his parents over this devastating turn of events made him agree.

"Give us a couple hours, please?" Gillette optioned.

The two shook hands. Gillette gathered his family still tending to the cook out. Mac strode Danny toward the wooden ramp leading to the lodge.

1982

It happened the same way every week day morning for the past year.

Two knocks on the bedroom door, followed by his father announcing, "Time to get up."

Danny rolled over in his bed. His legs tangled in the sheets and bedcover as he tried to glance at his clock radio which read three twenty-eight with the green neon light in the top right corner signifying it was morning.

He heard the heavy footsteps fade away as he lay his head back on the pillow for the remaining minute and a half he had left before his clock's alarm blared.

Those last ninety seconds or so meant so much to him. Not even registering as a nap, but he still dozed until the static beeping jarred him awake.

He kicked his legs from the covering, bouncing onto the carpeted floor. He took four quick steps to the small clock and tapped the top of the console gently before he sat on the edge of his bed.

He had thirty minutes to do his business in the bathroom before his father rose to take his shower. Danny couldn't be one second off schedule or his father, now a captain with the fire department, would rail into him.

The clock routine began nearly two years ago when Danny landed the job as a fitness instructor at the Merchandise Mart. His father's contribution happened after butting heads for eight months into his morning process. He joked that his father only had a ten-minute drive to work for a shift that started at six in the morning.

His old man spent no more than twenty minutes, tops, in the bathroom for the ole shit, shower, and shave routine, and came out with the area sparkling clean and Pine Sol fresh before Danny's mother made her preparations for work at four-thirty.

Not that she was demanding, but his father respected her enough to give her the time she needed, drive her to the "L" station on Des Plaines Avenue, then drive to work himself.

Danny, by that time, would have a light workout, have guests' clothes washed, but not yet dried, and be stretching his first group out for their "X-treme Cardio" workout.

Christmas had just passed, but the Downtown Chicago department stores still had their magically decorative window displays up.

As Danny was on Christmas break from school, this more than afforded him time to spend at his absolute love – interning at the top-rated radio station, WBHM.

Once his shift was off at the health club, he trudged his way toward Michigan Avenue by State Street southbound to the 300 South Building that housed the station on the sixteenth floor.

Most week days after he left the club, he'd head to his classes at Chicago City College for Broadcast Communications studies. A passion developed from his time at a college radio station in his one year at Cincinnati.

He fancied his knowledge of music and the artists down to the labels they recorded for, even knowing the names of their agents and their stable of talent.

He loved entering the elevators at the 300 South Building and being brought to the sixteenth floor. He'd get out and see the guests waiting in the lobby sitting on the plush couches as he sweet talked to Patty, the young receptionist to buzz him in. Many a time someone recognized him from his entrance, usually a record promoter, who would ask what he did there. He would proudly answer them with working in traffic.

That was all he would give them, no further details. By the next week, he made a new friend in the business as they handed him business cards.

He'd catch the glass door to enter. Sneaking away to a cubicle in the sales department, Danny would arrange all the commercial spots that needed to be broadcast that day or make a log of the "make goods" they had screwed up and now had to devote air time somewhere on the schedule. God forbid, paying clients removed their advertising and the tens of thousands of revenue dollars that went with them.

On Fridays, the thing Danny was extremely proud of was his role as "producer" of the Bobby Tower Gospel Hour show he would put together from reels of audio recorded from the Foundation Church of God, a Baptist institution on 43rd and Lowe dating back to the fifties.

For the past five months, Danny would head to the small kitchenette, make a cup of coffee from the large Brew Master loaned by one of the station's largest sponsors, then head to the station's production room. He would grab a canister of one-inch reels and play them back for two hours until he tabbed enough material to come up with an hour's worth of a show, sans the commercial breaks which were also logged and programmed during this time.

For his efforts, he would receive a mention as sole producer of the show during the final credits that featured the mellifluous vocal talents of his mentor, Dr. Jeffrey Allen Kent. As host of the station's midday show, Kent emceed the coveted 3 p.m. to 7 p.m. drive time slot. Second only to the morning show, Kent's slot took the station from non-existent to number five in the market in less than two years.

Earning his role as Jeffrey's specific intern during the week had given Danny the hunger to take the craft seriously. He started compiling an audition reel that featured sound bites of his time on-air during Kent's show.

His classmates took notice as well as some prominent teachers who virtually passed him with A's from his hands-on proficiency.

Earlier that day, he had checked his mailbox for a list of spots that needed to be logged in for the weekend's play. A manila envelope sat inside that he had left there the day before mailed directly to him. Normally, he removed such items and placed them in his briefcase for fear of the sales manager scrounging around his mailbox to follow up on any sponsors that may have been contacted on the side.

A classmate of his, Percy Arlington, had sent to his attention a promotional copy of a club song from a local group.

He'd met Percy in a radio production class the last semester. This tall, lumbering young man with strands of peach fuzz just approached him out of the blue after class. He had recognized Danny from the Tuesday record day for local promoters working for distribution or labels. He fancied himself as an independent promoter juggling no less than seven projects.

Percy was consistently either late for class or a no show but made sure he contacted Danny either for homework information or just to find out the programming for the station's music list that week.

After a few weeks, he propositioned Danny with a score of three hundred dollars if he could deliver a promo of an Indiana based artist. All Danny had to do was put the record in the music director's in-box and Percy would take it from there. Danny looked Percy directly in his protuberant eye not knowing how to address the proposal.

Danny hesitantly did what was asked and left a message that the request was addressed. Having nothing to do with the programming aspect of the station, Danny approached Jeffrey Kent with the record. Jeffrey, ever protective of Danny, advised him to not venture down the route he suspected Danny was heading. Danny nodded, told him he was right, thanked him for such sage advice, called him Obi Wan, then stuck the record in the music director's in-box for discovery the next day.

Friday's were reporting day to the trade magazines, specifically Radio and Records the key source for all information pertaining to business in communications. A radio station calling in a report on a record, leading to a charting was the way an independent promoter got paid.

While in class, Percy showed up, late as usual and plopped himself down in front of Danny. A small radio studio was partitioned behind a wall in the classroom. One student would be talent, while another would work the board. Danny, initially paired with a mousy girl who wanted desperately to be on-air talent, wound up trading her in to partner with Percy.

Behind the booth, Percy handed Danny a small envelope that was bursting at the seams.

"Another one of those can be yours real soon," Percy said.

Danny was holding that opportunity in his hands at that very moment.

While working on splicing the Sunday edition of his Gospel show, he tossed the single onto a Panasonic turntable. He placed the Magnavox headphones over his ears, with the black foam swallowing him up and turned the potentiometer up to ten.

Danny listened to a nasty baseline that came in three quarter measures throughout the entire song. In harmony, this South Side Chicago group exhorted the joys of roller skating at the local rink with the break delivered three minutes in. Danny couldn't wait for the next envelope.

He flipped off the on-air strobe that the studios used for recording spots on-site with his back to the door.

He bobbed his head to the beat that was so wicked he lost himself into the hit he was sure this would be. Percy had himself a hit.

A pair of hands covered his eyes from behind, nearly jerking him from the chair.

Bumping off the ear cover from his right side, a soft voice said, "Guess who?"

Danny spun his chair around, facing his big crush, Juanita Gaines.

"Did I scare you?" she asked with a giggle.

Startled, he quickly removed the headphones nearly ripping off his earlobe.

Sitting in the center of the console, Juanita shifted her legs to make herself comfortable.

"Hey, birthday boy," she cooed. "Got big plans for this weekend?"

Just looking at her made Danny salivate. Juanita was the fifteen-piece bucket meal at Kentucky Fried Chicken with the large mashed potato side and five hot biscuits.

Danny considered himself very fortunate to be on the good side of Juanita. While she was one year younger, she took him under her hefty bosom and showed him the ropes at the station, having been there roughly two months prior to his arrival.

When he first landed the internship, she avoided him like the plague. She barely acknowledged him to say hello his first two weeks in as he learned the ropes.

Danny was very focused when he got the job on Jeffrey Kent's show and as voluptuous as she was, he made every effort to keep his nose to the grind.

They covered an in-store appearance with the good "Doctor" at a Peaches Records one Saturday when Juanita's soon to be fiancé failed to pick her up afterwards. Desperately needing a ride home humbled her, and she inquired if Danny was heading her way.

He was not, for he only had a five-minute drive south to his doorway, but he was more than happy to offer her a ride home, as long as she had gas money. She had no intentions of paying for any gas, but she made him an offer. It was one he had yet to collect but made the cat and mouse game between them very rewarding. Danny believed he was wearing her down, until she laid that oversized rock that old fool finally plunked down on her finger.

Now she waved that thing around, showing it off to anyone who would notice. Many of their co-workers believed the diamond wasn't real, while others speculated she paid for it herself.

Danny knew the truth. Old boy had gotten it through a sponsor of the radio station that the good Doctor had taken care of with an appearance at one of the store's Chicagoland locations.

"I got something poppin'," Danny said. "But I'd rather be spending time with you on my birthday."

Ever the flirt, things intensified between the two after Juanita announced her engagement to a guy Danny classified as a low-level thug wannabe.

She was always flattered that Danny truly showed some measure of care for her. Their bond was platonic and messy with something always in the offing.

Juanita had tried to shake her feelings for Danny by serving up one of her thirsty cousins. Danny in his hope for otherwise, brought a wingman to offset anyone getting in his way. Danny's desire for Juanita was incredibly high. She had caught herself in the throes at one point and nearly caved in to surrender.

Here she was propositioning Danny at that very moment for a taste of adventure. Danny was resolute in the plans for this particular holiday weekend and there was nothing in those plans that said, "Let the biggest tease keep you waiting." She had it all though, but it was too late to back out of his plans now.

"Going to any clubs this weekend, now that you'll be legal?" Juanita asked playfully.

"Naw," Danny pondered. "Plenty of time for that."

He dared to put his hands on her thigh. She glanced at him, but he wouldn't remove it.

"When I get back," he said, "why don't the two of us just get away?"

She placed her hand over his, without ever removing it.

"Yeah?" she asked. "Where to?"

"I dunno," Danny said, at a loss for a response. "We can work that out. Please?"

She left his hand on her leg as he planted another on her waist. She leaned toward him. She could tell trouble was just around the corner with him.

"Maybe," she said.

She took hold of his hands and brought them to her lips and planted a light kiss on his fingertips, then a blew on them.

"Maybe," she repeated softly. She held his fingers for what felt like an eternity to him. "C'mon, Jeffrey needs you in the studio."

Danny's bubble was burst again. Danny's heart was defeated again. Another victory for Juanita.

He turned from her to not let her see she had crushed him again.

He popped a cassette out the dual deck tape player and grabbed his reel.

"Tell Jeffrey I'll be right there," his voice cracked.

"All right, sweetie," Juanita popped off the countertop and headed for the door. She pried the door open and turned to him, blowing Danny a kiss, then was out the door and once again, out of his life.

ENTERING THE STUDIO, Danny brought in a stack of carts to feed the meter-so to speak. Thirty and sixty second commercial spots that were logged to play for the next hour.

Dr. Jeffrey Raymond Kent had just shut off his microphone as Danny laid the tapes down on the desk.

Danny cherished his relationship with Jeffrey who treated him like a little brother.

While he had numerous reservations about Danny's desire to be on-air talent, he believed he aspired to belong to a radio family.

Eight months prior when Danny began to assist Geno Everett, also an intern from CC College on the show, Jeffrey gave Danny an opportunity to go on air after watching him prepare an air-check tape. Danny balked and left while the studio while the room was hot.

A stern lecture followed regarding no one opening the studio door when the "on-air" lights were on. Danny nodded, acknowledging he had broken a cardinal rule and promised to not make that mistake again. Thus far, he had lived up to the promise.

But he had been caught in the studio with Jeffrey when the show was live with Public Service Announcement readings. Jeffrey would turn to Danny and ask him, "Brother Danny, do you know what to do when the lights go out on your block?" Danny would stare at the mic like a deer caught in the headlights and say nothing leaving seconds of dead air, before Jeffrey would give out the number to Commonwealth Edison for emergency services.

Danny bashfully would back out of the studio once the light was off and dash back to the engineer's station, to hide out in shame.

Jeffrey really couldn't make out what Danny's true passion was about the station until he discovered Danny and Juanita in the breakroom. Innocent as their play was, he saw a kindling of true desire, if not lust between two kids, not yet adults, but thrust out of teen years.

Jeffrey began to coach Danny on the ways of women, never coinciding to the fact that he himself had two daughters and a failed marriage in his home state of Tennessee outside of LaVergne. Those lessons also came with a major warning – stay away from Juanita. She was going to eat whoever was in her sights alive, chew them up, spit them out, and move on.

Danny wanted Jeffrey to be wrong. It was him who put the two together on his show. Juanita just had a sophisticated flair and knew how to have everything set for his show before he even entered the building. Danny ran the logs, said the phones, and set the carts for every commercial that needed to be played or read live.

Jeffrey had them sit down and meet before a show to make sure everything was in place. Jeffrey just brought the magic.

Juanita was in love however, and that made things a little difficult for Jeffrey. He usually broke the cardinal rule that had been brought into his early radio career, don't shit on the plate you eat off. He had taken a lot of dumps in his fourteen years in the business, starting off at a little sixty-four-watt station that barely broadcast down the block to the 1,000 watts that he presently reached not only in the Chicagoland area, but central Gary, Indiana, and the border of Wisconsin outside of Gurnee. He was one of the top five rated afternoon drive time hosts in the market and he still occasionally dipped where he shouldn't, so he begged Danny to take heed and enjoy the fruits but don't mess with the crops.

As Danny was about to walk out the studio, he heard Jeffrey state, "And one."

The "on-air" prompt flashed red before Danny could reach the door. He turned and his heart palpitated as he knew what Jeffrey had in store.

"Before we get back to the music," Jeffrey said, "I'd like to take a moment to wish my man, Danny Alexander, a happy birthday."

Danny graciously nodded his head, trying to not embarrass himself and stay silent.

"Brother's been here nearly a year with the 'Kent Show' and I just wanted to say, thank you, man. I hope you have a fantastic birthday."

Danny softly thanked Jeffrey hoping the light would go out soon. He saw Jeffrey reach the square button for the cued cart to play, but instead he asked, "How old are you going to be, brother?"

Danny grinned, but said nothing. He knew there was no way out of this, but he had just been outed to all the fans of the show he had had the pleasure of actually meeting at promotional events, who took the time to write him letters, call specifically to talk to him, or sent him articles of clothing; used clothing from time to time.

"Twenty-one years old," Danny said softly. The meter barely registered picking up his voice.

"How old? I couldn't hear you," Jeffrey taunted.

"Twenty-one years old tomorrow," Danny said in a modulated voice.

Jeffrey turned from the mic, "You heard it, ladies. My man, Danny Alexander will be legal tomorrow. When you see him at our next event on Tuesday, please buy him a drink."

Danny feigned laughter, "Ha, ha."

"Better yet," the DJ said. "The first fifteen ladies at *Salacious* will have a chance to have a drink on us in the VIP next Tuesday."

Danny's eyes widened. He had no intentions of working, let alone attending that event. Jeffrey himself rarely attended the weekday promos unless he was taking off the next day.

Damn, Danny thought, it would be the first week back for his final semester and Wednesday's schedule was full.

"Looking forward to it," Danny threw out.

"I bet you are," Jeffrey stood out of his chair and swiveled it to grab Danny. He drew him in and gave a tight hug, as the cue light went dark.

"We're going to get you laid just yet, lil' brother," Jeffrey said as he towered over Danny. "Happy birthday."

They both stood in front of the studio door noticing Juanita on the other side of the door patiently waiting for an opening.

Leaning down into his other ear, Jeffrey said, "Don't forget what I told you. She will take you down."

Danny nodded again. They both turned and waved to the voluptuous figure that sauntered into the studio.

Juanita flashed a smile that was ominous and mysterious as if she knew she could eat both of their souls. Danny's heart pounded with the vigor of a young man wistfully in love. Jeffrey was reminded of how he wound up in his fifth market in eight years.

"Take him, darlin'. He's yours," Jeffrey gestured as he handed Danny off and bounced back to his seat to segue to another song in rotation.

The door closed behind them as Juanita did guide Danny to the management offices suite. There was a core of secretaries milling around two desks preparing to close shop for the weekend.

One of the office doors was wide open with a light glaring into the secretarial pool space.

Juanita slid Danny into the office of Jimmy Hollister, the program director of the station, who was in his favorite position, sitting in his leather chair, chewing on an unlit cigar, talking loudly on the phone.

Juanita positioned Danny into one of the chairs sitting opposite Jimmy. She waved to them both bidding goodnight, then walked out the room, closing the door behind her.

Jimmy Hollister's office was a shrine to the man Danny truly revered in the radio business. Photos of Jimmy posing with celebrities plastered the walls, but it was the dozens of plaques that commended the advancements in radio and broadcast achievements to Jimmy that always caught his eyes. Whether from trades such as Radio and Records, Cashbox, or Billboard, outlets such as Jack the Rapper, a soiree held annually in Atlanta for industry types nationally to converge and mingle for a weekend of business and debauchery, decadence, and just good old-fashioned industry love. Radio luminaries as well as record label big wigs met on neutral ground to discuss the changes taking place in the industry from both sides of the urban spectrum.

Danny looked at Jimmy in awe.

Jimmy wasn't much more than thirty years old, but in Danny's eyes he had accomplished more than a lifetime of achievement in the fifteen years he had been in the industry starting in a New York state's station mailroom in Albany.

Danny knew his story long before he met Jimmy having interned for a cohort of his at WCIN the one year he spent in Cincinnati.

Stepping in to stop that disc jockey from pummeling a partygoer at his university's campus, Danny quickly introduced himself and played up the two weeks he had spent at WVXU sounding as if he had been programming the station for more than a year. A slight embellishment on Danny's behalf. The DJ offered him a card if he was open to shadow him which Danny followed up on the opportunity within a week's time.

The disc jockey had him fulfill roles of no more than a go-fer, but while Danny tracked meals, opened fan mail, and even the occasional laundry pickup, he was privileged with stories of Denny Mack and Jimmy Hollister, two hooligans that ran the streets of Steubenville, Ohio with him.

When Danny decided to not continue his education at Xavier, but to stay home instead, he couldn't believe his good fortune when his Broadcast Radio class' first guest speaker was none other than James 'Jimmy' Hollister, program director of WBHM, that quarter's number one rated station in the Arbitron book.

When Jimmy fielded questions from the class, the job requests flowed from nearly every mouth except for Danny's. He had a plan that had to be executed immediately.

While taking a fifteen-minute break, Danny approached Jimmy about an in-store appearance he would be making close to his home. When it was confirmed that he would be appearing at said location, Danny thanked him for the time he took as a guest, then headed back to class.

It was at that promotional event that Danny seized the moment. Jimmy couldn't believe how Danny snuck through, but when he heard the story of the mail that got lost when Jimmy and Denny took early lunches one day that equated to a loss of over one hundred thousand dollars in clients' checks being stolen before they were unceremoniously shown the door. Jimmy corrected the story explaining it was only fifty-two thousand dollars.

By Monday morning, Danny had an office interview and was back with an application to intern from his school. But there was a problem with that paperwork.

Jimmy hung up the phone and smiled.

"Twenty-one, huh?" he opened. "That's going to be huge."

Danny smiled back at him.

"And you're about to graduate this upcoming semester, huh?"

Danny nodded.

"So, what are your plans afterwards?"

Danny couldn't answer. He didn't want to appear anxious. He'd been hearing for a while an overnight on-air position was going to open up. It was the very reason he had been working overtime on the air-check audition tapes.

"Look," the diminutive man stood up from his chair, standing no more than five feet and four inches on a good day. He waved his arms, pointing to all that he had accomplished. "Look around you."

Danny took his eyes off Jimmy's $500 three-piece suit with the pocket chained gold watch attached to gander at all the hardware that Jimmy had amassed.

"These are the signs of hard work," he said. "Radio is a very hard job. But it can be a very lucrative, rewarding one."

The speech, Danny thought, I'm getting the speech. He's about to tell me about the overnight position.

Danny's head was spinning. It was all too soon. Would he be able to get his degree when he accepted the job? He'd have to shuffle some things on his schedule around, but he was sure he could still handle one last eighteen-hour semester along with the job. Or he could finish school in the summer.

He would definitely have to drop the job at the health club. He was sure he could give Cary, the owner, a two-week notice. Surely, Cary would understand. This was everything he had worked so hard for. Those early mornings rising to his father's knocking to falling asleep at the kitchen table drooling on textbooks. Done!

He'd move downtown and get a studio apartment that he'd sneak Juanita to. She'd give up that punk ass fiancé once Danny brought her there. He'd spend late nights worming his way into listeners' hearts and early mornings worming his way into Juanita.

"I've had a conversation with your department's Chairman," Jimmy said as he walked over to a chair adjacent to Danny. "Know what he told me about you?"

Danny's smile faded.

JOB OFFER

Danny waited on the elevated train platform as the red headlights of the Congress Milwaukee train commenced to screech to a halt.

While it was a little later than the usual rush hour period, the train itself still had a minimum of seven cars attached. Some of the newer metallic silver air-conditioned cars shoved further ahead as the older green models with the push down windows stopped in front of him.

The doors slid open as a mob converged into the car hoping for an opportunity to sit on the hand torn cushions. Danny slowly walked inside and positioned himself as he grabbed a handrail above him.

The doors closed as the conductor muffled the next stop. Danny didn't care as he was riding to the final stop of Des Plaines Avenue.

He could hear the clackety-clank as the iron wheels rolled on the tracks. His leather satchel tapped his sides as the strap dug into his shoulder blade.

He messed up. Jimmy let him know how close he was to having it all, but a small - at least small to Danny - lie set him back.

As soon as Jimmy mentioned Al Parker, the Chair of his school's radio division, he knew he was screwed.

"People claw at the opportunity to intern here," Jimmy told him. "Every day we get all these qualified candidates throwing résumés in the mail, making obnoxious phone calls, bumping into staff members at promotional events."

Danny's eyes caught Jimmy's at that moment. Jimmy leaned in so close, he bet he could count his eyelashes.

Danny blinked incessantly trying to not let tears well up.

"I didn't want to work for some US99," he countered. "I told Parker where I wanted to go. I told him I had talked directly to you. I wanted his blessing since you and I were cool."

"So, you just thought you'd come in here and waste everybody's time? Is that it?" Jimmy asked.

"I wanted to be where the best opportunity was for me," Danny said softly.

Jimmy nodded. He understood. "But maybe it wasn't the best place for you. Did you think of that? Maybe Parker had your best interest at heart. He's been doing this far longer than either you or me." He poked Danny in the chest to accentuate his point, "Did you think of that?"

Danny closed his eyes for a moment. He could feel the tear ducts ready to flow. He was about to lose the most important thing in the world to him. A place he genuinely felt was home. A family of people who guided him and took him under their wing.

With his free hand, Danny brushed his fingertips beneath his cheek to catch the tear that finally fell.

He looked at the passengers on the train to see if anyone noticed as a long, loud snort ripped through his nostrils.

"Whew, damn allergies," he said as he pinched the bridge of his nose.

An older woman sitting near him took pity, "It's that season, isn't it? I can't seem to shake mine. Doctor says it's because I smoke like a chimney."

"Yes, ma'am," Danny respectfully said, "Just something in the air or so my doctor says."

She smiled at him, then turned her head. They both watched the traffic pile up as likely to happen on the Eisenhower on a Friday night. It was still early, only six-thirty p.m. and the lack of movement would continue westbound until Austin Blvd.

"School or work?" she turned back and asked.

Danny's attention jerked back, "Pardon?" he asked.

"Are you coming from school or work?" she asked.

Danny hesitated. She curled up her lips into a smile and the deepest dimples Danny had ever seen cut into her jaws.

He nodded as he reflected on his answer. "Work, kinda both, mostly work."

He wanted to be able to say that at least one more time before it was completely taken away.

"You remind me of me and Denny back then," Danny could hear Jimmy laugh. "More Denny, than me, mind you. Denny was always in trouble which is why we split up. We had to go our separate ways."

Danny sat in the chair tensed up trying to find the words that would change Jimmy's mind.

He couldn't afford to be at ground zero and start all over again. Not if he could help it.

The past year was ground work for the opportunity to be a part of something big. This radio job was that for him. And he certainly did not want to go back to Al Parker's office after this. He knew once the semester began, he'd have to address this with his office.

Most important, he'd lose Juanita. His heart was broken in more ways than just the toying around that she did. She had twisted him all around her fingers, but she never devastated him the way Jimmy was doing at that moment. Even that stupid ring that Danny was sure she bought herself didn't hurt him the way Jimmy was knotting him up that minute.

"Tell you what, my man." Jimmy tapped Danny on his wrist. "There's an opening in the sales division."

Danny lifted his head slightly. He was listening as his stomach groaned.

"Hear me out," Jimmy said thinking that sound was from Danny's throat, "My birthday gift to you. I'll talk to Parker on Monday if you like. We're on the same board for AFTRA. I talk to him all the time. He's good people."

Danny lifted his head further and nodded.

"See if we can work something out with you and Sam Goodman in the sales department. You have the weekend to think about it," Jimmy said.

Danny saw Jimmy stretch out his hand. For a small man, his hands were gigantic, with long fingers, not short and stubby.

Jimmy flashed an open smile that resembled a set of choppers that had thousands of dollars of work done on them to offset his thick brownish-red lips.

Danny took his hand out and watched as Jimmy's just swallowed his.

"Deal?" Jimmy asked.

Danny snapped out of that thought by the time the train pulled into the Des Plaines station. He had been seated since Oak Park Avenue two stops back.

He stared out the window as the car rocked back and forth in its final stop as patrons stood at the doors waiting for the conductor to open them.

The car was nearly empty when Danny pulled himself up after grabbing a handrail and walked onto the platform.

He stood with his satchel bag in tow watching the train pull off.

It was a long walk to the car parking at the station. Tucked far in the back, it actually was a half mile walk to an underlit lot that only allowed dollar bills for parking in a meter that resembled a mailbox for miniature cars.

Danny took his time as other lot patrons made mad dashes

toward their cars desperate to find if vandals had tampered with their vehicles, which the facility was well-known for.

Danny himself had his car broken into twice, the second time he was even ticketed because the security couldn't reach him and the wait for a tow truck took him beyond his allotted time paid.

He approached his car resigned that he had a decision to make over the weekend. He hated that it had to be this very weekend that such a decision needed his focus. He needed his trust fund to discuss issues like this.

He opened the hood of his trunk to his 1979 Firebird. The compartment was a mess. He shuffled items around until he was certain he had secured a place, then tossed the bag inside and slammed the hood shut.

He walked to his driver's side, slid into the car, and prayed that the cold hadn't shattered his glass starter. He turned the key and Barbara Eaton's show was jamming out his radio. The woofers darn near bled the bass was tweaked so high with little room for treble.

He hit reverse and backed out when the car cut off.

"No, no, no!" he screamed.

He turned the ignition and fired it up, fishtailing out the lot as quickly as possible.

HOME 1982

Using a large duffel bag he had purchased during travels to Cincinnati, Danny stuffed belongings for the weekend as he heard the back door to the house creak open.

"Yoo-hoo," sang Danny's mother into the backway reaching Danny's ears. "Who's that creeping in my house?"

Danny smiled every time he heard her voice.

Heels stomped on the back stairway followed by the door shutting close, then another set of footsteps somewhat softer but definitely more masculine.

The lights were on in the kitchen along with the lamp in Danny's bedroom to illuminate the way for his mother to make her grand entrance.

Her small cherubic face popped inside to peek Danny's cluttered bedroom, which he swore every weekend he would straighten up.

"Hello there," she beamed. Her eyes blinked in a Betty Boop fashion, "I'm home."

Danny put a pair of clean underwear on top of the bag as he stepped over two separate pairs of shoes, nearly tripping over one set as his ankle twisted briefly.

He hugged her tightly as if he hadn't seen her in years. She enveloped him in her arms and placed her head on his chest.

"Hey, mom," he said cheerfully. "How are you?"

His father walked briefly passed the two of them turning to offer a salutation, "Hello, son."

Danny said in kind, "Hey, dad. What's up?"

As he released his mother, she spotted the bag on his bed.

"Where you think you're going this evening?" she asked as only a protective mother could.

They'd been pretty protective of each other these last few years since Lamont's death. For Danny, it had become very smothering, but he knew it was coming from a very special place.

"I thought I told you," he realized he had stalled saying anything for so long, he hadn't even mentioned until this moment, "Darnell's family has a time share near Gurnee. We're just heading up there for the weekend."

He felt like an adolescent, giving half-truths to his mother knowing the reality of his trip would have sent his mother off the reservation.

"Gurnee?" surprised, she asked. "Where's that?"

"Right outside the Wisconsin border," his father barreled in.

His father understood the nature of what was happening. A rite of passage. Boy becoming man challenges man of the house.

His father was not threatened in the least, but Danny was losing the timidity he once had of his father. They had recently experienced a spate of arguments that Danny's mother wound up refereeing. Only one got physical, Danny's mother was not around to save the one punch that took him out. Neither said anything to her, but she sensed a competitiveness between the two unlike anything she had ever experienced when she grew up with two brothers.

"Which side of Wisconsin?" she asked.

Danny waited for his father to answer, but saw he was busy hanging his winter jacket.

"The Illinois side, mom," he lied, not about Gurnee being in the state, but the proximity to the town he was to which he was actually venturing.

They stared at each other. She looking at her only cherished son, all grown-up and about to get a college degree. While not the first to attend college, he would be the first in her family to graduate. Although she had reservations about his career choice, she was so proud of him in every way.

She stood in that doorway dressed in a full-length purple parka with every inch of her five-foot frame resembling a gift-wrapped elf with the matching beret. Her once black locks now gray and stringy. Danny loved her with all his heart, willing to surrender it for her if she needed.

His father's footsteps rapidly approached as he opened the refrigerator door.

"You making anything to eat?" he gruffly asked her.

She turned briefly as if snapped from a trance. "What would you like?" was her response, as she said, "I can make you a Spam sandwich."

Danny heard the door to the fridge slam, "I don't like Spam. You know that," as his father stomped away from the kitchen.

Danny's mother stood in the doorway gazing into space, then she turned toward Danny.

As only a mother could, she asked, "You going to eat something before you go? I can make you a Spam sandwich. Would you like that?"

Danny stuffed two pairs of sweat socks into the duffel bag and shook his head, "No ma, I'm good."

"You sure?" she asked. "I really think I want some Spam. Tired of leftover turkey. Aren't you?"

Danny chuckled, "I'll grab something on the way to the hotel."

"What's the name of the hotel?" she asked him.

Danny stopped for a moment, "Damn, I'm not sure, ma."

"You got a phone number?"

He had purposely neglected to collect such vital information although he had a clue to the whereabouts of his trip. "No, but I promise to call you when I get there. Give you all that info, okay?"

She observed him once more, her brown eyes scanning him, "Okay." She began to walk away, then said, "Let me know if you change your mind about the Spam, okay?"

"Okay, ma, you my girl," he said to his mother.

He was all packed at that point as his father stomped his way back to the kitchen. Danny was still lost in thought about Jimmy's offer and hadn't noticed his father standing there once his mother had walked away.

"Need to talk to you, real quick," the elder said matter-of-factly.

Danny was caught unawares as he saw the imposing figure of his father standing in the middle of the tiled floor.

"Yes, sir," Danny said.

Glowering with rage, his father said, "Downstairs."

Danny dared to raise an eyebrow, but nothing more as he thought to himself, *now what?*

With that all that was left was the sound of his father's footsteps pounding into the wooden stairwell.

Danny zipped up the bag and followed.

His descent on the stairwell was slow as it had always been nearly seventeen years ago. He had been afraid of the stairs, not because something was waiting to attack him, but because of Kim Novak and Jimmy Stewart's climb up the stairway in Vertigo. That nightmarish fall she made haunted him from the age of three. For years, he had illusions about falling to his death.

His most frightening moment was a trip to Mexico in 1968 during the Olympics. His father's youngest sister took him to the pyramids in Guadalupe. He raced up the uneven concrete steps only to have to be escorted by a band of girl scouts on the way back down when he realized there were no handrails or walls to cling to as he took one step at a time back down.

Here at home the worst thing that constantly happened was he bumped his head on a low overhang that separated the back door and five steps to the platform and the final ten steps down.

Standing behind a hand-built bar that his father constructed, tore down, and rebuilt three times in a fifteen-year span, Dan Sr. motioned for his son to have a seat in one of the six lounge chairs that surrounded the bar.

Danny's mind was on the time. He was expecting a ride very shortly and was one hundred percent packed.

"Let me tell you, son," was how his father always started a lecture.

Lately, it seemed his father imparted a lot of sage advice about life, but in Danny's mind, it always had the sound of disappointment.

"You might not have thought about this," he said as Danny took a seat, "but your mother had something really special for you on your twenty-first birthday."

Not that Danny hadn't given much thought to it, but he rarely saw his mother, or father with his crazy schedule, thus it never really hit him that she would have planned something.

"This trip just came up," he said. "I just found out about it this week. I didn't think..."

Lying through his teeth, it never occurred to him to pay a courtesy to inform his parents of his plans, since he knew about the trip around the Thanksgiving holiday.

"I know what you're thinking," his father said. "You're thinking you're grown, but you still live under my roof."

Danny knew where this conversation was headed. 'My roof, my rules.' Danny couldn't wait to move out, get a place of his own where it was his roof, his rules.

"Your mother made these dinner arrangements and was looking forward to getting out of the house for a trip to Chinatown. She's talked about this all week. Has the menu practically memorized, but now—"

Danny groaned a little too loud during the speech.

"Oh," his father said. "You got something to say?"

Danny knew this could go on for hours once his father got revved up. Danny thought how lucky his two older half-brothers were to never experience these 'talks.'

"I just didn't know," he said.

His father leaned into the bar. His most terse diatribes were generally in a low tone as if he were sharing a major secret to the world.

Lately, Danny had been the recipient of numerous father-son talks. Not just with his actual father, but Jimmy had spent a few late nights being introspective with Danny. Jimmy usually eschewed the business side of radio away from the glamor of meeting celebrities, hanging out at nightclubs, or receiving adoring listeners' undergarments. It became very clear, Danny had to learn, had to respect, and had to understand how to make it in the "real world."

These talks were getting "real" old, "real" fast. Not that he didn't appreciate the time these men were taking to help him find the proper course of direction for him to live his life, but damn, they could talk.

As his father settled in to really articulate how things were, Danny heard activity from the floor above.

"Danny!" his mother called out at the top of the stairwell.

Danny said, "Sorry, dad."

"Yeah!" they both said, father and son.

"DJ," his mother corrected.

"Yeah, mom," he cheerfully said, happy for the break.

"Your ride is here," she told him.

"Thanks, mom," Danny said as he rose from his seat relieved his friend didn't let him down. "Sorry, dad," he said as he put a on a somber face.

His father coolly erected himself and reached to pat Danny on the back.

"We'll talk when you get back," he said. "Tell your mother you'll make it up to her later."

Danny stopped at the foot of the stairs, reflected, and nodded as he began his ascent.

He felt a tug of remorse as his mother waited for him at the top of the stairs. When he reached the last step, she gave him a peck on the cheek.

"Have a safe trip."

"Thank you, ma," he said with a little anguish in his throat thanks to his father.

"Happy birthday."

"*Yeah,*" he thought as he could see a tinge of pain in her eyes.

WISCONSIN BOUND

*P*arked at the curb, Darnell Wilkins watched as Danny walked down the stairs of his family's house.

Closing the iron wrought screen door was Mrs. Alexander who waved at him as Danny approached his Fiero. He waved back at her as he hit the door locks.

Danny opened the passenger door with nary a smile, but grunted, "What up, man?"

"What up?" Darnell greeted back exuberantly.

Danny knuckling his duffle bag and hoisted it upward. "Where do I put this?" he asked as he realized the car was a two-seater.

The hood to the trunk popped open. Danny chuckled to himself as he walked to the back and tossed the bag inside the compact trunk.

Darnell flipped through a rack of cassette tapes tucked away in his arm rest and popped in Bob James Three.

Danny snapped the seatbelt in place as Darnell pulled off from the curb noticing Mrs. Alexander still standing in the doorway waving goodbye.

Danny threw a small wave from behind as Darnell wondered how long his mother was going to leave the porch light on.

"She knows you're not coming back tonight, right?" he asked.

Danny straightened up in his bucket seat and sighed, "I messed up big time, man. My moms must've had something planned for my birthday, but hey, that's what happens when you throw a surprise. Sometimes you get surprised."

Danny sighed again and looked out the passenger's window.

"Everything okay?" Darnell asked as he shifted gears in the tight confines of his car.

He cut a quick left at the end of the block, punching on the clutch, bobbing the stick like one would change channels on a Cox Cable box remote.

"It's been a day," Danny said. "I guess I just didn't think about my parents celebrating my twenty-first birthday."

As Darnell made a right turn a block further, he said, "I can always take you back if you don't want to go."

Danny shook his head, "No, I'm cool."

"You sure?" Darnell said. "I don't want you to feel guilty."

Danny pondered, hesitating for a moment before answering, "Nope, it's all right. Let's go before I change my mind."

Darnell was only blocks from the expressway at that moment. He glanced at Danny who was busy biting his lower lip.

"Heard you on the radio," Darnell said. "You've got a gift of gab."

Danny smiled, "Ha, ha, motherfucker."

Darnell nodded; glad he could get Danny back to earth.

"So, got any plans? What's going on with your job search?" Darnell asked seriously.

"I'm glad you asked," Danny said as he dug into his brown bomber jacket's right pocket procuring a cassette tape case and popped out Darnell's.

Carefully opening it like Indiana Jones exchanging a bag of sand for religious artifacts, he removed a cassette from its case and replaced it with Darnell's. He plopped it into the car's player and closed the case.

"Check this out," Danny beamed as he lay the plastic cassette housing in the car ashtray.

Grover Washington's "Mr. Magic" fades out when Danny's nervous screeching voice back-sells, "Grover – Mr. Magic – Washington with none other than, 'Mr. Magic' on WALX Alexander radio."

Darnell looks out his driver's window embarrassed for his friend and hoping to not let one ounce of air escape from the snicker he found himself trying to suppress.

There was suddenly a pause, no more than one second, but long enough to no longer conceal laughter coming from Darnell. He grabbed his passageway and applied pressure to his sinus cavity.

Danny turned to him instantly.

"What's wrong?" he asked as he turned toward Darnell in embarrassment. Danny reached for the eject button, but Darnell pushed his hand away.

"No, I want to hear the rest," Darnell said as supportive as possible while slapping the top of the console to stop from laughing.

"You sure?" Danny hesitantly asked.

Darnell nodded, "I'm sure – let it play." Danny kept his finger by the button as Darnell assured, "I'm serious, let it play. I have allergies. That's all."

Danny slowly moved his head back to the window as his radio voice cracked reading a public service announcement.

Darnell bowed his head trying to contain himself.

"So, what are you going to do with that?" he asked.

"Dunno," Danny said. "Got a job offer though."

Darnell merged into traffic on the Eisenhower balancing his focus on both the cars creeping by as he switched lanes and Danny's struggle to not stumble over the thirty second read which his errors easily added five seconds.

"Really?" Darnell asked. "On air?"

Danny shook his head, "Naw, sales."

"Sales?" Darnell asked. distracted by a BMW blocking his

entrance into the far-left express lane. He honked for the car to let him in, but the driver would not relent. Darnell shifted gears veering right instead, zooming a few feet then cutting left through two lanes finding himself directly in front of the black Beemer. The Bavarian Motor Works car flashed its bright lights as Darnell pushed the accelerator. Danny hit the top of the console in a fit of road rage as well.

"Do you want to work in sales?" Darnell asked. "I thought you were going for that late-night shift? What happened?"

Danny blinked not really knowing where to start.

"My internship is over," Danny said. "They found out I was never sent there."

"Never sent there?" Darnell asked with much confusion. "You've been there a year. What do you mean?"

Exacerbated, Danny tried to explain, "I was actually supposed to work at US99." Danny laughed nervously. "Can you imagine me working country music?"

"The school assigned you to go to a country music station?" Darnell asked.

"I switched some paperwork and submitted it for WBHM," Danny admitted. "No harm, no foul, right?"

"So how did they find out?" Darnell asked as he flipped the bird to the BMW in his rear. "This fucker is pissing me off."

Danny looked left but couldn't get a good look with the high beams glaring his vision.

"What's with this motherfucker?" Danny asked.

"Don't know," Darnell said. "Don't care."

Darnell found his opening and darted the car to the right lane veering toward the 294N signs. Its wheels skidded on the slick pavement as Darnell's wipers cascaded back and forth.

Danny looked behind to his left as the Beemer had to brake hard as its bright lights caused the driver in front to slow down.

"So, this sales job," Darnell asked, "It pays good money, right?"

Danny pondered the question before finally answering, "I get paid a commission based on accounts I bring in."

"Ohhh," Darnell flinched. "You're gonna die of starvation. That's worse than working for free."

Danny reluctantly nodded in agreement. He was very closed off regarding asking for advice on matters like this. Darnell had been the very first to parlay a job from an internship out of their group of friends and for all the hard work he put in, he made it look very easy.

As a transit engineer for Chicago's Transit Authority, Darnell spent nearly a year in the field. He had started near the end of summer when Chicago was experiencing 90 plus degree weather. The fall immediately cooled things off, but his job of checking the lines was still uncomfortable since he spent so much of the autumn in rainy weather. He had a cold that nearly took eight months to get over.

The winter of '81 was brutally cold and working with the switch operators to address concerns about the older tracks being operable also found him nearly a quarter of a mile-high working in the snow conditions as he approached his graduation. He was almost finished with the internship before he received a job offer, which turned into a lead management position on a lower tier, but out the gate making $75,000. By the time he got his second check, he was sitting in his '82 Pontiac Fiero with custom trim, classic rims, a Jensen sound system, bucket leather seats, and a gas account to travel back and forth to every end that the transit authority covered in the state.

Not bad for a twenty-one-year-old graduating top of his class one year early.

With his management position he had also created employment opportunities for family and friends who needed steady income that he knew were completely reliable. He had offered an opportunity to Danny, but 'Dan the Man' was gung-ho on making this radio thing work, even if it killed him.

To Darnell, it sounded like it had finally gotten Danny.

"Hey," he proposed, "I can see if there is a space available at work. You know there is always stability."

Danny was crushed. He knew his buddy was looking out for him as he had the last ten years they had known each other, but Danny had to remain vigilant, resolute, and hard head as ever in his quest for a radio position, especially at his favorite spot at the number one station in Chicago.

"Well, hey," Darnell said. "I'm just putting it out there. Think about it."

Danny nodded, "Yeah, maybe."

"Hey, man, you got to risk it to get the biscuit, right?" Darnell jokingly asked.

Danny stared at the highway ahead, wondering what the future held for him.

AM/PM

The ride itself went relatively smooth as the car pushed northbound to the Wisconsin border.

Darnell suffered through twenty more minutes of Danny's sound check before he was shown mercy through tears of laughter.

"Do I really sound like that?" Danny asked incredulously. He heard the nasal pinch that clogged up many of his PSA readings.

No matter how calm he thought he had gotten, the audio check just got worse, but so had many audition tapes of long-time disc jockeys.

While not finally settling into the idea of taking the proposal for the sales job, Danny was being lured to what Darnell joked was 'the dark side.'

Danny had popped the Bob James cassette back in the player and tucked away his own creation falling to sleep within minutes as he watched Darnell navigate through the wet snow. The flip flop of the windshield wiper blades finally lulled him into a trance, and he was out like a light.

The plan had been to rendezvous in Elkhorn at an AM/PM gas

station. The final destination would be no more than six miles from there.

Danny was still resting his head against the window when Darnell finally pulled into the station. His breathing steady as a stream of snorts erupted.

Darnell tapped him as he put the car in park sitting next to a pump.

Darnell's door blew open as he unbuckled his belt. The cold air stirred Danny back to consciousness. He shook his head to get his bearings.

"Where are we?" groggily Danny asked.

"Gas station," Darnell said as he climbed out. "Want anything?"

Danny squinted to see the red and blue neon sign. He unbuckled his belt to free himself.

"I got to pee," he simply said.

"Can't help you there," Darnell said. "You're on your own."

There was a crowd inside the gas station's mini mart. Danny wandered the store's aisle randomly picking up items, then discarding them in other areas.

Darnell walked inside the station wiping off the snow's remains. Heading toward a Slushee machine, he found Danny standing in front of the encased beverage refrigerator staring at forty-ounce bottles of beer.

"Which one you looking at?" Darnell asked.

Danny awakened from his trance. He reached for the handle of the door deterred by the twenty-one or older decal stuck on the glass.

Darnell opened the door and grabbed a bottle of malt liquor.

"Tomorrow it's on you," he said. "Happy birthday."

"Thanks," Danny appreciatively mumbled.

With the car nestled in a parking spot in the front of the store, Darnell and Danny sat facing the gas pumps listening to a smooth jazz track on WLUM.

Darnell's radio system illuminating a greenish neon light lit up the dashboard as the two shared a giant bag of Cheetos.

"Maybe," Danny thought aloud, "I should submit my tape to these guys."

He waited for some semblance of support from Darnell who could only offer, "Do you know anybody there?"

Danny smiled, as if he found his solution, "Yeah, actually, I know the music director there. She came from BHM."

He looked away momentarily, mentally mapping out a way to deliver a copy of the tape to his new found contact. He actually hoped they were still cool, given how little attention he gave her when it was apparent, he had designs on one particular spot. He'd blown off her farewell party at Bennigan's and only signed her going away card with some obnoxious sexually overt comment.

"Could you actually live down here?" Darnell asked.

"Up here," Danny corrected. "Hell yeah!"

He had been waiting for the opportunity to leave his father's house. His old man had been pretty hardcore since Danny came back to live with them. He didn't see the big deal. It wasn't like he actually left that one year, just went away to school, that's all.

He loved his mother dearly and a lot of time had passed to heal the wounds from Lamont's death. He still felt weighed down by guilt for letting his mother absorb the blame that neither really deserved to take. He'd watch her with that ever-pleasant smile always ready to discuss or listen to his future plans, but he also felt her overprotectiveness. She'd sat up late waiting for him to return home from a club event and ask if he wanted anything to eat before heading to bed, then rising a few hours later to prepare for work.

His father was cutting logs snoring so loud it reverberated throughout the house.

"Yeah," he said. "I could definitely move out here."

"Maybe," Darnell said, "You and Nick could room together."

"Hell, naw," Danny said without a second thought. "Your cousin is cool and all but, naw, man, that shit ain't gonna happen."

Darnell grabbed a handful of Cheetos and laughed. After washing the cheese puffs down with a Mountain Dew, he revisited the idea stating, "You should think about it. That's if you can get a job out here."

Darnell's cousin, Nick Wilkins and Danny had known each other since childhood living two houses from each other and meeting at the age of five at a birthday party.

The two had spent many years hanging out and Danny had been to Madison, Wisconsin on many a road trip since Nick had moved to the campus to finish his degree in medicine. Lifelong buddies that would die for the other but live together. Nope!

Nick was one of the crew they were actually waiting on parked at the gas mart. Nearly twenty minutes had gone by since they parked. It had been a long day from Danny and Darnell and the witching hour was fast approaching when Danny, the last of his group, became a legal adult at twenty-one.

"Anyway," Darnell said as he reached into the right pocket of his parka jacket, extracting a sheet of printed paper, "this is an early birthday present."

Danny took the offering as it was placed in his hand.

"What's this?" he asked as he accepted the sheet.

"A lottery ticket," Darnell said. "Maybe you'll have some good luck your twenty-first birthday."

Danny squinted at the waxy coating of the lottery ticket's design: a silver coin toss with Native Americans, shooting arrows.

Danny flipped the card around to its back with nothing more on it than fill out instructions and how to redeem winnings.

"What's with the silver?" Danny asked acknowledging the significance of the silver.

Darnell shrugged as he brought the bottle back to his lips, "Are you going to scratch it off? Maybe you'll win enough to buy a place down here."

"Up here," Danny corrected again. "Wisconsin is north of us."

A loud belch erupted from Darnell. Danny turned and almost swore he saw the gas rising from his esophagus.

"Damn. You alright?"

Darnell laughed, "Yeah, man."

Darnell wiped his lips with his right wrist as he grasped the bottle tightly with his left. Darnell was known as "Tank" earning the nickname for his explosive technique on the high school football team and shitting on those players he plowed through on the field.

"Got a coin or something I can scratch this ticket with?" Danny asked still reeling in the revulsion of the gas bomb.

Darnell tossed a penny from his ashtray to Danny. After fumbling around a bit, he finally controlled the coin and positioned it to rub off five gray circles.

Circle one – an arrow
Circle two – a feather from a head band
Circle three – two feathers
Circle four – a silver coin

Before scratching off the final circle, Danny asked, "What's a winner here?"

"Is it on the back?" Darnell's eyes roamed over Danny's head as he returned the volley of questions.

Suddenly, Darnell turned to hit his door lock as Danny's door swung open. A pair of large hands thrust inside and caught the unbuckled passenger off guard, dropping the penny and the lottery card to the wet pavement as someone snatched him from his seat.

The click of the automatic locks sealed the door for Darnell as another perpetrator jiggled the passenger door.

Grabbed by his jacket collar, Danny found himself standing on the tips of his toes.

"What up, birthday boy?" asked the man.

Struggling to maintain balance, Danny looked down on Larry Gardner, a 6'3" hulk of a man-child. When the "Family" first came together, Larry was already man strong back in their freshman year of high school. Ganglier back then nearly eight years ago, Larry didn't grow more than two inches, but what he bulked up to was the very thing of comic book superheroes who become villains.

Larry sneered at Danny watching him labor to get his footing. A smile spread across his face as he promised, "I'm getting them birthday licks tonight," he threatened as he shook Danny as if money would fall out. "Midnight, you mine."

"Let him down," a gruff voice said. "It's not his birthday yet."

Slowly, as the heels of his shoes touched the slushy ground the two stared at the sight of Baron Hawkins. Danny finally stood flat on his feet now looking directly at Larry's bandito mustache.

"What are you, ten?" Danny asked defiantly to the smiling brute.

A punch to the base of his back crippled his legs, as Larry caught Danny as he dropped down.

"Happy birthday, Brother Dan," came the rowdier gruff voice of Baron's brother, Carter.

"Muthafucka," Danny squeezed out as Larry helped him to his feet. "You, too, what's wrong with you?"

Carter stretched his arms out, not as an invitation to fight. Danny turned to him, loosening himself from Larry's grip, opened his arms out wide, and hobbled two steps to the small stocky man with a leather skull cap hugging his head.

They embraced, as two longtime friends were apt to do, even with the silliness of being boys at heart.

"That shit hurt, man," Danny said to a mugging Carter. "What's wrong with you?"

Carter smiled, "Just giving you a taste of what's to come." He tightened his grasp of Danny testing the raw strength of his college football against that of Danny's physical fitness instructor physique. Nearly bear hugging his friend in the one-sided challenge.

"You done?" Danny grunted, straining in the hold of his buddy. "People might talk."

Danny leaned close and blew Carter a kiss after which Carter immediately released him.

Inside the car, Darnell was startled by the jiggling of his locked door. He grabbed the inside handle and bolted out coming face to face with a dark skinned, tall young man that resembled a forty-pound lighter version of himself.

"You've gained some weight," Darnell gestured patting his own belly, then embracing his cousin, Nick Wilkins.

"Still not as big as you," Nick said as he wrapped his hands around his cousin's girth. "How's the family?"

Darnell released his hold before answering, "Yours or mine?"

Snow fell furiously on Nick's curly mop of black hair giving it a greasy look.

"Yes," Nick said.

"They're fine," Darnell said. "Both of them. You missed Uncle Joey's birthday party. Everyone asked about you."

"What'd you tell them?" Nick asked as he stepped toward Danny.

"Told them you were doing okay," Darnell said. "What should I have told them?"

Nick and Danny clasped as if they hadn't seen each other since they first met in 1965. Seventeen years didn't seem so long ago. But Danny had ridden to the University of Wisconsin less than two months ago to drop Nick off at the campus. Ever since Nick transferred to the school two years prior, Danny had been there at least every semester. Good friends to the end, but they both knew they could never be roommates.

"How long you guys been here?" Baron asked.

"Not long," Darnell said. "Just twenty minutes or so."

"Where's everybody else?" Danny asked.

The roar of *La Cucaracha* blared from a car horn at a pump as two heads emerged from a brown Ford van.

"What up, baby!" yelled the passenger standing on the van's ramp.

The van bounced up and down as the driver, slight in height, not in size jumped up and down on his side to be seen.

"Happy birthday, dog!" the driver shouted.

The least nonplussed, Danny immediately ran to the passenger's side of the van to hug his two friends, Clinton Hodges, the passenger, and Wynton Pryce, the driver.

"Hey, there, Booboo, boy!" Danny shouted at Wynton, the shorted stout driver.

Clinton jumped from the van, nearly hoisting Danny off his feet with jubilant affection that was mutually returned as the two young men hugged. Danny winced at Clint's two hundred fifteen pounds of brute force, but only from his recovery of the fist pump he received earlier from Carter in the small of his back.

"Happy birthday, brother!" Clint yelled at Danny even though his face was in his chest.

"Thank you," Danny mumbled.

"You ready?" Wynton called out as he walked around his van to join.

Danny's heart was filled with elation. He couldn't think of a greater bond than the cohesion between these men. No one made him feel truer to himself whether good or nefarious than these young men. Brothers in every sense of the word, but something was missing.

"Where's Marshall?" he asked.

"He's riding with Mike and his girlfriend, RaShonda," Carter said.

"RaShonda?" Danny asked, "Who the hell is RaShonda? What happened to Pam or Vicky or...?"

Carter rolled his eyes, "You know Brother Mike."

Danny nodded, but he really wasn't that close to Mike Campbell, his bond was with Marshall Whitacre.

In Danny's eyes, the formation of the Family started at the house of the Hawkins, but it was Marshall Whitacre who had forged the nucleus of the Family a group of young men who came together via academics and sports at school who rode together from 1974 until that very day.

Through the slush in the gas mart's lot rode a tan 1978 Cadillac Eldorado coupe. As it pulled into the empty lane next to Darnell's.

Baron and Larry immediately swarmed upon it. Baron to the driver's side and Larry to the passenger's attempting to jump the driver and passengers trick again.

The passenger door popped open before the car engaged in park bumping Larry to fall on his backside in the snow.

Offering a hand, Marshall's light shone against a dark green hooded down jacket contrasted Larry's berry-colored jacket. The thickness of hands and the sizes of their features were extremely complimentary as a bond between the two surpassed even that of the relationship between Danny, Nick, Wynton, and Clinton.

Pulling Larry up from the snow, Marshall dapped his fraternity brother.

"What's up, brother?" Marshall asked Larry nonchalantly.

Larry wiped himself off after returning the handshake.

Baron leaned into the driver's side looking toward the backseat.

"Good evening, Madam," he greeted RaShonda Wallace.

RaShonda Wallace may have been in the long line of girls that fell under the attraction of Mike Cantrell, but none rode as hard as she. She had the quality of an Ebony Fashion model, but she was one of the toughest cookies any of the guys had ever encountered due to her army brat upbringing.

Mike, fully bearded, sitting in a military camouflage jacket with dog tags dangling from his neck punched Baron off, "What do I look like, nigga?"

Baron opened the car door and embraced Mike whose hard demeanor was the glue of the members, even those who never made it.

"What's up with them over there?" Mike asked.

"Recruits," Baron said.

"Really?" Mike set up with full attention. "When, tonight?"

Marshall said, "Naw. Tonight's Danny's birthday. Tomorrow, we break them in."

"Cool," Mike said. "What we waiting for? Let's get this party started."

BOOK 2 — TO THE LODGE

The trek from Kenosha to Dodgers Lake was no more than a twenty-minute ride under normal conditions. As the snow continued to pelt the streets it made driving conditions treacherous adding an additional thirty minutes to the trip as the driving lanes shifted from four to two.

Darnell led the caravan now with Nick in his car as Danny shifted over to ride with Wynton, Clinton, Carter, and Larry in the van who were trailed by Mike, RaShonda, Marshall, and Baron in the El Dog.

"Shit, how far is this muthafucka?" Mike asked. "I could be in Minnesota any minute for how long it's taken to get to this place."

"I hope we didn't pass it," Baron said. "We should have been there a while back."

"So, what's the game plan for tonight?" Mike asked. "These snacks ain't gonna cut it."

Mike had settled into the driver's seat leaning so far back his head could barely be seen past the dashboard. His chair pushed back leaving little leg room for Baron to stretch out his.

In the back seat of the Cadillac, nestled between Marshall and Baron were three white plastic bags of chips, candy and assorted cookie treats. Enough to hopefully hold down a vat of liquor they all intended to imbibe that night once they were tucked into a safe environment.

"We are going to get Danny boy tore up from the floor up," Baron said. "He is never going to forget his twenty-first birthday."

"We got enough?" Mike asked.

"In the van?" Baron asked. "More than enough."

The wiper blades moved feverishly back and forth on the van's windshield. Numerous times Clint had offered to replace the shredded right one that left a smeared streak of water residue on the window blurring his view. Wynton had forgotten to check the automotive section in the gas mart, beelining instead to grab handfuls of beef jerky and canisters of nuts.

They were barely on Springfield Road heading to the resort when Wynton popped the aluminum container for salted cashews that he generously shared with his buddy.

Danny sitting in a bucket seat directly behind Clint reached for a handful from the can as well.

Clint swiveled his chair and turned toward Danny.

"What up, dog? How's the job?" Clint innocently asked.

Danny lowered his head as he slowly chewed cashews.

"Long story, short," he said. "I have to make a decision on a job Monday."

"Really?" Wynton eagerly said. "You're going to be on the air?"

"No."

"But you're going to be working for the same station?" Clint followed up.

"Yeah," Danny reflected aloud. "Actually, two stations. They have an AM outlet that I would also sell for."

"Sales?" Wynton asked.

"Yep," Danny said.

"How much money you gonna be making?" Larry chimed in.

"Yeah, that's the initial problem," Danny said pensively as the van fell silent. "No salary. Commission only."

"What?" came the collective response.

"That shit is foul," Carter blurted out. "How they expect you to survive when you starting out?"

"I gotta earn my keep," Danny softly said as he wondered how his father would respond if he chose that direction.

What was the point of four years of college with a Broadcast Communications degree when he could have gotten a sales job out of college? Hell, he could have done that in Cincinnati at WCIN.

It wasn't like his parents expected any money back from his education. Not at all, but the least he could do was give them the satisfaction that their hard-earned money went to a career that they had sustained.

As Clint turned back to navigate in the front passenger seat, Danny became aware of a small clinking sound from behind him.

He turned his neck to catch Carter sitting behind him rustling inside a duffle bag.

Carter eyed him and produced the wooden handle to a paddle with an engraving of the fraternity whittled on it.

Danny rolled his eyes toward Larry sitting next to him nodding his head ecstatically.

This had been a problem for a while now. Initiating Clinton and Wynton into the "FAMILY" had been in discussions for over a month. Danny and Nick had fought feverishly against the idea of an initiation of any sort citing that none of the so-called original members were ever treated to such a barbaric indoctrination.

They had banded together from football at Proviso. Larry and Danny actually transferred from a private school in their sophomore year. Danny landed on the sophomore squad while Larry was elevated within days of enrollment to the varsity team due to just raw instincts and spectacularly innate abilities.

Danny was on special team squads with Carter and Nick, while Baron, Marshall, and Mike welcomed Larry to the offensive line of the varsity team. Larry was elevated to co-captain before his first season of school was completed.

Larry actually had received a scholarship to play ball for Oklahoma but couldn't sustain himself in his junior year as the need for money became overwhelming due to family constraints. By that time, he and Marshall had rushed it was well after becoming freshmen. Both were deemed natural born leaders on their teams as well as the campuses and were accepted everywhere they went.

When both came home, their frat ways nestled into the 'Family' dynamic with everyone except Danny and Nick. Even bringing Darnell into the fold presented an initiation for which the two were sidelined until a more peaceful resolution was presented.

Danny and Nick also argued for Wynton and Clinton when hazing possibilities were presented such as slapping Icy Blue on their genitalia. Danny wanted to know which genius was going to be holding either's balls and if they'd like to hold his as well.

Icy Blue was out the window as was anything else remotely associated with hazing concepts. No whips, no chains, tapes, tether balls, or paddles. This wasn't Animal House. None of them was Neidemeier or Chip Miller.

Agreed.

But now, Danny saw the paddle.

"Put it away, now," he said.

Carter was his boy. He may have been gambling as he zipped the bag up, but he and Danny had been close friends since fourth grade. He had no problems acquiescing.

Danny's tolerance for Larry's brand of crazy had its limits. They had come close to tussles before. This was an issue Danny was willing to get his noggin cracked for. He wanted no parts of that fraternity lifestyle in the 'Family' with no disrespect to his 'frat brothers.'

Danny turned forward trying to catch a glimpse of the Gold Fiero which Wynton rode bumper for close to a mile not to lose him.

Inside the Fiero, Darnell followed the taillights of a truck until he could see to his right, the illuminating beacon of the resort.

"The entrance must be close by," he informed Nick who sat just taking in the blizzard like conditions with nary a worry in the world. "Let me know when I get to the gate."

"Right," Nick yelled, "now!"

The car fishtailed onto a small pathway that was completely covered with snow.

The van behind nearly careened into the sports coupe as Wynton almost bumped the car as he cut to the right. His headlights blinding Darnell's vision as well as illuminating a path for him to follow. Darnell cut the rays of the van's lights from intruding on his sightline by cutting the glare from the rearview mirror.

The Eldorado kept its distance as it tracked behind the two vehicles but keeping pace with both until they cleared a forest of trees and saw the gray tiling of the lodge's roof.

Darnell edged the car passed the entrance offering enough room for the van and the Cadillac to park.

Turning to Nick, he smiled. "We're here."

Darnell shut the ignition off and popped his door open. Nick did the same, slamming his door shut to bolt up a flight of snow-covered steps that led to the lodge's entrance.

The van idled a moment after Wynton shut the engine off. Danny was out the side door as Carter jumped out the back with the display tire. Snow descended upon their heads within seconds. Both raced to stand next to Nick.

Mike and RaShonda covered up and slowly took the stairs to the lodge like the king and queen of the ball, with Baron and Marshall in quick tow.

Wynton, Clinton, and Larry caught Darnell at the stairs and made their way up as the others were already entering the quaint low-lit lodge.

CHECK IN

*D*arnell and Nick pulled the Oakwood doors open to enter the lodge. A sign posted above welcomed all to the Dodgers Lake Resort.

Patting themselves off, free of the remnants of snow dropped on their bomber jackets, they stopped immediately to locate the front desk which was tucked away in a corner nearly twenty yards from where they stood.

The rustic look of shiplap wood covering nearly every wall against the marble floor popped out at them creating a crisscross accent wall.

There was a woodsy smell to the place like fresh pine and wintergreen.

Wynton was next to enter followed behind Clinton and Carter.

"What's up?" Wynton asked Darnell as he dapped him. "Long time, no see."

Darnell nodded, acknowledging, "Yeah, been like a few months. What's been happening?"

"Oh, you know," Wynton said nonchalantly. "Another day, another oil fire."

"Another one?" Danny shouted as he entered catching the tail end of the conversation. "You trying to lose another job?"

"This one wasn't my fault," Wynton said defensively.

"Yeah," Clinton chimed in. "It's those darn gas lines that can't seem to shut themselves off."

The five men burst out laughing much to Wynton's expense. Since college, it wasn't his first incident attributed to malfeasance. He'd had three charges levied against him since he got his degree in chemical engineering. He prided himself as a hands-on learner which was his strong suit as his academic GPA record was barely 2.5. He was book smart, just not exactly exam savvy. Trouble shooting had become his expertise since he entered the workforce and it was an invaluable shell in his arsenal. He was mostly loved because of his self-deprecating humor which he shared with Clinton, Danny, and Nick.

The registration desk made also of the oak with a blend of cedar as its pattern sat barren until emerging from a side door, a cadre of three maroon blazered clerks appeared.

Congregating around the front desk one male and two females straightened up materials on the desk as Larry, Baron, and RaShonda entered the confines of the lodge's entrance. Larry stood at the door stomping his tan bucks removing the snow and slush off his heels and onto the marble floor.

Marshall and Mike entered the building engaged in a mildly passionate discussion.

Baron walked casually toward Darnell and Nick taking a stutter step as he approached them.

"What's the hold up?" Baron asked.

He continued to walk past them as he acknowledged the front desk ready to take charge having been cooped in a vehicle of mostly Cheeto-breath young men, himself also included.

Following suit, Darnell and Nick found themselves in step with Baron as Darnell patted his pant pockets, searching for paperwork detailing the resort reservation.

Danny stood awestruck by the layout of the lodge. Transfixed as one would be by the realization of familiarity.

"No shit," he said to himself aloud.

Clinton turned his attention toward Danny's odd demeanor and asked, "What's wrong?"

Danny shook his head trying to wake from his trance as he said, "I've been here before."

Clinton tapped Wynton as he approached Danny.

"Really?" Clinton asked. "When? I thought this place was new."

"Naw, not new, dog," Danny replied. "This is where Lamont died."

"Here?" Wynton challenged. "Impossible. This is their grand opening."

Danny walked toward a ramp that led to a suite of rooms.

"Not a grand opening," he observed. "More like a re-opening."

RaShonda broke away as she watched Danny zombie walk toward the ramp. "Is he alright?" she asked as she joined Clint and Wynton.

Clint explained, "He thinks he's been here before."

RaShonda nodded as she followed up, "Like déjà vu?"

Wynton also nodded, "Kind of. He thinks this is the hotel where his cousin died."

RaShonda, frowning, took this bit of information in quickly and said, "Oh, my. But isn't this a grand opening?"

"Ya think?" Danny asked facing the three of them. "I know this place like the back of my hand."

RaShonda had not been long with the group since meeting Mike, but she was like a den mother to them even though she was no more than twenty-two years of age.

She'd also played matchmaker to a couple of guys. Baron and Marshall had been fairly successful, but Danny was too silly and immature. Her girls were not impressed, but she was drawn to him like a big sister.

"You okay?" she asked.

Danny snapped out of the trance he was in. The place had a new interior design from the cold metallic Euro look it once had, but he was certain of its layout. He'd gotten lost to be sure.

"Yeah, I'm good," he assured her as he walked back to the main floor toward her.

She wrapped her arms around him and gave him a peck on the cheek, "Happy birthday, huh?"

A sheepish grin cut into his face.

"Yeah."

"Twenty-one, huh, big man," she chided.

"Yeah, finally legal," he said.

She pulled him closer and looked him in the eyes. He had two inches on her even with her heels on, but she was staring dead at him.

"What happened with Darlene?" she asked as she hit him hard.

He wanted to let go of her, but he couldn't resist her. She was going to be there all night.

"I fucked up," Danny said.

"Uh huh," she scolded wagging her index finger at him. "You sure did."

Her eyes burned inside his soul. He wanted to look away like a child.

"I can fix things for you, but you have to want this," she said. "Do you want me to fix this?"

Danny hedged, he didn't really want to commit, and he was relinquishing his decision to her and answered, "I don't know."

"Tell you what," RaShonda relaxed her position, "I'm going to give you the weekend to think it over, okay?"

Danny nodded with relief. No pressure for at least 24 hours.

"So, what's bothering you?" she asked.

Danny released her.

"It's nothing," he said. "I just thought for a moment...It's nothing."

Her eyes rested on his face surveying him as she looked for

cracks. She let him go, then headed toward the desk joining Baron, Darnell, and Nick. Mama Bear coming through.

Darnell had spread out the sheet he retrieved from his back pocket. A male clerk seemed solemn as RaShonda rested her elbows on the desk.

Turning toward Darnell, she asked, "What's going on?"

Darnell, confused, tried to keep his composure, "It appears there is some confusion on our arrival."

The clerk kept his head down to remain professional.

"I am so sorry for this inconvenience, sir," the clerk said. "We tried to communicate to everyone that our opening was going to be delayed. Some of the suites aren't fully prepared."

Darnell, always level-headed, tried to find reason.

"Are there any rooms open tonight?" he said. "We've driven from all corners and just need a place to stay for the night."

The clerk turned to a blond-haired counterpart for an assist. Her eyes were as blank as his, she relented finally resorting to the stock answer, "Let me check in our office to see if there is something we can work out."

The male clerk brushed his name tag, Chad, and nodded extensively, "Thank you, Katie."

Katie nodded in return and she headed for a door adjacent to the desk. She knocked twice on the door, opened it, then she disappeared while the door shut behind her.

Mike and Marshall glided toward the desk passed Danny, Clint, and Wynton.

"What's going on, guys?" Mike asked loudly with no care about his voice level.

Baron whipped around but noticed RaShonda already hushing him.

"What?" was his response.

The two clerks, Chad and his other counterpart, Kylie were boxed in by the desk, management door to their right and a mirrored wall to their left.

Baron tried to explain the situation to both men as Danny walked toward them. The door swung open as his eyes fell on the mirror when he thought he saw sitting at a desk facing the door a mirage; the ghost from his past, LaMonica Haynes.

He rushed to the desk as the door shut and Kylie walked to the desk a little flush. She stepped to Chad and whispered for him to push away from the desk.

As they converged by the door, Kylie placed her hand over her face as she explained the plan. Chad rolled his eyes at their audience and nodded understanding his role. Katie stood alone with the guys trying to surround her.

Chad approached the desk and cleared his throat.

"It appears, we may have your suite available very shortly," he said.

"How shortly?" Baron asked. "We're very tired and very hungry."

Chad, distracted, tried to regroup, "Well, we should be able to get you in within the hour. However, the restaurant is closed until six tomorrow morning."

Katie offered copies of a folded brochure, "But we do have a late menu you can order off of."

The crew looked at each other.

Baron grabbed the brochures, "How many of these do you have?"

FAITH

"Would you like to touch me?"

Danny sat on the couch holding the forty-ounce tightly when those words came to him.

"Jimmy says he feels close to God when he touches me."

Danny clung tightly to the sweating bottle taking small sips to wash down the dry turkey club with the rubbery bacon and wet lettuce. The chips had nearly cut his gums they were so rigid. The alcohol from the beer stung a little when it hit his teeth.

Using the small dinette table, the guys had broken out a game of Spades. The teams consisted of Marshall and Mike against Baron and Larry. RaShonda stood over Mike as he occasionally showed her his hand careful to block it as Larry tried to sneak a gander at the cards he held.

Playing to a hundred books, Baron, the score keeper etched hash marks to run the tally. Marshall and Mike had a comfortable lead of seventy-one to fifty-two against Baron and Larry.

"No cross talking!" Larry shouted as he himself kept trying to engage Baron due to his very own inconsistent play.

"I got next," Ricky said to the players. Ricky glanced toward

Danny, cognizant of the glare that alternated between him and Trudy.

"I'm with you," Carter said. "I'm Ricky's partner, y'all. What's the score?" Antsy, Carter looked over his brother's shoulder and shook his head. Baron lowered his card hand as he could feel Carter breathing down his neck.

"Do you mind?" he asked warily.

"Don't you want to feel good?"

Danny closed his eyes as the beer took effect. It had been a very long day and he just wanted to forget what he knew he needed to focus on. Would he take the job offer or would he go back to Al Parker's office and take the internship that was initially offered? Try again. What if it held him back from graduating until summer? His father would flip.

"Here, take my hand."

Danny's eyes darted back and forth between Trudy with the biggest brown eyes just batting them as if she idolized Ricky. Ricky who was no better than Jimmy Reese.

Thank God, Jimmy, wasn't there. Danny felt for sure he would smash his face with the bottle he was clutching to for dear life.

While he had only lived five blocks, south of the Reese family, Danny hadn't met Jimmy until his freshmen year of high school on the porch of the Hawkins family.

The family itself had been initiated on the very steps of 2402 S. 2nd Avenue where everyone converged after the second day of the two-a-days regiment they were forced into that August summer.

Danny had known the Hawkins since 1971 when the family transferred from Paw-Paw, Michigan to Maywood for Mr. Hawkins' job with Loyola Hospital system's analysis.

The Hawkins boys entered his fourth-grade class two weeks after school began. Danny became friends with both brothers within days, loving the symbiotic bond the two just had as siblings.

Baron and Carter, while uniquely different, just had a presence in their own right and Danny fell under their spell.

Their mother was somewhat apprehensive of friends they attracted and treated all of them including Danny like stray cats she needed to shoo away.

Their father was more open, happy to see his sons had adjusted so readily, so easily, progress as the true charismatic leaders they were.

Baron was extremely bright, intelligent, athletic, and just a natural leader. All through grade school, there was rarely any activity or event he wasn't taking the lead on. Generally, receiving ninety-eight percent participation to all he reached out to.

Carter was more introspective, pensive at times, immature, but he had an artistic eye that every one of his peers gravitated toward by the sheer genius of his work. His creativity knew no boundaries and every day it changed as he adapted to the medium placed before him. He, too, showed a rare gift of athleticism, but was usually overshadowed by his older brother.

Danny also had the privilege to endeavor their baby sister, Faith, a precocious little bubbly spirit of a girl who was without a doubt the apple of her parents' eyes, a companion to her eldest brother on occasion, and a pain in the ass to her middle sibling.

Faith had entered high school in Danny's senior year. She joined the Pom-Pom Squad and was a much an honor roll student as her eldest brother. That was when Jimmy fell for her.

Danny missed a portion of the football season after the injury to his knee and Lamont's death. He had also stepped away from the church vowing that he had no need to believe in a higher power that would take the life of such a good kid and create the mental anguish his mother went through. He let his position be known and it was with the Christian healing hands of the Hawkins family that let Danny have a place to grieve knowing that he would find his way back to God in time.

"Jimmy says he feels God when he touches me. Don't you want to touch me and feel good?"

Danny had found himself at the Hawkins doorstep during the

Christmas holiday. He had left the basketball tournament early and just wandered by the house. Given he lived slightly over a mile from the school, he stopped there to break the chill on the seven-degree winter day.

Faith opened the door much to his surprise. She had the widest, most perfect smile no dentist had ever had the opportunity to tamper with. Sunshine on a cloudy day, and effervescent from the good nature she exuded. If Danny had a baby sister, he wanted one just like Faith.

Informing him of Carter's presence in the house, Danny entered cautiously always mindful of Mrs. Hawkins cardinal rule of no guests in the house alone with Faith.

He followed Faith into the living room where the Magnavox 19" color television sat on a wooden table with the pane window behind it.

She offered him a seat on the family sofa where he sat on many a visit. She was the spitting image of her mother. As if she had been cloned from her mother's genes. Even her laugh was the same. She asked if she could get him anything, to which Danny politely declined except for letting Carter know he was there.

She smiled and walked in her bare feet down the hallway to a door. She opened it and said, "Carter, someone here to see you."

There was no reply as she shut the door and returned to sit in her mother's recliner.

Danny sat on a couch and turned his attention to the television. On the screen was a WTTW cooking show. Faith in every way had outstanding culinary skills much like her mother.

She watched everything her mother did in the kitchen and not only mimicked her but emulated her cooking to perfection.

Danny had been privy to many a meal at the Hawkins household as had Marshall, Larry, Mike, and Jimmy. The original members of the "Family." The Hawkins family shared what they had, always. Mrs. Hawkins had embraced these young men over the years as they transitioned. She became their mother, their counsel, their confidant.

She fed their hearts, as Mr. Hawkins fed their minds. Not one of the boys ever went hungry, nor without high school degrees.

Faith intently watched the screen taking mental notes on Julia Child's preparation of a roasted chicken.

"I can do that," Faith exclaimed. "I know I can do that."

Danny turned to her, impressed, "You can do that? It looks awfully..."

Lost for words, she gave him, "Frilly?"

Danny nodded, "Yeah." He tilted his head rocking it left to right. "Not exactly the word I would use. More frou-frou. Way to 'exotic,' that's the word, way to exotic for me."

She laughed, "Not if I make it for you."

Danny was astounded at how cocksure she was of herself.

"Really? You can make this?"

She boasted. "In my sleep. But I wouldn't use the paprika. I've got other seasonings I would substitute."

"Damn," Danny blurted. His hands immediately went to his mouth. "Sorry."

"I could make it for you sometime if you like," she said rather empathetic.

There was a blast of silence as she looked to him.

"Would you like that?"

Danny was unsure what she meant, "You making it for the family?" he asked.

"Maybe, but I could make it for you if you'd like."

Danny was thick as mud at that moment.

"How are you Danny?" she finally asked as if she had been holding onto that for an eternity.

Awkwardly, Danny said, "Fine. I'm fine. Why?"

She stood and suddenly commanded the presence of her mother to take over. She slowly walked toward him; the floor creaked as she gingerly took a step.

"I sometimes cook for Jimmy," she said. "He's tried my cooking many times."

Danny laughed, "That fat pig would eat anyone's cooking."

"Uh-uh," she said as she slowly moved toward him. "He especially likes my cooking. More than anyone else's."

Danny felt a twinge. He was confused. Was she talking metaphorically? He truly doubted it.

"We haven't talked much, you and me, but I have known you the longest," she said as she sat next to him on the couch. There was a quilt that covered the seating that suddenly rose and slid off the back.

She grabbed his left hand, "Take my hand."

Danny's palm was sweaty as she wrapped it between her two.

"Jimmy likes to hold my hand after I've fed him."

"Jimmy some boy you met at school?" Danny asked with much trepidation.

She laughed lightly and put her head on his shoulder.

"I want you to know, if you need anything from me, you can ask," she surrendered. "I want you to feel good. I want to see you smile again."

"I smile," Danny said as he slowly withdrew his hand from hers.

She placed her hands in his lap and lifted her head, "Jimmy says he feels God when he holds my hand. Jimmy says he feels God when he touches me." Her eyes fell onto Danny's as she began to lean her head in. "Don't you want to feel good?"

Her lips parted as she moved closer.

The door to the basement squeaked as it opened. The clomping footsteps followed behind it, then a slam as it closed.

"Hey, DJ?" Carter's voice called out. "Gimme a second, I got to go to the bathroom."

Danny's eyes widened as he stood from the couch and ran to greet Carter who stood groggy eyed in boxer shorts and a ripped t-shirt.

"Take your time, blood," Danny said with relief.

Trudy sat on Ricky's lap almost like a victim with nowhere to go as Ricky clamped her face with one hand and turned it toward him for a kiss.

Her eyes dejected, came upon Danny's.

"She's fucking seventeen, man," Danny shouted as he rose from the couch. "Get your fucking hands off her."

Ricky stood up tossing Trudy off his lap as he saw Danny change his position with the bottle of malt liquor ready to attack.

Grabbing a bottle off the card table to defend himself, Ricky held the neck in his palm ready to strike as Nick and Clint held off Danny's mounting and Marshall and Mike took hold of Ricky.

"Bitch, nigga," Danny said. "Go find someone your own age."

RaShonda wrapped her hand around Trudy's wrist and swung her toward the guest bedroom as Trudy screamed at Danny, "You ain't my daddy. I'm tired of you." Tears flowed from the confusion she felt.

Clint lifted Danny, sweeping him off the floor as Nick guided them both to the main bedroom with Danny kicking frantically for freedom, but unable to get out of Clint's grasp.

Ricky reached for his coat and shook off Marshall and Mike's advances.

"I'm tired of that nigga!" Ricky shouted. "If he tries to put his hands on me again, I'm gonna knock him the fuck out! Believe that!"

Ricky headed for the door and flung it open.

"Bitch, nigga!" Danny's voice came muffled from behind the bedroom door.

Ricky reached for the door to slam it closed, but a spring load wouldn't allow it.

"Where you going?" Baron asked as he lay his cards down.

"Out," Ricky growled letting the door close on its own.

RICKY

Ricky found himself outside the compound as snow gently fell upon him. He pulled the fur lined collar of his bomber jacket up to save his drip curl from the giant flakes that billowed downward.

His intention was to run to an AMPM, get a dog and a beverage. When he cooled off, he'd probably go one-on-one against Danny, and shut him up once and for all.

He found himself mumbling. He couldn't believe he could get so riled up over something that happened nearly eight years ago. They were in eighth grade for goodness sake, he thought. He wasn't that kid.

He'd show them. After he put something in his belly. Probably have to buy Trudy a candy bar or some chips as well. He had some plans for her that night. And to hell with whether she was eighteen or not. She looked eighteen, said she was eighteen, and felt like she was eighteen. She might as well be eighteen. She had no reason to lie to him. But what if she wasn't eighteen? What if Danny was right? She was here with him, though. She had to know why she was there. She wasn't going home without him getting those drawers. They had driven over two and a half hours to get here through the wintry snow. Damn right, she knew what time it was.

She better be eighteen, he thought.

He looked in the parking lot and was suddenly unsure where he had parked. He pulled his keychain out and hit the alarm on his remote.

Nothing. He hit it again as he looked for the '80 Riviera. Certain he had parked on the side overlooking the main lodge next to Darnell's Jack-in-the-Box Fiero.

He saw no sign of that car nor did he have a view of the lodge.

He hit the remote again, and still nothing. He walked row after row in the expansive lot.

The snow began to fall harder. He was the only soul outside. He believed he had been walking in circles for at least fifteen minutes further away from the time share units.

He tried to remember some landmark, but nothing came to him.

He decided to walk back to the building and retrace his steps. He must've parked on the other side.

As he began to trek back, he noticed fresh footprints from a rather large set of boots that were not matching the treads on his Chuck's.

Odd, he hadn't seen anyone outside the entire time he chased his tail looking for his beater. But these tracks were deep and lay next to his trail of footprints.

As he approached the steps to the entrance, he pumped the black remote once more. Just the sound of the winter gale at his back whooshed over him.

He reached for the door to pull it open, and found it locked.

"Damn!" he shouted.

A small sticker displayed on the window gave hours that the door was open. Otherwise, to enter through the main entrance on the other side.

He shook on the metal handle hoping it would unlatch. Nothing.

"Shit!" he exclaimed loudly.

He banged on the door in hopes of someone hearing him. The glass rattled. He feared he'd smash it.

He believed he saw a shadow down the end of a hallway. His hand was freezing, but he continued to knock with his palm.

His eyes were locked on the figure as it shifted his way. He released a series of slams that he was sure could be heard.

The figure turned away and disappeared.

Grabbing at the door handle, Ricky ferociously shook it.

"Hey!" he yelled to no avail.

His hand hammered away at the glass plate. He stopped as he saw a reflection behind him. He turned, but no one was there. His attention went back to the glass plated door. He cupped his hands to try to peep inside.

His hands were freezing. Snow had layered itself on his shoulders and began to wet his collar.

Again, he saw a reflection behind him in the glass. He turned, but only saw a fresh set of boot prints.

He backed away from the door and decided to walk to the other side.

The building's length was easily a block long, but he felt he had to have parked in another lot. The lodge had to be on the other side.

He moved to the right to walk with the wind currents that swirled around him. A light non- accumulating drift fell onto his back tickling his neck.

He quickened his steps as he found himself walking in a few layers of fresh snow coming up to his ankles.

He turned the corner of the building as a strong gale slapped his face. The lights overhead illuminated brightly casting his shadow forward.

Each step appeared to find itself deeper in the trenches of snow as he began to see the crest of the lodge ahead. He breathed a sigh of relief knowing he was heading in the right direction.

A crunching sound came from behind him. He turned but was met with a dose of snow.

A shadow fell upon the building's side, but he couldn't make out what could be creating it. Before he could turn back, he heard his name.

"Ricky," the voice said softly. He shook it off to just the wind blowing.

Before he could turn back toward the lot, a bulb exploded. Glass shards shattered blowing toward him. Another light blew out. Sparks fired down as another light went out.

Ricky began to dart toward the parking lot lifting his feet high, kicking through the snow.

Another light flared out, outpacing Ricky as he headed to the lot.

He cut off the path to avoid the broken glass and fragmented filaments. He picked up his pace aware that his heartbeat pounded in his ears, but so did the return of the footsteps behind him.

He never turned to look behind him as he hit the remote on his car. The chirp of the alarm and the flash of his brake lights were a source of comfort.

A few cars down to freedom.

His strides got longer as he stretched toward his navy-blue cruiser. He reached for the door with his hand on the door handle, only to slip and fall.

The car keys left his hand and slid under the chassis. Bumping his head hard on the pavement, he slit his ear on the run of his back-left tire.

The warmth of the trickling blood on his chilled ear sent him into a frenzy.

"Shit," he spewed. He turned onto his stomach and searched for the key set as the snow-covered pavement froze his stomach.

He opened his left hand and stretched to find the keys under the darkness.

He was beginning to lose feeling in his fingertips when he decided to pull back. Coming off his hands and knees, he ran to the passenger's side of the car.

Dropping down again flat on his stomach he reached again. This time his fingers grazed the remote. He just needed to change the angle and wriggle a little more underneath.

He did his best to see where his digits roamed, but while he could make out the outline of his hand, he saw nothing else but snow on the other side of the car.

A pair of brown buck-skinned boots appeared on the other side, jolting him.

"Hey," he asked, "can you give me a hand?"

The feet stayed in position as Ricky finally felt his fingers wrap around the key ring. His finger enclosed on the loop and he slowly dragged the key set toward him.

The boots never moved.

"Never mind," he said, "Got 'em."

He felt a pair of hands grab his ankles and pull him from under the car as his gaze fixed on the pair of boots.

His car alarm began to blare at an ear pitch scream, muffling the cries he emitted simultaneously.

No more than ten seconds for the alarm's screech before it shut off.

The entire lot went silent...

Ricky was gone.

PARTY TIME

~~~

She sat on her knees bouncing off the mattress as RaShonda opened her Samsonite traveling suitcase.

Pulling the cover off, RaShonda did her best Carol Merrill showing her the contents inside.

"Girl," Trudy said, "why you got all this stuff with you for an overnight?"

Slightly older than Trudy, RaShonda carried herself as worldly or at least well-traveled. An army brat, she was always packed and ready to hit the road. She just upgraded the material.

"We're going back home tomorrow to hit the Water Tower," she said. "I have some things I have to return to Lord and Taylor."

Gingerly, RaShonda dug into the travel case and shifted toiletry items to remove a crimson colored cocktail dress. She pulled at it with help from Trudy who found herself at odds, afraid to even touch it daring herself to not let it rip one little bit.

Ankles crossed, Trudy rose on her knees as she passed the garment over to RaShonda who hoisted it the rest of the way, twirling around with it clinging to her.

"It's Armani, girl," RaShonda said gleefully as she displayed the tag in the collar of the dress as well as the price tag that she had tucked inside. "Guess how much," she said to Trudy like a striptease dancer.

Trudy, accustomed to long shopping sprees with her older sister smiled and guessed, "Four hundred dollars."

RaShonda stopped mid-twirl, twisted her head to glance at Trudy, "Lucky guess."

She moved to a full-length mirror sitting next to an Oakwood chest of drawers.

Admiring herself, she positioned the dress in front of her holding it on her tall frame.

"I love this dress, but," she said.

"It looks fantastic," Trudy admired. "Why are you taking it back?"

She smiled at her reflection as she said, "Already wore it once. Gotta return it in less than thirty days to get my money back."

RaShonda twirled on her bare feet once again letting the shag carpet dance between her toes, tickling her. She pivoted back as the amusement wore off. She stared at her image, then shifted her gaze to Trudy.

"How long you been with Ricky?" she asked.

Trudy sat up after peeking into the luggage case holding a bottle of Chanel No. 5 in her grasp.

"I'm not with Ricky," she said. "Not really."

RaShonda craned her neck and curled her plump lips, "Girl, you with him now. You rode all the way out here with him. Whatchu think you here for?"

Trudy placed the bottle back into the bag next to a pair of strapped heels.

A light knock came upon the door startling both young ladies.

"You alright in there?" Baron asked.

"Yeah, we're going to need a couple minutes," RaShonda said back.

"Let me know if you need anything, okay?" Baron asked.

"Okay," both said. They held themselves for a moment to suppress laughter. The tension had been broken and both were tentatively relieved.

"You with Ricky," RaShonda said to Trudy much to her chagrin.

Baron crossed the hallway and grabbed the bedroom door's brass handles. He barged right in as Danny sat on the edge of the bed, with his fingers wrapped around the forty-ounce.

Clint and Nick stood side by side against an accent wall staring at Baron. They had gone to battle to contain Danny with exhaustion written on their faces as sweat poured down their cheeks.

"You okay?" Baron flatly asked Danny.

Danny raised the bottle over his head and nodded. "I'm good," he said.

"Cool," Baron said as he walked inside. He glanced back at Clint and Nick who moved aside heading toward the door. "How about you two?"

They nodded in unison.

Clint turned to Danny and asked, "What was that all about?"

Danny looked up at Baron, standing before him, shrugged his shoulders as he said, "She's a baby, man. A little girl."

"She's almost nineteen, Danny," Nick said. "How old did you think she was? We've known her since we were five – six years old. C'mon."

"Really?" Danny questioned. He shrugged.

Larry peered inside to assess the possible damage. "Y'all good?" he asked.

Larry stepped into the room and headed toward Danny. Clapping his hands together, he smiled at Danny adding, "It's time, my brother."

Nick and Clint were already out the door walking into the suite's living room.

Baron looked at his watch. "It sure is."

Danny raised his head.

"You're officially legal," Marshall said.

Larry patted Danny on his back to get him up. "It's that time. C'mon."

Danny jumped up from the pounding Larry was consistently delivering to his shoulder blades.

He half jogged to the doorway. Across the way Trudy and RaShonda were also stepping out of the guest room. As RaShonda waddled toward Mike, Trudy stood and gave a stink-eye to Danny. Danny let it go.

Following behind the two women, Danny found himself stopping in front of the card table, which now became the center of twenty-one shot glasses filled with different colored liquids in each one.

"Happy birthday, partner," Marshall said patting Danny on his back.

Others chimed in except for Trudy who stood by amused.

"Y'all gonna drink all these shots?" she asked innocently.

Baron grinned. He couldn't hold it in. "No, Brother Danny is going to drink each shot."

"Or whatever is left," Larry chimed in, "is how many licks we give him." Like the mad man he actually was, he turned toward Danny as he reached for a shot glass.

"Drink up."

Danny took the glass in his hand. He saluted everyone before bringing it to his lips.

His hand brought the liquor to his face, he scrunched his nose at the smell of the pure grain alcohol and asked, "All twenty-one shots?"

Marshall, Mike, and Carter cheered him on.

Wynton and Clinton stood back to watch along with Nick and the girls.

Larry and Baron stood on both sides as the first sip was chugged down.

The burn in his throat shut down his passageway for air. He coughed immediately as he wiped tears from his eyes. He surrendered the shot glass to Baron, only to receive another one from Larry.

He stood incredulous as Larry wrapped an arm around him, "C'mon, Brother, twenty more to go."

PARTY UP

Trudy wondered, *what was she thinking?*

She sat on the love seat and watched as he took – what was he up to now – five shots. Taking a breather but looking more like he needed a nap.

How on Earth did she allow Ricky to lure her to this?

She sat with a Pepsi in her hands. The can was starting to sweat as it perched in her hands.

She watched as RaShonda played hostess, getting bottles of beer for Mike, Marshall, and Baron, but always with an eagle eye on Danny who just folded onto the other couch surrounded by Nick, Wynton, and Clinton as they pushed Larry away while he circled Danny like a vulture waiting to feast on him.

Sixteen shot glasses lay on the card table serving no other purpose than for Danny to prove himself a man.

Stupid ritual, Trudy thought. This is what being a man was all about, she was glad she was not one.

Where was Ricky? How could he just leave her like this? And what was Danny talking about, like he was her daddy or something?

She was ready to give him a good piece of her mind. Not that it would do any good now.

Danny's eyes were glazed over. She couldn't imagine he could hear anything any of his friends had to say.

A draft blew in and nearly froze her arms off as Darnell stood on the patio slab smoking a cigar. She could barely make him out until he puffed, and she saw the orange glow.

There was a radio on playing loudly in the background. Trudy made a big mistake when she began to sway to Evelyn "Champagne" King's 'Love Come Down.'

She closed her eyes and just let the song take her away:

> *No sleep last night*
> *Been dreaming of you*
> *Please hold me tight*
> *'Cause I can't help the way that I feel*

She got to the hook of the song when she felt the presence of someone looming over her. As she opened her eyes, to her horror, Larry stood in front of her, holding a beer bottle asking if she wanted to dance.

She tried to be polite and shook her head. She glanced over at RaShonda who was feeding potato chips to Mike.

She was trapped as the big man didn't seem to get the message the first time. She stared at him, not wanting to be rude, but he was about to be introduced to *Gertrude Patrice*.

Trudy peaked around hoping for a savior, someone to just poke their head in and rescue her.

She reached in her front pocket trying to locate a stick of gum. If Larry was going to spend all that time in her face, the most she could do was offer him a Juicy Fruit to revive whatever it was that died in his mouth and took two dumps before retiring.

She'd done the same with Ricky. She just had to be subtle. Her fingers felt for the pack, but either her jeans were too tight, or she was sitting in a position where only two fingers could get in as she pecked and hunted.

Larry was relentless. Every time Trudy was sure she had deflected his advances, he just pushed even harder. She needed him to understand she wasn't interested.

Hell, when Ricky showed up, she was letting him know she was ready to go home. She wanted out of there in the worst way.

Danny stood up. Her eyes widened as she thought for a moment, he was contacting her. His head rolled back, and he was up. Nick tried to dissuade him from making the attempt, but Danny was being the Danny she thought she knew; pigheaded to the end, even when he was in a near-liquor induced coma.

Larry was suddenly distracted.

"Yeah," he crowed as he turned toward Danny. "C'mon, get this."

Darnell and Carter came in from the cold and migrated toward the card table.

"I'll have a shot with you," Carter said. He lifted a glass as Danny stumbled to them.

Larry was licking his chops, waiting for his "brother" to fall.

Trudy saw this as her opportunity to break away from Larry, but as she traveled closer to RaShonda and Mike she moved toward a trajectory of colliding with Danny and Nick, who was trying to coax him out of taking the shot.

Clint and Wynton, in tow, quietly held the rear.

Baron, Marshall, and Mike sat but cheered Danny on as Trudy somehow found herself right next to Danny as his hands trembled reaching for the shot glass of Peach Schnapps.

Their eyes met again. She felt pity for him as the glass shook while he brought it to his lips. He steadied it to his mouth but did not immediately drink. He took deep breaths and closed his eyes as Larry and Carter chanted, "Shot, shot, shot."

Others looked on, but Trudy caught RaShonda shaking her head.

Men being boys, Trudy was sure they were both thinking.

Danny pinched the glass as he tipped it back, taking it down in a gulp.

Trudy watched with sorrow in her heart at the immaturity she felt she was witnessing.

The guys cheered him on, then headed back to their places.

Nick grabbed Danny who stood frozen in his place.

"You alright?" Nick seemed to be asking time after time.

Danny set the glass down onto the tabletop but didn't seem to want to move as Nick tried to usher him back to the couch.

Larry also appeared ready to get back to the business of that dance when Danny collapsed onto Trudy. His weight on her as she wrapped her arms instinctively around him.

"I got you," she said.

His breathing was labored, as he placed his hands around her waist.

Nick helped her move him taking small steps as Larry sneered at the block Danny threw.

Danny's head was on her shoulder and she could smell the reek of liquor. The sweetness overwhelmed her like someone wearing too much cologne.

"I'm sorry," Danny said.

"For what?" she asked.

Danny's eyes widened again in uncontrollable anguish. He bumped into Nick, as Trudy watched his Adam's apple bobble and she knew.

In the rush of excitement, she and Nick tried to get Danny to the guest bathroom.

Drool leaked from the side of his mouth. They were entering the doorway, when Danny turned toward her.

It was too late as he released himself on her side as he fell to his knees in front of the toilet.

First on her, then into the bowl.

The right side of her sweatshirt was a mess, but she held onto Danny as he spit his birthday prayer to God.

RaShonda dashed into the bathroom and immediately found a white face towel. She doused it with cold water from the faucet, wrung it out, moved Nick out of the way and knelt beside Danny resting the towel on his forehead like a compress.

"Get me another rag," RaShonda ordered Nick.

Frantic, Nick's eyes roamed the bathroom wall before reaching for another face towel. Once he followed her directive, he made a handoff and the two exchanged cloths.

"Girl, how bad did he get you?" RaShonda asked Trudy.

"It's okay," Trudy reluctantly said feeling the gook stick to her side. She felt horrible and gross as Danny's retch dripped from her side onto the floor.

"I've got a change of clothes in my bag," RaShonda said. "Go try something. I got him."

Trudy hesitated, not wanting to leave RaShonda alone as Nick stood passing face rags. Clint and Wynton blocked the doorway waiting for orders from General RaShonda.

"Come over here and get your boy," she said.

Trudy moved out the way as Clint stood over Danny whose arms wrapped around the porcelain commode.

Clint handed another to RaShonda as she showed him how to keep it against Danny's forehead.

"I'll be back," she said. As she assessed what damage she had incurred while handling Danny.

She found Trudy rummaging through her small duffel bag. She had one change of clothing that she lightly tossed on the bed.

Larry stood in the doorway when RaShonda caught sight of him.

"Uh, uh," she said as she grabbed her travel bag and took Trudy by the hand, barreling past Larry as she led them both to the master suite. She slammed the door behind them; making sure all could hear her lock it.

PARTY DOWN

*D*arnell was entering the suite with two buckets of ice. He placed one on the card table, then headed to the guest bathroom.

"RaShonda, you said you needed some ice?" Darnell asked.

The guys were tiptoeing around as RaShonda had let them know her displeasure at their immature rites of passage challenge. She had issued a list of items she thought necessary to reduce the amount of fluids Danny had been losing for the past hour.

"There wasn't any Ginger Ale or 7-Up in the pop machine," Darnell said. "I brought a couple of Pepsis though. Will that do?"

Pointing to the countertop of the double sink, she told Darnell, "Put that down here."

Darnell placed the items down, then backed out the room.

Danny was resting limply on Trudy's shoulder, unconscious and sweating profusely. He seemed to slip in and out of awareness. Whenever he awoke, he dry-heaved into the bowl. For whatever reason, he would lean toward her voice. Not that it was anymore soothing than RaShonda's, maybe more direct and less commanding. It was clearly more familiar, like home.

She sat on her knees dressed in maroon sweatpants and a hoodie from the University of Wisconsin, matching RaShonda's.

Her chest was soaked from Danny's perspiration as well as tears that seemed to flow just before he could pass out begging for the Lord's forgiveness.

She had lightly chuckled at one point and before RaShonda could take her to task like she was the boys, Trudy tried to explain, "He doesn't believe in God."

RaShonda laughed, "He sure do now, huh?"

They shared a quiet laugh at Danny's expense as he lay slumped at Trudy's bosom.

"You know," Nick said, "this is the very place that caused him to lose his faith."

They both turned toward the doorway, feeling a little guilty for their titters.

"What do you mean?" Trudy asked.

Nick walked in but keeping a distance as the odor of Danny's bile had filled the atmosphere.

"He believes we are at the hotel where his cousin drowned," he said.

"Get out of here," Trudy gasped as she wrapped Danny tighter in her grip instinctively. "This is where Lamont died?"

RaShonda, at a loss in the conversation tossed out, "Wait a minute. Who is Lamont?"

"Four years ago," Trudy said, "Danny's cousin drowned in a swimming pool while on vacation with Danny's family."

Baron popped his head through the doorway, "How's he doing?"

RaShonda shook her head, "A lot better if you all didn't act like little boys."

"Did you know this was the hotel where Lamont died?" Nick asked Baron.

A quizzical look fell upon Baron's face as he was at a loss, "Who's Lamont?"

"Danny's cousin!" RaShonda said, then modulated the pitch as her softer voice stirred Danny, "His cousin, Lamont."

Nick turned to Baron, "The one that drowned four years ago."

Baron's face went flush. "No?" he asked as he backed out the doorway and called to Darnell.

"Yeah?" Darnell called back.

"Did you know this was the place Danny's cousin drowned?" Baron asked.

"Can't be. They barely opened this place," Darnell said.

"You went to the same church, right?" Trudy asked.

"With who, him?" Baron said. "He hasn't been to church in ages."

Baron stopped. The light came on.

"Something about if the devil could stop someone from saving his cousin from drowning, then there was no God," Nick said.

"That was this place?" Darnell said. "Can't be."

Nick said, "He's been talking about it since checking in. He said something was different, but he was sure he knew the place."

Danny raised his head alarmingly, "Oh, God!" he cried out as he stuck his head back in the bowl.

His retching brought a moderate amount of bile followed by a series of spits. RaShonda grabbed the face rag again as Trudy kept his head up.

Handing the towel to Nick, RaShonda said, "Help her!" She walked out the door frame and found Mike chatting with Marshall, Carter, and Larry.

"Get your coat and your keys!" she yelled to Mike. "We got to get some things for that boy!"

Mike raised up and grabbed his jacket asking, "Where we s'pose to be going?"

As she wrapped herself in her parka she volleyed, "Whatever's open."

THE PARTY'S OVER

"Oh, God," Danny moaned as Nick and Darnell lifted him off Trudy who was finally able to stretch her legs out and reawaken them after having Danny's dead weight lean on them for the last hour.

Clint laughed lightly. "For someone who doesn't believe in God, he sure is calling his name a lot."

They dragged him toward the guest bedroom as Marshall moved bags from the guest room suite.

Trudy was flexing her thighs to get blood circulating as she followed closely behind.

"Oh, he believes in God," Nick chimed in. "He's antagonistic."

Baron laid his beer down onto the card table, chortling, "Agnostic. Not antagonistic. Although he will debate you about anything."

"Ain't that the truth," Marshall said. "And he doesn't even know half the stuff he's talking about but can make it sound good."

They sat Danny on the bed as Trudy bent down to remove his shoes.

"What's the difference?" Wynton asked.

"Means he believes in a higher power, but in Danny's case, his problem is with the denominations," Marshall said.

"What's money got to do with it?" Wynton asked.

They all pulled their heads back as Trudy peeled the shoes off Danny's feet.

"God damn, what is that smell?" Carter said.

Covering his mouth not to choke, Baron said, "His feet."

Trudy coughed as she tossed the shoes to the side. Her eyes welled up as she stumbled to get out the bedroom.

Danny fell back, gurgling as he lay face up.

"Turn him over," Baron said. "And get his socks off."

They all declined the challenge covering their faces either inside their shirts or by their sleeves.

The aroma of rotten cheese curls filled the room as each filed out immediately, laughing at the embarrassing moment they would be adding to the legend of Danny Alexander.

Carter standing by the card table still holding his collar over his nose joked, "Luke, I am your father," getting a good laugh from all except Trudy.

Darnell acknowledged Trudy's mood, "Not a *Star Wars*' fan, huh?"

Trudy shook her head, "Is that with Doctor Spock?"

The boys looked at her incredulously as she spoke the sacrilegious words.

"That's 'Star Trek'," Carter admonished her. "Mr. Spock, not Doctor."

"Sorry," she replied.

"You're forgiven," Carter said.

"So," Trudy turned her attention to a more serious topic, "when did Danny find God again?"

Nick felt her eyes on him, but he deferred to Baron, "You hung out with him during this time. When did Danny find God again?"

Baron stroked his goatee and pondered, "After his first mid-term exam in Cincinnati. He had a GPA of 1.7 after being in AP for the last two years of high school."

"Really? Wow!" Trudy said astonished. "What happened?"

Larry interjected, "Pussy!"

Taken aback by the response, she stammered, "Excuse me, what?"

Marshall cleared his throat, slightly embarrassed by the response. "What he means is, Danny discovered the pleasures of a woman when he got on campus."

"He got sprung," Larry said. "That girl put it on him good."

"What girl?" she asked.

"Some sophomore who was supposed to be his tutor," Nick contributed.

"Yeah, she tutored him alright," Larry tossed in, "In the art of love."

He put his hand out as Carter slapped him five.

"Disgusting," Trudy mused.

Nick said, "He came back home, and his father let him have it."

"Is that why he is going to school back in Chicago?" she asked.

Baron shook his head, "No, he got his GPA back up to about 2.5, but he wound up in some trouble on the campus."

"His wing got in trouble," Marshall corrected. "His name was tossed in, but he said the university never proved he was guilty in trashing a girls' dorm."

"He did what?" Trudy was astonished. She truly had no idea about Danny at all. "So, what about him being ag…"

"Agnostic," Baron said. "He found God during his finals. He was whooped by this girl whose grades went down as well. Her mother told her to drop him and she did."

"His GPA went back up when he hit those knees and prayed his father didn't beat the brakes off him," Marshall said. "He's on the Dean's List at his school now."

"Yeah," Nick said, "and you can't tell him nothing now."

"Huh," Trudy said. "Wow."

She walked back to the doorway to watch Danny who lay in the center of the bed in a fetal position.

"Can someone help me move him?" she asked.

Most of the room gave a resounding, "No," in unison.

"I'll help," Clint said.

"Me too," Wynton said. "What do you want us to do?"

"Can someone find an aerosol spray?" she said as she entered the room slowly. "Lysol or something?"

Her voice trailed off as she entered the abyss pinching her nostrils, only to dart out briefly.

Baron laughed, "That bad, huh?"

She shook her head, "No, I need some cologne. I know one of you brought some."

Darnell dashed into the main bedroom declaring, "I'll be right back. I got something."

"I think you're going to need some Holy water," Carter said.

She turned as she heard Darnell yell, "Got it!"

He bounded into the room with a black bottle of Drakkar.

Wynton laughed, "You, too? Did you get it for Christmas?"

Darnell nodded as he handed it off, "My grandmother gets it for me every year. I hate the smell, though."

"So does everyone who's with you when you wear it," said Nick. "She gets me the same thing. I refuse to use it."

Removing the cap from the bottle, Clint sprayed the second he entered the room. Wynton and Trudy followed behind.

After dousing some of the liquid on Danny's feet, the bottle was placed on the dresser's countertop.

With the bedroom smelling like an explosion at a fragrance factory, Trudy directed Clint and Wynton to lift Danny up while she peeled his shirt off. They tossed it in a corner along with his undershirt which also stuck to his side.

Goosebumps popped onto his skin as Trudy tried to warm him up. Clint gently laid him onto the pillows and tucked him under the covers with just his pants remaining.

The three walked out victorious as Wynton handed Darnell his bottle back.

"What time is it?" Nick asked.

"Why, where you gotta be?" Larry said.

"I have to be out of the dorm today by ten o'clock," Nick said. "I'm moving into an apartment off campus."

Nick waited for a response, then said, "I can use some help moving. I'll buy pizza."

Trudy turned toward them and asked, "Has anyone seen Ricky?"

GILLETTE

His galoshes squeaked on the tile floor as he walked through the lobby.

Chad was still at the front desk, smiling as he greeted him, "Good evening, sir."

The old man handed him his snow-covered parka and said, "It's eleven-thirty-two. What's so good about this evening?"

As the desk clerk took the coat, he dashed off to find a hanger, responding, "Nothing, Mr. Gillette, nothing."

He careened around the desk and burst through the office door much to the surprise of the occupants at the time.

"Show me what you got," he ordered.

A tall young blond stood from the office desk and walked to a workbench that housed monitor screens to the lodge's premises as well as a one-inch playback machine that erased material every two hours on a continuous loop.

The blonde's name tag said plainly, Eric, who proceeded to take a beta tape and shove it into the machine after replacing the tape already recording.

Hitting rewind on the playback allowed Dr. Paul Gilbert Gillette to see all the activity that took place merely an hour and a half earlier.

"Stop!" he yelled.

Eric tapped the pause button as the monitor displayed three faces it had captured of Darnell, Nick, and Baron.

Gillette shook his head.

"Hit play," he said.

The noise lines vanished from the image. There was no audio and the picture was a grainy black and white.

Into the frame, Danny entered looking intently at the mirror on the wall adjacent to the check-in desk.

A smile fell upon the bearded face of the good doctor.

The office door swung wide open catching Gillette's attention as she walked in.

"Did you see this?" he asked.

Molica Phillips looked directly at the screen of the nineteen-inch monitor.

"It's why I called you so late," she said.

"Good decision," he said, pulling her close to him as he wrapped his arm over her shoulder.

Molica had shoulder length curly black hair that belied her mixed heritage. As her grandfather kissed her on the forehead, she asked, "What do you want to do now?"

"We're going to have to figure out how to dispatch his friends first," he gleaned.

She took a long look at him, "What?"

"I told you he'd be back," he mused. "Something brought him back."

"You're sure that's him?"

Scoffing, he bent his head toward the screen, "Aren't you? After all, you called me at this ungodly hour. And he, my dear," the old man asserted, "is going to put an end to our search."

MIKE AND RASHONDA

⚜

The Cadillac's wiper blades roared furiously as they lashed back and forth upon the windshield cutting through the snow and ice.

The high beams cast shadows on the limbs of the trees covered with frozen water.

Mike still leaning in his car, pushed beyond the fifteen miles-per-hour speed limit by at least twenty as he took a backroad from the parking lot.

RaShonda still stressed about the excessive shots Danny had taken, raged on as they broke through the unpaved path.

"Children," she said. "Y'all still actin' like children."

"No one said he had to drink," Mike said. "It's not like he couldn't say no."

"Or what?" RaShonda asked.

"We would beat his ass, that's all."

"That's all?" she asked.

Mike shook his head. She didn't understand.

"It's birthday licks. That's all," he futilely tried to explain. "Ain't nobody trying to kill nobody."

RaShonda cocked her head, "You sho'?" she countered. "What about Larry's crazy ass?"

Mike could see where she was going with that point as he semi-nodded. Larry was over the top which fueled Carter.

"Look, look," Mike said, "We gon' get this Ginger Ale and what not and he gon be good as new. Just another story for him to tell."

He hoped he had calmed her down as she sat back in her seat.

They had driven nearly a mile and a half on the resort's property.

RaShonda restlessly groaned, "And why you choose to go out the resort this way?"

"It looked like it would be closer to the road than the way we came in," he said.

"Well it ain't," she said.

A blanket of snow fell upon the windshield, causing them both to tense up.

"Be careful, Mike," RaShonda said.

"I got it," he said. "I got it."

The wipers crossed a few times before removing the debris from the trees overhead.

As Mike's vision cleared, a white figure appeared in the road as if crossing darting out of nowhere.

"Mike, watch out!" RaShonda panicked.

Mike hit the brakes. As the car tried to respond, the figure stood almost paralyzed in its footsteps.

Mike swerved to dodge it as his tires had trouble gaining traction due to his speed.

RaShonda let out a banshee's cry as the car flipped over.

THE AFTERPARTY

Moving in silence was not in their vocabulary as they prepared to ship out to move Nick early that morning.

"Anybody seen Mike or RaShonda?" Baron asked in a deep husky morning voice.

Darnell was wiping sleep from his eyes as he ventured to the drawn curtains on the sliding door. He flipped it partially open to inspect the car lot in the back of the lodge, squinting as rays of sunlight seared through the glass pane. A blast of arctic air pushed him back.

"What time is it?" Darnell asked no one in particular.

"Almost eight o'clock," Baron said being the first to rise and shower when the suite was still encased in darkness.

Carter and Larry had run to the second-floor scavenging for additional towels, soap, pillows, and linen before retiring around three-thirty.

They secured Trudy in the main suite bedroom while others slept on the couch, recliners, or floor.

Carter had enclosed himself in the guest bedroom's closet, sleeping comfortably on the shag carpeting.

Mulling around, the goal was to be out by nine that morning, return afterwards to handle some "family business," then head back home.

Danny still knocked out in the guest bedroom wouldn't be able to travel with them after all the activity from earlier.

They didn't expect to just nod out before Mike and RaShonda had returned. Now that it was daylight, they had to address that concern.

Marshall, dressed in a University of Missouri t-shirt and sweatpants to match, sat up from the bed he made on the loveseat, and reached for the phone perched on a small table next to him. Placing the receiver by his ear, he tapped at it a couple of times.

"Hello? Hello?" he said into the phone's receiver. He checked the phone a few times, then repeated calling out again. Finally, he hung it up and checked the cord.

"What's wrong?" Baron asked.

"No reception," Marshall said.

"Did the snow knock it out?" Darnell asked hesitantly.

Marshall, still fighting sleep, shrugged his shoulders, "Maybe."

"Who you tryin' to call?" Darnell asked.

"Any of you seen Mike?" he asked.

The two looked around performing a mental head count. Baron walked briskly toward the guest room and saw RaShonda's travel case still sitting outside the closet.

Ambling toward the suite's door, he opened it looking for some signs of an attempted entry.

"Could they be in Mike's car?" Baron pondered. "Maybe they knocked, but we didn't hear them."

Darnell went to the master bedroom and pushed through his jeans. As he tossed on his sweatshirt from the night before, he headed for the door, and said, "I'll check the parking lot."

Like a shot, Nick buzzed past all three as the door closed on Darnell. Bee-lining toward the guest bathroom, Nick shut the door.

The click of the door's lock popped into the air followed by the sound of methane gas whistling beyond the door.

"Guess we won't be going in there any time soon," Baron said.

The rollers on the guest bedroom closet whirred as Carter, shielding his eyes from any light source, hobbled out wearing a torn t-shirt and Proviso sweatpants.

He walked into the bed, bruising his shin, then hopping into the hallway muttering little curses.

He saw Baron and Marshall staring at him. He stood and returned their gaze with his own squint.

"S'up?" he asked nonchalant sounding like a frog was caught in his throat.

Marshall laughed, "What up, man? You didn't hear anybody knock on the door last night, did you?"

Carter pouted, then shook his head, "Nah, why? What's up?"

Baron said, "Trying to figure out if we missed Mike and RaShonda trying to get in."

"Or Ricky," Marshall said.

"Yeah, or Ricky," Baron said.

"Man, I forgot about Ricky!" Carter exclaimed. He walked to the doorway of the master suite and looked in on Trudy sleeping in the queen-sized bed knocked out after playing nurse to Danny most of the night. "How's she getting home?"

A loud groan emitted from the guest bathroom startling Carter.

"Who's in there?" he asked alarmed.

"Nick. Who else?" Baron said.

"Are you alright in there?" Carter said as he banged on the bathroom door.

"You could hear that?" came the muffled response from Nick.

"Hurry up," Baron said. "Other people have to pee."

Larry shuffled toward the living room followed by Clint and

Wynton. Larry popped his head in the master bedroom to gaze at sleeping beauty.

"How is he?" Wynton asked with genuine concern.

Larry, still leering at Trudy sleeping on her back as her chest rose while she breathed, returned, "He, who?"

Clint and Wynton stood behind Larry to peek in, suddenly realizing who he was looking at.

"Other room," Marshall said.

"Oh," Clint said.

The door pushed open and Darnell looked like the chill had gotten him as he pounded snow off his shoes.

"I didn't see Mike's Caddy, but Ricky's car is still out there," he announced.

"That doesn't make much sense," Larry said as he turned from the bedroom. "Where is Ricky?"

"Maybe, he's with Mike and RaShonda," Darnell said scratching his head trying to make sense out of the disappearance.

"Do ya think something happened to them on the way back?" Carter asked.

Baron grabbed the jack to the phone, picked up the receiver and walked to another wall unit. After plugging it in, he tried to get reception. With all eyes on him, he shook his head.

"Nothing," Baron said.

Marshall walked to the guest bathroom door and knocked on the door.

Nick grunted.

"Hurry up!" Marshall said as he talked through the door. He turned to the guys and issued, "Let's get dressed and go to check in. See if the hotel is having phone problems at the front desk. We need to place a Missing-Persons report for the three of them."

"What about Danny?" Darnell asked.

Marshall nodded his head, "Who wants to stay with Danny?"

From the corner, Trudy's sleepy voice rang out, "I will."

The guys turned and watched her. She looked just as fresh in sweat pants and a hoodie. Her hair somewhat frizzier than when the night started, and freckles danced all over the bridge of her nose now that the makeup had faded. She looked like an angel of mercy.

"Cool," Marshall said as Nick opened the door to a crack.

"Anybody got some air freshener?" Nick asked.

The guys moved quickly to the front of the room to escape Nick's intestinal gases.

BOOK 3 — MOM AND AFTERMATH

Four years ago, those investigators were thorough, methodical, and as far as Danny was concerned, too damn slow. Would they have been any faster ten years earlier in 1968?

While they didn't spend much time interviewing Danny and LaMonica, it was the short interrogation of her "sister" that burned him the most.

Mac Watley and he stayed by the pool at the officers' request since Danny was connected to the incident.

Danny was jarred when the sheriff's patrol car arrived on the scene.

What was going on? Danny wondered to himself.

The questioning was fairly routine as far as Danny was concerned.

What's your relation to the deceased? When did you last see the deceased alive? What was his mood?

Huh?

Did he seem okay when you were with him last?

What did that mean? Yeah, he was fine.

Uncle Mac knew how to talk to the deputy in charge. He interpreted every question then turned to Danny with a "What they are asking you is" or "what they mean to say." For Danny, the investigator's verbiage was confusing and darn near accusatory.

Guilt was all Danny felt. He most certainly did not like the prodding, especially since he was not there to witness the accident. He was not there to protect Lamont the way his mother wanted him to.

There was a sinking feeling in his chest that he had let his mother down. It was a feeling he had felt before. Like the time he broke a porcelain dish that had been given to his mother years before he was even born that he broke with his belt trying to imitate Bruce Lee's swinging his nun chucks. The buckle just crashed down on top of the bowl-shaped plate and shattered it. He spent two hours trying to glue it back together, but his father – who's work schedule he could never get a handle on – walked into the house hours before he normally would and somehow beelined directly to the dish. As his father picked it up, glue dripped from its center onto the cocktail table and crumbled in his grasp.

His father made him confess to his mother within ten minutes after she walked into the house. When he explained his mistake, she hugged him and cited it as old anyway. She'd replace it later. But he could tell it had value to her, a very special place in her heart. She forgave him and moved on like nothing happened.

Writing in his steno pad, the deputy took a report from Dr. Gillette regarding how he came to aid the drowning Lamont when he heard his granddaughter scream out.

A rottweiler, chained to an iron spike nailed to the ground by the barbeque pit barked furiously as it waited for morsels to be tossed its way.

Danny was lost. He felt the knot tighten inside him as he knew he had to go back to the hotel room and face his parents. His uncle could only do so much to save him. Plus, Mac as well as other members of the club had families to go back to. Uncle Mac's wife and daughter were waiting for relevant news.

As he watched the officer conclude his report, Mac Watley asked to be excused to get Danny back to his family. Danny was fully cognizant of the respect the cop showed to his uncle as much a professional man, as the good doctor Gillette and his family who watched a young black kid drown in a pool no less than ten yards from their gathering.

The officer kept eyeing Danny, making him feel somewhat responsible for this entire incident. Gone would be the excuse that he wasn't even there. Exactly, and that's how this mess happened in the first place.

The summer heat turned up a notch as Danny perspired in his tank top and swim trunks. It had been a while since he had eaten, and yet, Danny felt a pang in his stomach. The knot grew tighter, constricting his breathing. His chest felt like it would burst as the crashing of that stupid dish hit him.

His mother accepted the news of the destruction of the treasured plate with grace and acceptance. "Accidents happen," she said casually. "It was an old thing, something cheap picked up by your grandmother when she vacationed in Mexico."

She'd gone to retrieve a White Way grocers paper bag that was folded in three sections. She increased it and gently placed the dish's contents into the bag as if it were a small pet that had perished.

The Elmer's glue did not hold as the dish splattered in the bag. Danny felt horrible as he could hear the five separate pieces jangle about.

She folded the creases back into the bag creating a tri-fold before carrying it off.

Danny followed behind, but never made it past his bedroom, which at the time sat right off the living room. A much tighter space than the room he now had off the kitchen which a relative occupied at that time.

His father sat on his bed with a long face of disappointment etched into it.

"Come in, son," he gestured.

Danny hesitated. He could count on his two hands all the times his father had actually entered his room since Danny officially took sole possession of it after sharing the room with his cousin in bunkbeds for three years.

He took cautious steps into the room with his eyes diverting his father for fear of Playboy magazines he had hidden directly between the mattresses of his twin bed set.

The room was dark save light that cracked through the window blinds Danny usually kept down, not wanting to emit light in his hiding place.

Panic set in. If his father knew he was hitting his stash, it was all over for him. He would do more than move his hiding space, but probably move it to a completely different location, as in a different address. DAMN!

Danny moved forward to tighten the distance between the two.

His father sat up erect. Waiting for some semblance of an attack. Danny tensed, froze before getting too close, but close enough to get his foot on the magazines to shove it further under the recesses of the bed.

"That dish was more than just some ashtray that guests use for their cigarette butts," he pressed on. "That dish belonged to your grandmother."

Stunned, Danny said, "That's not what she told me. Mom said—"

"I don't care what your mother told you," the senior Alexander hissed. "It's the last thing your mother had of her mother's. Something she vowed to take care of and never let anything happen to it."

Danny reeled from that piece of information. He felt devastated that he had taken that away from his mother.

"She's got nothing, but memories now," his father said.

Dan Alexander rose from the mattress, towering over his son at 5'8" in height. He bent to his son's ear and said, "Think about that."

He watched his father walk out the room and head toward the living room.

"And clean up your room by tomorrow!" he said. "It looks like a pigsty."

Danny said, "Yes sir." Without any thought, relieved his father didn't find the stack of magazines.

He felt an urge to relieve himself before he started the task of cleaning his room and headed toward the sole bathroom spotting his mother in his parents' bedroom sitting on the edge of the bed holding onto the paper bag.

Mac Watley wrapped lightly on the door to The Alexanders' hotel suite.

Danny's eardrums pound as his heart beat rapidly. There was no response as they waited patiently at the door.

Mac raised his long bony fingers, ready to knock again when they both heard a woman's voice.

Danny wanted to turn and run away as far as his legs would take him for as many days as they would carry him even with his hobbled leg.

The door swung open as Lou Thomas' wife, Margie, stood in front of them. She wrapped her arms around Danny before he could even look inside. But he heard her wailing. It was more disturbing than watching her sitting on that bed holding tightly to the last item she had from her mother.

Danny froze as he embraced the tall, thin woman. Burying his head in her chest, his tears soaked the shoulder of her shirt.

She slowly dragged him inside to console him as he heaved long breaths into her bosom. She whispered softly in his ear to ensure him it wasn't his fault.

Unable to contain his weight, she allowed him to pivot around her. He saw a small cabal of women on their knees in a corner of the suite's bedroom. A hand reached up in anguish and a shriek trembled from the room. The women collapsed onto Carroll Alexander to bring her down.

It was then, Danny saw the owner of the hand. His mother,

balled in a fetal position, rocking herself as the wives of the golf club tried to give her strength.

Danny sank to his knees. Margie lost her grip on him and called for Mac Watley to help her.

Danny had no words for the pain he believed he had wrought his mother.

Why had she made such a stupid promise to Lamont's mother assuring his safety?

All Danny could do as he was wrapped up by Uncle Mac and Aunt Margie was cry out.

"Mama! I'm so sorry!" Danny cried out

Watching her sit up, then fall back to her knees as the three women held her, Danny couldn't help but feel he had hurt her, broken her heart again.

He accepted the blame but knew he couldn't take the pain from her. She would not be the same, ever. How could God have let this happen to this woman he worshipped?

There could only be one answer to that question.

Daphne had it wrong. No devil stopped her from saving Lamont. That would mean there was a God. At that moment, Danny was certain of one thing absolutely.

There was no God!

AFTERSHOCKS

*D*anny awoke. Just like that. The nightmare ended and he was awake. Like before. Like so many times before.

He was staring at the off-white ceiling and the shiplap columns that crisscrossed when the urge hit him.

He sat up and swung his legs to the floor.

In his groggy state, he reached for the alarm clock on his end table, but his hand never found it.

His head throbbed like there was no tomorrow. A pounding sensation he hadn't experience since the first time he got drunk off Boones Farm Strawberry Hill.

And how did that end?

With his father cleaning the bathroom wall at two in the morning.

He slowly lifted his head trying to open his eyes. He shielded them from the brightness in the room, but he didn't understand why it was so bright.

And the urge raged on.

A soft rumbling came from his mid-section as his tongue felt like sandpaper had been wiped across it. His mouth was dry as he attempted to create saliva to swallow. His throat ached from an aridness he couldn't determine.

He needed water.

But first, that urge.

Under wobbly legs, he rose from the bed, partially opening his eyes. Once again, he reached for his alarm clock, but as he cocked his head, he realized it wasn't on the end table.

There was no end table for the alarm clock.

What the hell? he thought.

He forced his eyes open, as he realized he was not at home. But where was he?

He took a step toward the door frame. His right leg buckled as he applied pressure. He caught himself on the mattress and leaned into it as his knee throbbed.

He gathered himself and slowly stood erect.

He dragged his leg to take steps to the door still piecing together his whereabouts.

He stumbled into the hallway and glanced at the suite's living room. He had never seen this place, but the layout looked so familiar.

He was filled with a sensation to call out for his parents but suppressed it as the urge called out to him to find the bathroom.

He moved as stiffly toward a closed door. He grabbed its handle and turned.

His loins jackhammered to let him know he only had seconds left.

He shut the door behind him.

After flushing, he shuffled through the hallway again. Finding his way back to the bedroom, he grimaced in pain as he flung himself onto the bed.

He groaned softly and gripped the top of his forehead as the pounding became muffled by the down pillow he lay face down upon.

His free arm rested upon her ribcage under her breast as Trudy breathing vibrated beneath his elbow.

"Did you wash your hands?" came from the pillow.

Danny opened his eyes in horror realizing his arm rested upon Trudy's torso as she lay on her side.

He shrieked nearly pushing her out the bed.

He jumped up only to come crashing down as the weight on his leg caved once more.

"What the hell are you doing here?" he asked.

Rolling over, still half asleep, but alert enough to hang on to the edges of the bed, Trudy said, "Chill out, birthday boy."

"Where the hell am I?" he stammered totally out of sorts.

"We're in Wisconsin," she said dryly, amused by his disorientation. "You don't remember anything, do you?"

He took a moment, shaking his head as a throbbing raged in his temples.

"What time is it?" he finally asked.

Trudy, still dressed in sweats, rolled over to view the small Timex clock on top of the dresser.

"Eleven o' six, sleepy head."

Damn, how long was I out? he thought to himself.

A fog was starting to part as he recalled the drive to the resort.

"Where's everybody?" he asked as he wiped sleep from his eyes hoping that would alleviate tension on his pounding headache.

"They went to help Nick move," she said. She sat up in the bed with concern, "How do you feel?"

A moment flashed in front of him languishing over the toilet bowl and he had a glimpse of the passing hours.

"How bad was I?" he asked.

Drolly, she said, "You were in bad shape. You better hope I can get your gook out of my clothes or you're going to owe me."

Startled, more than embarrassed, Danny said the probe, "I threw up on you?"

"And RaShonda," she said. "You threw up everywhere."

He sat down on the mattress trying to account for the time he lost. "How many shots did I take?"

She laughed, "You didn't make it to twenty-one. That's for sure. More like five, maybe six."

She reflected, "No, you didn't make six. That's the one you threw up on me."

Danny gave a blank stare. He vaguely remembered hanging onto the toilet with his arms stretched far and wide, but beyond someone stroking his head, he was at a loss.

"RaShonda, too?" he lamented. "I bet she's furious with me. She went with them, too?"

Trudy shook her head as she moved off the bed and stood to stretch.

"No, she and Mike went to get some Ginger Ale for you at the AMPM, but we haven't seen them since," she said. "Mike and RaShonda left here shortly after three."

"Three? They haven't come back for eight hours? Did they call or something?"

Trudy shook her head once again. She explained how Baron and Marshall attempted to call the police, but the phone didn't work in the suite.

Danny lay on the bed. The room wasn't spinning as much now, but he was still in a fog.

He grabbed his right knee and felt a tenderness to it that made no sense.

"What's wrong with your leg?" Trudy asked.

"What?" he sat up and stared at her. "Why?"

She said with much concern, "You couldn't put pressure on it while you were praying to God this morning."

"Praying to God?" he asked amused.

"You know," she mockingly mimicked, "Oh, God, please save me. Oh, God, help me. Oh, sweet Jesus, Mother Mary of God, take me now."

Embarrassed, Danny shot back, "I didn't say that."

"Yes, you did," Trudy smirked.

He released his swollen knee and crawled back under the sheets sliding his head back to a pillow. "How come Ricky ain't take you home yet?" he chortled.

Trudy, said seriously, "He hasn't come back either since you tried to attack him."

Danny's face went blank as he turned toward her.

"Darnell says his car is still here," she commented. "I told your friends I'd watch you until they came back."

Trying to block the light, Danny turned away from Trudy, "You can go now, Hamhock. I'm alright. I just need to get some sleep."

She watched him for a moment trying to block her out. She crawled to the other side of the bed rising over him.

"Did you wash your hands?"

He groaned; appreciative he didn't have a baby sister. Otherwise, he'd strangle her.

A FOOL RISES

Trudy stood in front of the sliding door watching as small snowflakes descended softly falling onto the step-out patio of the suite.

She had bored of watching television, flipping through the channels with nothing more than special interest programs on. She had hoped ABC would present a boxing match like it once did on Saturday afternoons, but those were becoming less frequent from the days her family would sit around the tv watching Muhammad Ali box. Even his losses were exciting because everyone knew he was coming back and triumph. He was the ultimate black super hero.

She was tempted plenty of times to turn the radio on, but she didn't want to wake Danny.

She had checked in on him three times to monitor progress on his recovery. He had gotten up once to find aspirin. She had none, but RaShonda had a bottle of Pamprin. After explaining its usage, Danny relented and took two. He had also stumbled back to the bathroom to "drain the lizard." His words, not hers and she wasn't really interested to know what 'the lizard' looked like.

She had tried the phone a couple of times and the results were the same. Nothing but a dead line.

She was desperate for a shower and eventually found an appropriate opportunity to do so, but she didn't feel as clean as she felt she should have since she didn't take advantage of the usual twenty minutes she would have spent languishing in the hot water. Her sister was much worse, and their father spent each month screaming about the water bill. The boys had actually cleaned up the area as best they could, but there were short hair strands that circled around that bothered her as well as she tried to avoid them heading for the spigot.

Without another change of clothing, she went back to the sweats thankful that Danny hadn't baptized her a second time.

Of course, none of this would have mattered if Ricky had returned or told her to grab her bag so they could leave together. *But no, he stormed out and...what,* she wondered. If Darnell was telling the truth and Ricky's car was still in the lot, where was Ricky? When he showed up, she was definitely going to give him a piece of her mind.

They were supposed to only be coming up for a quick stop to a birthday party. She made sure Ricky understood, it was a quick stop and not a quickie. But she packed a bag. What was she thinking? She really wasn't sure. Her stomach had been in knots the moment she retrieved her sister's overnight get away bag. It had been sitting in the closet since her sister came home for Christmas break from the University of Iowa.

Her mother was going to go ballistic if she didn't attend the last service of the year at church. Ricky's whereabouts aside, the weather itself looked to be the biggest hindrance to her getting back home.

As she watched the snow fall, she thought maybe she could get a cab at the front desk to take her back to Maywood. Surely, they had some kind of transport service to get her to a bus station or train, maybe a horse & buggy. Something to get her out of there and on her parents' doorstep in time for the eight o'clock service the next morning.

She should have enough money to cover the expenses.

"What're you doing there?" she heard Danny's voice faintly. Trudy jumped, so deep in thought it scared her. She nearly considered running through the plate glass in that split second, she heard his voice.

"Nothing," she said. "Feel better?"

She turned as Danny limped into the suite's living room.

"I'm hungry. Is there anything here to eat?"

A few of the paper bags had remains of the food they had retrieved when they checked in. Trudy had rummaged through the bags two hours earlier and extracted a soggy BLT and a wilted quarter of a pickle. It did tide her over, but the pangs of hunger were striking now.

"There's something in these bags," she said, "But you should really have some soup or something. Nothing heavy."

He was dragging his right leg. She could see it was really bothering him. He tossed himself on the couch hiking the leg up gently.

As he rolled his pant leg up, he asked, "Anything good on tv?"

She moved closer as curiosity encouraged her to peek at the damage as she said, "No, not really."

The knee was puffy with inflammation. She saw a scar that crowned the knee. The stitch marks protruded as if the bone would pop out. She winced but was fascinated by the surgical cut.

"Really?" he asked as he poked at the buildup which popped up like cake dough still baking. "No boxing or anything?"

"No, nothing, right?" she said. "There is usually always a boxing match, right?"

"You like boxing?" he asked finding it amusing.

"Yeah," she said. "Daddy and I watch it all the time on the 'Wide World of Sports.'"

He laughed and did his best impression, "This is Ho-ward Co-sell."

She stood over him examining his injury. "What happened?"

"This?" he said. "Believe it or not, boxing."

"What? You got hurt in a fight?"

Danny still pressed on the knee as fluid moved around, "No, knocked out in an exhibition. I actually hurt it here. Or somewhere near here, but I think it was here."

Trudy looked at him quizzically, "I don't follow."

"I believe this is where my cousin died," he said solemnly.

"Here? How could that be? I thought this place just opened."

Danny toyed with his knee enough and rolled the pant leg down.

"This part we are at didn't exist, but I am certain this is the place. I just haven't had a chance to walk around."

She sat down next to him still focused on his bum leg. "I don't think you're going to get the chance at all today. It's been snowing off and on since last night."

He stood up briefly to test the leg out. Spotting the paper bags on the card table next to two full shots of liquor, he gingerly walked in that direction.

"We still have food?" Danny asked.

Trudy nodded, "Yeah, but not much. I left you about a sandwich and a half. I can put my boots on and walk to the lodge. That's where you guys got the food, right?"

Danny screwed up his face, "You mean the phone still doesn't work?"

"Yep," she said. "Line's still down."

He scavenged through the remaining bags and bounced back to the couch with a shot in his hand. Trudy scowled at him as he said, "Hair of the dog."

"Okay," she said perturbed.

He was only two bites into the sandwich before he gulped the shot down. He coughed and hacked, then pounded his chest trying to beat the meal down around the alcohol burning his throat.

"This ain't gonna cut it," he said. "I'm hungry as fuck."

Trudy stood up and walked toward the bedroom.

"Where you going?" he grilled.

"I'll go get us something to eat," she said resigned to having to brave the weather. "Your knee is way too messed up. Maybe you should soak in the tub and let the jets take care of that."

Danny was struck by that. "There's a hot tub in the bathroom?"

"Yeah," she said. "Or you could go to the sauna. But you should take a shower or something. You smell like vomit."

"Damn," he said. "It's like that?"

She scrunched her fingers like she was squishing a bug, "Just a little."

He laughed, "The only sauna is attached to the pool if I remember this place and that's at the main lodge."

She shook her head, "No, Darnell said there was one in this building. He said he saw it."

"Really," he pondered. "I guess I'll have to take a look. I need it." He glanced at her, "But first, I'll take a shower."

"Sounds good. I'll go get food," she suggested.

Danny shook his head, "No, I'll get the food. Just let me knock some of the rust off this knee first."

"Sounds like a deal, if you let me go with you," she said. "I've been cooped up in here since I got to this place."

Danny hesitantly said, "I don't know. If this is the place I think it is, there are ghosts haunting this place."

Trudy asked. "What ghosts?"

Danny chuckled to himself before answering, "The ghost of Chief Black Hawk."

"Chief Black Hawk?" she asked.

Danny clapped his hands while replying, "You never heard of Chief Black Hawk? Well, he wasn't really a chief, more like a tribal leader," he explained. "Our hockey team is named after him and the Black Hawk War of 1832."

"You're making this up," she said unamused.

"No," Danny said emphatically. "Real deal. Black Hawk didn't like the deal made for Illinois land and demanded retribution. He slaughtered a militia, then headed north. The legend is he looted various areas buried what he took from the militia in these parts, then surrendered somewhere near Mississippi or St. Louis or something like that."

Trudy looked at him suspiciously, "Do you believe it?"

Danny slowly walked to her and said to her honestly, "I don't know what I believe, but I believe I am hungry and will die of starvation if I don't get a move on."

"That's cool," she said quietly.

Danny walked into the bedroom looking for his travel bag. He rummaged through the closet until he found it. As he backed out, he bumped into Trudy who seemed to shadow him.

"Excuse me," he bashfully said.

She stared at his bag and saw the sleeve of his 'Family' jacket.

"Are you guys a gang?" she asked cautiously.

He shook his head with disbelief, but she could see he understood the question.

"No," he exhaled. "We are a group of respectful young men who value what brotherhood - and sisterhood – is about. Just because we wear jackets with the name 'Family' on the back doesn't make us a gang."

She nodded, "So who's getting initiated?"

He closed his eyes. She could see his mind racing before giving a response, "No, no, no."

He dropped his bag and began a search for specific carrying luggage. First, Carter's which lay next to where he retrieved his. Grabbing it, he flung it on the bed and unzipped the boy-scout backpack. He tossed out a large Dungeons and Dragons handbook.

"Pathetic," he grumbled.

His fingers dug deeper into the bag until his eyes opened wide. Yanking hard, he extracted a plastic bottle of Watkins Icy Blue Ointment. She could see the relief in his demeanor as he flipped the jar onto the bed.

"Silly motherfuckers," he mumbled.

He was finished with the contents of the pack and headed back to the closet tossing items around until he found Larry's University of

Idaho bag. Just the oblong shape gave Danny pause for consolation. He unzipped the top and they both could see the fraternity insignia etched on the long piece of plywood that created Larry's greatest weapon. He pulled it out and produced it for Trudy to inspect.

"The Widow Maker," he announced as he handed the paddle to Trudy who was engaged with the bottle of ointment.

"What's this for?" she asked holding the bottle like it was a precious jewel.

"You don't want to know," he said still shaking his head as he watched her screw the cap off the jar.

She stuck her nose over the open container and sniffed it.

"Menthol?" she said as she drew her head back.

Danny dipped his finger into the waxy ointment and swiped his index finger on her nose.

The coolness caught her off guard as her nostrils just opened up. The sudden warmness turned to hot.

"I don't get it," she said as she tried to wipe the smear off the bridge of her nose.

"You don't have to worry about it, Hamhock, as long as you don't have the crabs," he dismissed.

Taken aback, she slugged Danny in his shoulder. He flinched but accepted the punch.

"No one's called me that in years," she said petulantly.

"You might need it, hanging with Ricky Williams," he said coldly.

As frustrated as she was with Ricky's disappearance, she was still extremely concerned.

"Are you jealous?" she asked.

"Of Ricky? Hell, naw," he said. "You want to be with that loser, it's cool with me."

"Isn't he a member of your precious 'Family?'"

He turned away from her replying, "Not my choice."

She tried to read Danny as he examined the paddle. Joining in, she thought its thickness was a bit excessive as he tossed it onto the bed.

"So, you're not friends?" she asked demurely.

He shook his head, then turned to give her his full attention, "Not since the eighth grade. He's just somebody I went to school with."

The dab of ointment was beginning to take effect as her nose turned a soft violet. Her skin was warming up like someone had dropped wax on it. She rubbed it unaware she still had some on her fingertips as she spread the smear. She took her sleeve and attempted to wipe it off as the aroma was watering her eyes.

"What is this stuff?" she cried out frantically.

Her vision was blurring when Danny knocked her arm down. She was prepared to retaliate until she felt him place a dry face rag over the bridge of her nose and wipe away from her eyes. The downward stroke alleviated the very cool sensation she was feeling.

She wrapped her hand around his and noticed how tight it was.

From his fist to his forearm, he was much harder than she had ever envisioned. She had a similar thought earlier that morning when he rested on her in the bathroom and she wrapped her arms protectively around him with her hands on his mid-section. She had memories of him with a little paunch in the middle, but this morning his stomach felt flat as an iron board.

When he was put to bed and Nick and his friends tried to straighten Danny out to lay on his back, his shirt raised up and she saw the abs shocked that he kept himself in shape. She was impressed.

He stroked the towel once more, before he tossed it next to the paddle.

"My fault," he apologized as he caressed her face holding her cheeks lightly in his hands as he examined her, "I didn't think I put that much on you."

"It burned," she whined. "What is that?"

"One of the station's best clients. It's 'Icy Blue Ointment.'"

She grabbed his wrists in her hands as he maintained a gentle grip. She didn't struggle as she looked into his eyes.

"What's it used for?"

A small laugh escaped his lips as he searched for an answer, "I'm just glad it can't be used for what Carter had in mind."

He was finishing his inspection of her, while she never stopped looking at him.

"What happened to you and Darlene?" slipped from her lips. She regretted it immediately. She so wanted to retrieve it like someone would a pet python let loose at a friend's house.

His eyes connected with hers as he set her jaws free from his grasp.

"You okay?" he asked avoiding her question.

She surrendered her grip on his wrist and nodded.

"Think I'll try to find that sauna," he said quietly as he turned his attention to the bed hunting awkwardly for another towel.

He lowered his head to sustain the throbbing pain still in his head.

INSIDE POOL

Danny stepped into the hotel hallway, wearing Carter's shorts which were tightly hugging him in the hips. He tossed a white hotel towel over his shoulders across the white-t and hobbled out the door giving it a hard pull with his right hand. The door swung quickly then within inches of closure slowed due to the spring reflex in the door causing it to shut softly.

Trudy giggled on the other side further infuriating him. Danny grabbed the knob and slightly pushed the door open then with a mighty force pulled it toward him again only to be thwarted by the spring action.

"Shit!" he said.

Trudy walked to the door. Hair flayed over her face. "Stop acting so silly," she said. "Wait for me. I'll go with you."

"For what?" he asked.

She opened the door wider.

"I told your friends I'd babysit you. I'm not going to let you out of my sight."

Danny growled in frustration. He bowed his head and relented.

She studied him. "For real?"

"Yeah," Danny sighed as he walked back in.

She slipped into the second guest room. Giddy to get out of the room. Cabin fever was taking a toll on her.

"I won't be long," she said. "I think RaShonda brought something. I'll dry the swimsuit off before she gets back."

She turned to make sure Danny honored his word.

He moved toward the couch retrieving the remote control from the foot table.

She watched him seat himself among the corduroy pillows, then closed the door behind her.

Hurriedly, she dashed toward the pink overnight bag and began to unzip it open.

Carefully, she removed items of clothing, toiletries, and various feminine products.

Piling up the material gingerly on the bed, she acknowledged the task at hand and walked back toward the bedroom door.

"This might take a while," she said as she pried the door slightly and took a glance into the living room.

He was gone. The television was on some old western. The remote on the cocktail table.

Danny was nowhere in sight.

Furious, she roared, then slammed the bedroom door.

THE BUBBLING warm water soothed Danny as he sat in the jacuzzi with a beer by his side. He took a swig nearly chugging a quarter in one gulp. He lay the bottle on the base of the whirlpool tile and released a belch that rattled the swirling waters by its force.

Closing his eyes for a moment took him back to that night.

She had the most beautiful hazel eyes. Very much emerald colored, but real, no contact lenses.

For a seventeen-year-old, she is very much built like a young woman in the blue and white floral patterned one piece. Her thighs are round, but don't slap together. Her arms are toned, but not cut; and as she slowly took steps into the jacuzzi, into Danny's arms, she is ready to become a full-fledged woman.

Danny flexes hard, trying to shore up his thin arms as he cradles her in them.

Her chest against his. She moves forward whispering softly in his ear. He damn near swallows her face as he turns to meet her pursed lips.

He calms down within seconds as he backs up to take a look at her.

From behind, he sees a silhouette. He shoots a glance over her head toward the pool's entrance.

The outline of a male stands there watching.

"Lamont?" he calls out.

There is no response.

LaMonica gazes at him, quizzically. He pushes her to the side and calls out again, "Lamont."

The figure stands there in front of him in the doorway.

Danny backs up and turns to LaMonica. "Don't you see him?"

She stares, then sinks. Only the black curly locks of hair float on top of the bubbling water.

"'Monica, Monica," he calls out.

He looks down in horror as the follicles disappear amidst the swirling waters.

He looked again and the pool's door was wide open, but no one was there.

"I ought to beat your ass," she said in his ear.

Startled, he reached behind him and tossed her body into the water.

As arms flailed, swinging wildly, her head popped up. Trudy struck at him defensively trying to get out of the way of the jets.

Her head popped up and she kicked him in the right leg. He immediately released his grip.

"What's wrong with you?" she screamed. Turned her back and said, "Mother fucker."

She shoved a handful of water at his face to defend herself.

Danny wrapped his arms around her to calm her down.

"I'm sorry," he said, "I was having a bad dream."

She shook to break free from his embrace.

"Let me go," she cried out, "Something's wrong with you. Very wrong with you."

Breaking free from him, she pushed herself out the pool and began to walk off.

"Wait up!" Danny yelled. "I said I'm sorry!"

Danny hobbled out of the pool area chasing after Trudy.

WITH A TOWEL WRAPPED around her head and a hotel bathrobe draped around her, Trudy emerged from the bedroom.

Danny, already dressed in jeans and a sweater, sat on the couch pretending to be engrossed in some skiing event.

As she moved to the small refrigerator, she briefly opened the door, then slammed it shut.

She stomped back into the living room area blocking Danny's view of the television.

"You are so stupid."

Danny sat and took in the view.

"What are you staring at?" she asked.

"I said I'm sorry," he said. "I'm only gonna say it so many times."

"I don't care how many times you say it. You ruined my hair," she pouted.

Danny smirked, "What the fuck you talking about?"

She ripped the towel from her head. Her locks were gone, replaced by a frizzled flaxen gob of black hair. Somehow to Danny, more pleasing.

"Do you know how much it cost to get my hair done?" she said. "You are going to pay for my next trip to Gladys'."

"Sheeit!" Danny said as if he were taking a long one.

"Sheeit, my ass," she said. "Seventy bucks."

"For what?"

"My hair," she said back.

Danny stood up, defiantly.

"Sit your cripple ass down," she said. "Ain't nobody scared of you."

Danny walked over to her. Face to face, he lowered his head and eyeballed her.

She matched him as she looked up. They were less than an inch from each other.

"I'm hungry," she said. "Get me something to eat."

Danny growled at her.

"Please," she changed her tone. "I haven't eaten all day."

"I got something for you to eat," he said.

"Later," she said unwavering. "I'm really hungry."

She moved closer. Guard down.

"Please?"

Danny didn't take long to weigh what that meant.

She kissed him. She took charge. Held him. Pulled him closer. Then pushed him back.

Looking for a key, Danny snatched the piece and dashed to the door.

"Anything in particular?" he asked.

"Surprise me," she said softly.

Their eyes met, then Danny swung his jacket over the shoulders, shoved his arms through, and picked up his black knit skull cap that popped out his sleeve.

He opened the door, then turned again.

"Anything to drink?"

She thought about this, peaked into the opening of the bathrobe, and with a frown said, "Diet Coke."

He nodded and began to pull the door open, repeating, "Diet Coke."

"Two Diet Cokes," she said.

Danny stood in the doorway, "Two Diet Cokes. Gotcha."

The door began to close.

"And a bag of potato chips."

Danny swung the door wide open, "Bag of chips. That's it? You done?"

She stood and faced him.

"What are you getting?" she asked.

Danny stood in the doorway and pondered the question.

"I'm not sure. I guess when the guys get back, they'll bring a pizza. So probably some wings and fries," he said.

"Cool, I'll have some of yours."

He pursed his lips as he acknowledged her request and said, "And two cokes."

"Diet Cokes," she corrected. "Two Diet Cokes."

"Gotcha," Danny said and quickly tried to shut the door only to watch it spring load close.

The flip-flop shoes she borrowed, shuffled across the floor as Trudy headed back to the guest room. As she crossed the threshold, a soft knock carried itself to her.

She turned around and headed back to the door. She reached for the brass handle as a second wave of light raps vibrated the door. She pulled it open and found Danny standing there, sheepishly.

"What now?" she laughingly asked.

Danny raised his head slowly and gave a slight smile.

"I'm sorry for dunking you in the jacuzzi. I'll make it up to you," he said.

She stood and stared at him.

"That's it?" she asked.

Danny, taken aback, said, "Yeah!"

"Boy, go get me some food," she pushed the door to close as he stood there with puppy dog eyes.

"Two Diet Cokes, right?" he asked as the door created a schism between them.

"And a bag of potato chips. Stop playing," she returned. "I'm hungry."

"Okay," was his last word as the door clicked close.

"Sorry," he said once more into the door.

"I'm starvin' like Marvin," she said.

Danny turned with a smile on his face that quickly faded as he began to walk the long corridor.

INITIATION

Swigging a beer, Marshall sat on the bowling alley bench. His plaid pants corresponding with the blue and yellow checker pattern of the seat. He patiently watched as Clinton palmed his bowling ball, anchoring the weight in his right hand.

"C'mon, Clint, one more strike and we win!" he yelled out.

Focused, Clinton began his march to the black stripe. He cocked back, then moving his arm forward, gently released the ball.

Marshall and Carter both held their collective breaths as they watched the ball glide from kissing the gutter alley to pirouetting toward the center pin.

Clinton turned away with a broad smile toward the scorer's table, mouthing the words, "Strike."

The ball struck left of the lead pin and tore its way through the rest. The pins ripped apart, falling nearly in unison, as Clint's prediction became fact.

Wynton raised his hand to Clinton for a high-five.

Larry seated next to him, nudged him in the ribs, reminding him, "They just beat us out of one hundred dollars."

Wynton immediately tried to lower his hand, but Clint had already slapped it.

Larry turned to Baron who was removing his rental shoes, and asked, "Do you believe this guy?"

Baron stood up from the other end of the bench and patted Larry on his back.

"Let's see how he comes out of the initiation," was his reply.

"Initiation?" Wynton crowed. "What initiation?"

Larry stroked his muscle man goatee and grinned, "Yeah, initiation."

Marshall wrapped his arm around Clinton's shoulder and brought him closer, "You, too."

BROUGHT into the bowling alley's lounge blindfolded, Clint and Wynton were seated on opposite sides of a corner booth.

Larry slid in next to Clint to anchor him in with the only way out being a plate glass window. Baron placed himself opposite Larry keeping Wynton in check as well.

Two large glasses of water and a pitcher of beer sat on the countertop along with two piping hot bowls of what looked like chili. From the smell alone, anyone could sense the extras of hot sauce, apple sauce, a variety of chips, and a large, heaping spoonful of dog food buried underneath.

Blindfolds were removed as Marshall lauded over them. Carter giddily stood by his side.

"All right," Marshall said, "this is your initiation night into the family."

The two inductees' eyes widened as they saw the individual bowls.

Wynton nervously looked across the tabletop to Clint who nodded his head gamely.

"So, you mean," Clint asked, "everyone who joins the family has eaten this?"

Darnell shook his head, "I didn't. They made me do some other stuff."

"That's because we knew you'd eat anything," Carter said.

Wynton wore a concerned look unable to contain himself. "Can we opt to do something else?"

"Oh, we had something else planned, but Danny, Darnell, and Nick voted it down," Marshall shared.

"I didn't vote it down," Larry said.

"Me, neither," Baron chimed in.

Clinton turned in Larry's direction. Pound for pound, each man matched, but Larry was structurally more muscle as well as not mentally complete.

"Oh, we can discuss the options," he said.

Neither recruit liked the sound of that.

"Well, boys, what's it going to be?" Marshall bartered.

Both young men narrowly looked at each other. They both reached for spoons and dug in, egged on by the rooting of the other man.

As the first spoonful touched their palettes, Wynton immediately gagged. Clinton paused but gulped that bite-full down.

Larry wrapped his arm around Clint and beamed, "Good, huh?"

Clint smacked his tongue as Wynton reached for the cup of water before him.

Unable to read why tears were forming at Wynton's eyes, Baron slowed down his intake of the water.

"Is it too hot?" he chortled.

Wynton shook his head. Trying to navigate through the taste, he said, "It tastes like dog shit."

A round of sniggers came from the onlookers.

Larry poked Clint's arm, "Keep going, partner."

Clinton dipped his spoon into the bowl again. He quickly took another gulp. His eyes closed, but he managed to get the plastic utensil back into the bowl for another round.

Clint had two more spoonful sliding down his gullet, as Wynton finally pushed the second down.

Larry, ever the instigator, said, "I like this man." He pounded Clint on his back.

He pointed to Wynton, and said, "I don't think this one is going to make it. Maybe we should have just stayed with the Blue Ice for him."

Carter leaned over the countertop and said, "C'mon Wynton. I got faith in you. C'mon, man, c'mon."

His hands trembled as he reached for another gulp of water. A slurping sound signaled that the cup was empty. He reached for the beer mug only to have Larry slap his hand down.

"That's only if you finish this."

"Fuck you," Wynton coughed up. "Fuck all of you."

Clint chortled. A stream of snot blew from his nostrils as he shoved another round of spoonfuls into his mouth. Clearly, he treated this like it was a chance at a million dollars.

Wynton's eyes widened as he watched his best friend with one spoonful left in his bowl.

Clint smiled back and pushed the water to his buddy. Wynton grabbed the cup two-fisted and began to gulp it down.

Clint closed his eyes. The burning in his chest catching up to him. He grabbed a napkin and wiped his face.

"You can do it, Clint!" Baron said.

Clint looked down into his bowl. One small morsel sat.

"I can drink the beer when I finish this gulp, right?" Clint asked.

"Absolutely," Marshall said.

His face became bloated. He closed his eyes, then opened them. His best buddy was already tanking. Wynton had nothing left. He closed his eyes again, squeezing them tight. The he slowly opened them and scooped up the last helping. His lips barely moving to accept the concoction, but the spoon pried his mouth open.

A loud yell came from the group as Clint reached for the beer mug. His grip so tight, he nearly smashed the glass within his grasp.

"You okay, Clint?" Baron asked.

Nary concern for his health, but the amusement of his actions preceded that question.

Clint rolled his eyes and slid the glass closer. It took a lot of energy for the husky man to bring the glass to his lips, but once the frothy coolness reached his tongue, he had to wash every ounce of his sins.

He slammed the empty mug down, staring each of the men down as his compadre lowered his head trying to accept the challenge as well.

With labored breathing, Clint pushed his way out of the booth, nearly shoving Larry to the floor as he clambered to his escape.

Clint stood wobbly, crouching over the countertop. Relief washed over him as he succeeded in the challenge.

He opened his eyes and could see them talking him up, but he couldn't hear anything beyond the beating of his heart banging hard in his eardrums.

Clint turned and spotted the sign pointing to toward the restroom.

He took a final breath. His eyes fell on Wynton, defeated, but gearing to be a part of something special.

Without that cup of water, Clint knew Wynton couldn't succeed.

Clint's insides were bubbling. He needed to get to the bathroom in a hurry, but he couldn't leave Wynton there alone with that mob.

He reached for the spoon in his empty bowl and took a scoop into Wynton's bowl. He closed his eyes and shoved it in like it was castor oil. He believed his heart stopped for a moment. Wynton looked at him in disbelief as his very own spoon found its way into the bowl.

Each took a turn at the mixture until there was only two scoops left.

Clint's breathing was loud and clogged as he looked at his buddy, and uttered, "You're on your own."

With that, he stumbled toward the bathroom.

Baron turned his attention to Wynton, eyeing the bowl.

"You've got a little left."

Wynton closed his eyes and said a prayer. The little strength that fueled his body came together as he wrapped his hands around the bowl. He cupped the paper and drew it to his mouth and poured the remains down his throat.

Another thunderous roar from the group as he blinked, tossed the bowl to the side, and grabbed the mug of beer.

In the tiny men's bathroom, Wynton took a stall next to one housing Clinton.

"We made it," he weakly exclaimed before finally purging the remnants.

"Yeah," was all Clinton could muster.

TRUDY AND THE GHOST

*P*eeling out the clothes from RaShonda's travel bag was a little daunting to Trudy. For a three-day getaway to a winter time share, this woman packed like she was going to a Vegas convention.

Trudy stood in front of the mirror just marveling at the array of dresses, two pieces and even the haute nightie that was stowed away in the suitcase.

She felt naughty and guilty all at once as she tried on a red low-cut dress – cut a little lower than she expected. It was snug in a tawdry way, but she felt excited as it hugged her in a special way. While Trudy was a little shorter than RaShonda, she realized she was wider in the hips. But this dress accentuated her full grown-ness in a unique way. She suddenly wished she had known this girl on her Junior prom night. She would have slayed in this outfit.

The patent leather pumps while also a little tight just added heft to her.

With her head still wrapped in the hotel towel, she felt incredible. She stood and looked at herself in a different way in the guest bedroom.

It was the third outfit she had tried on and it was perfect.

God, she wondered, what else has she got in her closet.

She stood there longer than she had intended when she heard the knock on the door.

She jumped. Shit. How would she explain going through RaShonda's clothes? This was embarrassing.

But it was a knock. Clearly it couldn't be anyone who was with them. There were keys aplenty amongst them. Danny even had a key.

Another soft knock came from the door.

She walked out the bedroom. The pumps were tighter than she realized. She crept to the middle of the living room area, then stopped, waiting to listen for another knock.

Maybe it was housekeeping. It was almost midnight but given the size of the lodging complex maybe it just took a long time for the service to come around. They had originally waved off the cleaning crew as Danny laid wasted.

Marshall had stolen a handful of towels from another floor afterwards to address the clean-up they had refused. He absconded a couple of days' worth when he and Baron came back with armloads of white cloth towels and soap. Even little bottles of shampoo for her and RaShonda, and miniature bottles of Scope. She commented they should have gotten some sanitizer for the putrid smell Danny left retching in the bathroom. She and RaShonda were left handling that.

Danny cried in her arms that he would make it up to her when he unloaded on her sweater. She just knew it was ruined, but RaShonda got Wynton and Clinton to go out at the beginning of the snowstorm and purchase a bottle of Wool-ite at the AMPM a few miles from the resort.

After all that mess about her age, and fake IDs, and whatever that was with him and Ricky, damn right he was going to make it up to her.

Where the hell was her damn sandwich and chips?

The knock came again. It was harder. Heavier. Still she didn't move.

Then, faintly she heard, "Trudy?"

She began to move to the door as the sound came again, "Trudy, it's me."

"Ricky?" she asked herself out loud.

She moved toward the door. Relief swelled up inside of her that her ride had returned. More than that, but she really wasn't sure what that was. But to hear his voice after last night; what a relief.

She grabbed the doorknob then hesitated. She stuck her eye in the peephole to get a look at him. Did he have a change of clothes in his car? Could he possibly still be in the same outfit he left in? Where'd he go? Where'd he been all this time? Did he get any sleep? Did he bring any food?

She saw nothing. No one. Just canned light burning on an orange carpet.

She turned the doorknob and swung the door open.

The lobby was empty.

She turned around in the opposite direction. Still nothing. Someone was playing games with her.

She stepped back inside and began to shut the door.

"Trudy," she heard again.

She popped her head out. She could make out a silhouette further down the hallway.

"Ricky is that you?" she called out. "Stop playing."

"Help me," the voice said.

A knot tangled up in her gut. She wanted to believe it was a hunger pang. She nearly doubled over.

She went against her better judgment and threw the metal latch across the door so it wouldn't shut her out the apartment.

She slowly walked toward the end of the hallway with RaShonda's tight shoes on. She had to get them off. Cute as they were, they just weren't working for her.

She got to the end of the hall and turned the corner.

No one was there.

"Trudy," she heard once more. "Help me."

One of the canned lights blew out. Sparks shot from the recessed can.

"What the ...?" she thought.

Another blew out. Then another. She flipped out. She began to head back to the unit. As she rounded the corner, she could see more bulbs flaming out from the other end.

She made a mad dash for the apartment, as mad a dash as one could make in high heels.

She nearly tripped, but she caught her balance on the wall to keep from falling.

She pushed forward as she heard her name once again.

Darkness enveloped the hallway as she made it to the door. She pushed her way in and slammed the door, only to have it spring open to close. She leaned into it to force the process.

She could still hear someone calling her name.

She sobbed as she struggled to get the spring to shut. Finally, the jamb clicked, and the door closed. She immediately dead bolted it shut.

She leaned against the door and took deep breaths. Her temple throbbed as adrenalin kicked in. The rush was overwhelming.

There was a bump at the door. She whimpered and moved away.

The door handle began to jiggle as the metal frame shook. She shouted and looked around for a weapon.

Larry's paddle still sat on the table. She picked it up and swooshed it in the air.

The door rattled more as she backed away.

"Trudy, let me in," the voice said.

She stayed crouched in the corner, no longer hungry. Just wishing Danny would hurry up.

The heel caught in the floor vent and Trudy fell. With the paddle still in her hand, her head hit the wall as the rattling continued.

She screamed once more, then the shaking stopped.

Tears streaked down her face. She wiped them away and tried to pry herself from the shoes. She had broken the stiletto heel on the left shoe.

JUST A CLOSER WALK

⚜

The freshness of the cold Midwestern air was quickly clearing his head.

Danny had zipped the bomber jacket completely to the top as he ascended upon the lodge.

The direction he was coming from elicited no memories that he thought would flood his brain once he actually had an opportunity to see everything with light on it.

The final hour of sun that remained buried behind gray clouds was all he needed to find his way the quarter of a mile he had to travel from the time share to the main office. Something was off, but it may have been that the only time he'd ever driven through the land was nearly four years and possibly from another direction.

Nothing was coming to him. Nothing.

A buzzing caught his attention to his left. He glanced at the redwood building and pictured a horse barn that he was sure had been in its stead. The sound was like a giant blender or maybe a pressing machine. Danny couldn't be sure, but it raged for nearly twelve minutes intermittent as he soon approached a wooded ground that had numerous snow-covered picnic tables and an open pit cover with iron railings.

His thoughts bounced around as he tried to recall the actual location of the swimming pool he was approaching. Surely, not the size he remembered, and its design was much more oval than the rectangular Olympic size he recalled. A sheet of ice covered it and he was curious why the pool would be filled this time of year.

As he drew closer to an entrance to the lodge, he was careful to not slip on the icy concrete slab as he made his way through the hotel's spa.

His sense of direction was of no use as he twisted through the hotel's hallway following lighted signage showing the way to the front lobby.

Unlike the time share unit, the guys were staying at, this building appeared to actually have lodgers as he bumped into a couple lugging a cart full of baggage.

There was a scent of cleaning products as he followed the brown patterned carpet through wooden doors that led to other lobbies pointing to the exit only to lead to another hallway of hotel rooms.

Damn, lost again.

He was the last Boy Scout you wanted to get lost in the forest with. Danny had a horrendous sense of direction whether he was outside or in. His inner compass always pointed in another area. There was no true north for him, and the North Star and the constellations were just part of mythology to him.

But he had a keen sense of smell followed by an above average ability to hear things. Once he cleared his mind, he could hear plates clacking together. Using that, he changed course ignoring the exit posting ahead.

His head sensed a clamoring of people gathered together which really piqued his interest as he pushed through another inner lobby hallway. He began to scan door numbers as they moved up.

A brief memory told him he was in the building's third tower as he counted a series of doors in the 3240 range. He was on the second floor of the third tower.

How much walking had he done?

Now he believed, if this was where he thought he was, he needed to be in the first tower, or he could look for the hallway leading to an elevator bank.

He opted for the elevator bank. He moved forward not trusting the way back.

His leg hurt immensely even after that brief jaunt in the sauna. He flinched every other step, but his stomach was roaring. He couldn't quit.

And yet, he could still hear dishes stacking just as clear.

He entered the next lobby over when he distinctly heard the bell of an elevator door opening straight ahead.

Tucked away near the bank of elevators was a figure dressed in a black blazer and red blouse that clung just above the knees.

Danny realized he was a long way from the hotel employee but decided to give it his best shot.

"Hey, hold up," he said. The words cracked from his throat which was still raw and shredded from tossing his cookies throughout the night.

The lodge employee boarded the elevator, then turned in Danny's direction as he was only a quarter of the distance from the conveyor.

His vision was still fogged as he tried to gain the attention of the uniformed patron.

He noticed she immediately attacked the bank of buttons. He thought she was punching to maintain the open door, but the metal dividers began to shut close.

He exerted himself to move quickly hoping that she accidently hit the wrong button.

As he made his way down the corridor halfway from the elevator, he watched her stand in the center of the box and back up toward its wall.

Before the door could completely seal her inside, he caught her face as she stared directly at him.

It was LaMonica Haynes!

The elevator door closed as he approached mere feet from the metal box.

"LaMonica!" he shouted. The door shut closed as he watched tears fall from her eyes.

He glanced at the bank of numbers as it descended from the second floor to the first floor.

Confusion set about his heart as his mind furiously pushed past the cloudiness. Not quite angry, for what, but murky on why she would be there dressed in the hotel's uniform.

His hand ripped hard against the wall as he pressed for the elevators to appear.

Another elevator was up to the ninth floor.

Danny found another exit sign to a fire escape. He attacked the door and bound down the two flights of concrete stairs.

A sign read, "Do Not Open," but Danny be damned at that moment. He'd explain how he got lost to anyone willing to listen. His palm hit the knob, twisted, pulled, nothing.

Another lobby, but he heard the hinges of a door close on his left and saw no hotel rooms. He ambled briskly to the door and as he opened it, saw her going through the one ahead.

Hobbling, he moved quickly down the hallway catching a glimpse of her head.

His hand reached for the door and he flung it wide open.

A cacophony of sound blared at him from all sides as he found himself in the hotel's lobby.

Guests arriving moved to and fro with ski gear, ready for the inclement weather that surprisingly delivered in time for the season.

Danny's turned his head every which way trying to identify the uniform to go along with the thick shoulder length, curly black hair, the hour shaped-glass figure, and the caramel colored skin of LaMonica Haynes.

The front desk was occupied with two families catered to by one lone figure, a blond-haired male trying his best to juggle both groups.

Danny's attention was drawn to the mirrored wall opposite the closed office door. He approached the desk with the agenda to inquire about phone service until he realized he was witnessing the clerk on a landline phone.

His brain scrambled as he positioned himself behind a family of four that was being handed keys and a laminated map of the lodge.

A male dressed in a black pea coat took two steps back and bumped into Danny. He apologized profusely and assured Danny that he was finished with his transaction before wishing him a happy holiday. As awkward as the exchange was, Danny smiled and offered him the same.

He moved up and stood at the desk, hoping the office door would just be open, just a crack. No such luck.

His mind raced when the desk clerk turned to him and surrendered, "Please, excuse me. We're short-handed. I'll be with you soon."

Danny nodded, then said, "It's cool. I'm just looking for LaMonica."

The clerk gave a faint smile, but never actually looked Danny's way. Danny thought about repeating the name, looking at his name tag which read, Joseph with an add-on anchored underneath which said, "Trainee."

Joseph turned to apologize to the family at the desk as he handed a map to the lodge along with a set of keys as he pointed to a bank of elevators down a corridor on the other side of the mirrored wall.

Danny stepped back to get a glimpse of the elevators. He recalled using that tower one year before Lamont's death.

He also remembered that LaMonica and Daphne stayed in that tower the year they met. It was his family that shifted towers.

He wondered if LaMonica was still in the same area. But wasn't she wearing a hotel uniform?

"How may I help you, sir?" the 'trainee' asked in such an accommodating voice.

Where to begin?

Danny wandered back to the front desk, giving his best "Boom-Boom Washington" smile.

"Hi, there," he said slyly as he leaned on top of the desk. "I was wondering if LaMonica was available."

The clerk twisted his face, alerting Danny his strategy didn't work.

He thought to take a different approach.

He raised his arm to his neck, "She's about yay high, black curly hair, and an a..."

He caught himself, not wanting to appear crude.

"She's a very beautiful, vivacious woman of about twenty-one years of age," he rebounded.

Joseph still didn't register any connection.

"You say she works here?" Joseph said.

"I believe so," Danny tried to contain himself with his answer realizing the clerk was about to be diligent in his position.

"Give me a second," Joseph said. He walked to the office door and lightly knocked.

The yowling of a dog seeped through the wooden door startling both Joseph and Danny.

Fear rose in the clerk's eyes as he was told to enter. Danny averted his attention to the mirror as the knob was slowly turned and Joseph cautiously stepped into the room.

Danny saw the black beast rise, approach the door almost inspecting the clerk, then turn away as if called back. It wagged its stubby tail, then lay back down in its spot.

Danny examined the reflection of the office as best he could, but only made out another male roughly in his early thirties.

The other male rose and walked toward the door. Danny turned around to view the café remembering the actual purpose for his trip to the building.

He needed to know if he saw her. He'd thought about her so often. So much so he felt guilty as he recounted their encounter in the sauna. Guilty that he often wondered if anyone would have taken his head off if he had arrived even later after Lamont's drowning as he tried to get a better look down the front of her one-piece bathing suit. He truly believed he could have lost his virginity that night, but chivalry and that damn bruised knee stopped him cold. Nervous as he was, he believed he could have 'pulled' her.

The trainee exited the room somewhat sheepishly. Danny could only imagine what the other guy could have said to him.

"I'm so sorry," Joseph said rather rushed. "I'm afraid we don't have anyone with that name here."

"Really?" Danny was astonished, sure it was her. He shifted gears, "Was that Ace in there?" He was surprised he remembered the dog's name.

Joseph was jolted, he smiled, "Why, no, it's his son, King. How do you know Ace?"

Danny thought to himself, a breakthrough as he said, "I stayed here years ago. I thought that was LaMonica's family dog."

Joseph's smile faded, "I don't know anything about that." He paused and moved to the other half of the desk motioning for another guest. "Is there anything else I can help you with, sir?"

Danny felt the agony of the brush-off.

"Yes," he said, "One more thing. We're having problems with our phone service. Can you send someone to take care of that, please?"

MISSING PERSONS

It had become a series of miscalculated events as far as Marshall was concerned, but it still irritated him to no end.

Maybe it was the lack of sleep, having to watch over Danny, then boosting the towels and toilettes that he oversaw on the second floor. He found it quite odd that the floor was as quiet as it was and how fully stocked the hotel's service cart actually was. Carter and Larry carried back armloads of face rags, throw rugs for the shower, soap bars, and miscellaneous candy bars. All that was missing were the miniature bottles to stock the bar.

Maybe it was the twinge of pain in his lower back carting Nick's furniture down two flights of stairs to load into the rental U-Haul. Why on earth Nick had a four-poster bed was beyond him. Dismantling it was a chore as they had to borrow tools from the Resident Monitor on the wing.

Nick was ill prepared for the move. It was as if he thought everything would magically pack itself. There was obvious tension between Nick and his roommate with accusations flying about clothing borrowed and never returned and the lack of privacy.

Marshall laughed at that. They were in a dorm. What privacy? Where did they think they were staying?

Nick was no different than the rest of them having shared a bedroom with two brothers after sharing a room with his grandmother. Marshall himself had to share a room with an older brother for most of his teen years, having the bedroom to himself finally in his senior year.

No, this was clearly an issue of the roommate's with problems stemming from his boundaries and borders invaded by Nick who just broke all personal space without giving a second thought.

Marshall knew Nick well enough to understand the frustration he could bring when he just saw a necktie that matched his outfit. Or socks that were handy when the laundry was stacked up. Even loose change lying around on laundry day. Nothing was safe around Nick, which Marshall clearly understood was troubling the roommate.

What they had was acrimonious.

Marshall had split from girlfriends with less beef than the tension that was being thrown by this guy.

And Larry was about to give the roommate a beating for some side comments made about Neanderthals.

Larry didn't take it lightly when someone compared him to a caveman or ape. Sure, Larry had some Cro-Magnon characteristics with the large protruding forehead. He had a football helmet specifically designed to fit his head because of the size of his melon in his sophomore year of high school that had to be retrofitted when his head grew larger. This happened three times.

Baron assured Larry the roommate wasn't specifically talking about him, or anyone else with the exception of Nick. But it was clear, the sooner they vacated the premises the better everything would be.

They discovered the new roommate was no more hospitable than the first. Marshall was ready to get out of the joint the minute they arrived.

There were certain terms to the living arrangement that both parties clearly had not formally mapped out.

The utilities being the foremost at the moment.

The water department had not been informed of the new tenancy thus a pipe to discharge their hot water had not been arranged.

The heat in the unit was delayed due to setups during the holiday, but Nick and his roommate were assured they would have a resolution within the hour.

Ma Bell was in-route but that was hours after the guys had arrived.

Marshall felt it was imperative a phone call be made to the Dodgers Lake police department regarding Mike and RaShonda immediately. Baron, too, had his concerns.

There was a battle to get Nick's furniture into the apartment building as they struggled to get certain items, specifically that stupid bed up two flights.

Nick owed them big time with Larry vowing not to be available when the time came from Nick to leave his new abode. Larry was adamant about this as well as the certainty that a move would be forthcoming shortly.

Wynton, Clint, and Carter were sent to round up food, which was supposed to be a payment from Nick, but two-thirds of the money to buy the pizza from a joint Nick's new roommate swore was only a few miles away came out of their pockets. Marshall was furious.

The telephone installation couldn't happen soon enough. Exactly two hours after the pizza had been consumed, the buzzer to the apartment rang with the announcement of the phone company's arrival.

An hour later the phone was wired, but there was a problem with Nick's portion of the down payment. Nick argued that there had to be a misunderstanding on how the payment was to be billed, leading to a conversation of no service until a resolution occurred.

Meaning more money out of the guys' pockets.

Five minutes and sixty-two dollars later, there was a dial tone.

Marshall didn't even wait for the telephone service rep to exit; he was on the phone with an operator to reach the police department.

He experienced a series of holds before he found himself talking to a detective.

"Rossi, how may I help you?" the North Midwestern voice on the other end of the line asked.

"Yes," Marshall said, "My name is Marshall Whitacre. My friends and I are staying at the Dodgers Lake Resort and we'd like to file a missing person's report."

There was a pause on the other end of the line. Marshall wasn't even sure if he was still on the line.

"Hello?" Marshall called out.

"Sorry about that," Rossi said. "You say somebody is missing? How's that again?"

Marshall was unsure where to start. "Yes, sir," he said. "We have been guests at the hotel staying in the time shares there."

"Really," Rossi said sounding bemused. "Didn't know they had finally opened that area. Thought they were still delayed."

"No, sir," Marshall said. "They are open as far as we can tell. We are staying in the bungalows," Marshall paused, then said, "Can you give me a moment?"

He called out to Darnell for the actual suite number before returning to the phone.

There was a discomfort about the call. Not with the cop, but the comment about the time share and the viability of its opening.

He explained most of the events to the officer on the line excluding the events of Danny's birthday.

The officer seemed to take his information in stride before he finally asked the most obvious question.

"What time did you say your two friends disappeared?"

Marshall thought about this and tracked by his account the estimated time.

"Three o'clock this morning, sir," he said.

MISSING PERSONS | 173

"What's your name again?" Rossi asked.

"Marshall Whitacre, sir," Marshall sucked his teeth with aggravation.

There was another long pause on the phone before the officer finally said. "Sir, usually we don't take calls on missing persons until twenty-four hours."

Marshall was flummoxed. Marshall asked suddenly feeling a sense of rage, "You mean I have to wait until three tomorrow morning before I can report the disappearance of my friends?"

"'Fraid so, sir. If your friends are still missing around that time, feel free to call us back. The desk officer will file a report."

With that the phone went dead.

Marshall held the receiver helplessly looking over to his friends.

"Ain't that some shit?" Marshall commented to himself aloud as he slammed the receiver down.

"What'd he say?" Baron asked.

Marshall, perplexed, said, "We got to wait until 3 a.m. before we can file a report. You believe this bullshit?"

Marshall watched as the rest of the guys were tossing around the boxes of pizza and bottles of beer they had picked up along the way.

The roommate moved toward the phone, asking Marshall, "Do you mind?"

Marshall took hold of the receiver, raising his hand gesturing one minute.

"Who you calling?" Larry asked as he tossed an empty beer bottle into a garbage bag.

Marshall wagged his finger at Larry as he said, "Hello, yes, Dodgers Lake Resort? I'm looking for the suite of Darnell Wilkins."

A young man's voice said, "We are trying to get service to the suite. Maybe you'd like to leave a message?"

Marshall thought about it.

"When do you think you'll have the service back up? It's been out all night," Marshall said.

The voice of the clerk was cool and assuring, "We're on it. I will talk to the manager right away. She's coming my way right now. Feel free to check back."

Marshall accepted the answer resolved he'd done all he could at that moment.

Now all he could do was wait.

She approached the front desk having heard mention of needing her assistance.

"Everything, alright, Joe?" she asked.

The trainee smiled.

"There appears to be a problem with phone service at Bungalow 115," he said. "A guest walked all the way from over there to inform us of a similar problem, Ms. Phillips."

LaMonica Haynes smiled back at the clerk and said, "Maybe I should take care of that."

The clerk acquiesced, "If it's no bother, otherwise, I'll be more than happy to handle it."

"No problem at all," she said as she entered the office. The Rottweiler rose guardedly before relaxing upon acknowledging her presence.

BLACK HAWK

⁂

Formed during the tail end of the ice age, Clark Street had been a key trail for thousands of years.

Stretching back as far as 14,500 years ago, the terrain of Chicago was shaped by the ebbs and flows of melting ice.

The process of littoral drift, small bits of sand and organic matter shifted from place to place on the tide where small but distinct ridges were etched into the land.

Rising no more than ten or fifteen feet above the terrain, those natural high grounds became some of the pathways used by Native peoples as they began to inhabit the area about eleven-thousand years ago.

For the indigenous tribes, these high points held obvious value due to most of the land being swampy and very little stayed dry year-round.

Passing down their understanding of the land's natural features through oral traditions greatly helped incoming European settlers traveling to the area during the seventeenth and eighteenth centuries who depended on this knowledge for survival as they quickly came to understand the significance of the trails which they adapted for commercial and military purposes.

This was the first land that Doctor Gillette's family encountered those indigenous footpaths which for centuries were not wider than five or six feet across before widening and normalized to become Chicago's first roads.

It was the Northwest Ordinance of 1787 that not only brought George Rogers Clark, brother of William, one half of the Lewis and Clark expedition, but the Gillette's as well when Corporal Michael Gillette traveled to the territory after the American Revolutionary war.

Their roots followed a route north of the Loop from North Avenue on the path of an Indian trail called Green Bay trail that ran all the way to Green Bay, Wisconsin while in pursuit of the Sauk war chief, Black Hawk.

Black Hawk, a Sauk leader and war captain had fought against the United States in the War of 1812. He emerged as a leader of the Sauk faction in 1829 when he was well into his sixties.

While not a civil chief, he had influence within his tribe.

As head of eight-hundred Sauk, roughly one-sixth of the tribe, he chose to resist American expansion after disputing an 1804 treaty that was signed insisting that what had been written down was far different than what had been discussed at that treaty conference, believing that whites were in the habit of saying one thing to the Indians and putting another thing down on paper.

After the Battle of Stillman's Run on May 14, 1832, Black Hawk's "British Ban" attacked a militia camp at Stillman Valley, thus killing twelve Illinois militiamen with only forty warriors.

It was in June of 1832 that Black Hawk wound up in South Wayne, Wisconsin when his band of thirty warriors attacked a group of farmers, killing and scalping four in an attempt to lead the Americans from his camp at Lake Kosh Konong.

By June 25, 1832, Black Hawk's last military success in war at the second Battle of Kellogg's Grove, finally saw him take his tribe back across the Mississippi before he finally surrendered to American troops after the Battle of Bad Axe in Tonah, Wisconsin.

It was here that rumors, and legends had birthed a tale of a treasure that Black Hawk had his people bury near the area now known as Dodgers Lake.

Doctor Gillette had recounted that story numerous times to his granddaughters as he began his pursuit to purchase land at various sites along that trail opening three resorts from Gurnee, Illinois to the very site Molica now found herself cursed to reside as the doddering old fool chased the ghosts of a legacy filled with more bloodshed than perhaps the very silver her mother believed existed.

The hunt for this treasure came about from her maternal great-great grandfather who served in the U.S. 86th Infantry Division otherwise known as the "Black Hawk Division," under the direction of Frederic McLaughlin, who ironically became the original owner of the National Hockey League's, Chicago Blackhawks.

SHE WAS BORN Molica Alicia Phillips. Told her first name was French for 'angel,' she earned her middle name from her maternal grandmother whom she never met. Nor did she ever meet the good doctor until one month after her fifth birthday to celebrate the birth of her half-sister, Veronica. Her father had disappeared nearly three years prior, replaced with the likes of Chad Beecher.

Upon the appearance of Gilbert Gillette, Molica immediately understood why there were no visits to his first grandchild. The disdain that he looked down upon her made her cognizant of the fact that even her stepfather never initially brought into her home. As she was a black child that never mattered.

Veronica, by then was the third of the doctor's grandchildren. He shared many stories of his family's lineage, especially their involvement in the surrender of Black Hawk.

His eyes glistened whenever he talked about the lost treasure that the Sauk chief may have looted and hid in the outskirts of Tonah.

She only heard the stories around the holidays when he came around to see his 'pure' granddaughter.

She became impervious to his malicious standoffishness. He pushed her away for so long, she stopped even bothering to care, always asking to be excused whenever his company was present.

An odd relationship also came into being with her stepfather, who would offer her potential visits with the father she barely remembered. By the time she was ten, she realized he was threatening her. She knew she would soon have to turn the tables on him. Her mother was of no use in this matter, but her grandfather became a stalwart ally especially when she hinted at possible malfeasance to his precious 'Roni.'

While never fully comprehending the little tune-up that occurred, old boy Chad never remotely looked at either cross-eyed.

Her grandfather eventually "rewarded" her five years later by acknowledging her birthday. Her antennae soon raised, knowing the old man well enough. He took her for a solo ride to the Wisconsin border for a trip to the Botanical Gardens in Green Bay.

For the first time, he talked to her one on one about his dreams for his family. He shared with her a vision, then asked if she wished to see it.

She was painfully eager, but she still waited for the shoe to drop.

They drove another thirty minutes north finally pulling into a small resort with lush greens that led to a nine-hole golf course.

A valet parked the car and called her grandfather by name which struck her as odd. How did this attendant know to call him "doctor?" How often did her grandfather travel to this resort?

As they entered, many clerks and bellmen also acknowledged the old man by title.

They walked to the small grill buried on the side next to an elevator bank. They were seated immediately as business appeared slow.

Molica was handed a menu but found nothing close to her liking on the trifold brochure.

Doctor Gillette asked her what she'd like, and she said as innocently as possible, "Grilled cheese, please?"

The old man laughed, tucked away the menus, and grabbed her hand leading her to the kitchen.

As they moved past the swinging door into the cook house, Molica was overcome by the array of metal. Counters, cutlery, cooking utensils, just a sea of sterling silver consumed her.

The chef immediately ran over to the tour pleading to remedy whatever it was the good doctor's guest requested.

Gillette asked for two aprons, the block of cheddar, petals of butter, and the largest pan in the house.

Gillette spent nearly fifteen minutes sharing his skills in the delicacy known as the grilled cheese sandwich.

They ate at a booth in the back of the restaurant sharing grilled cheese sandwiches made from one of the largest providers of dairy products in Cambridge, Wisconsin. Along with a plate of special cut French fried potatoes that they shared.

This was a magical moment for Molica who thought her grandfather never gave two shits about her. Hurtful things always came out his mouth about how dirty she looked with her naturally frizzy locks.

As she dipped her fries in a splash of ketchup, the old man reached in the breast pocket of his dress shirt and produced a silver coin.

Holding it up in front of her, he asked, "Do you know what this is?"

"A silver dollar," she said nearly spitting chunks of the fried potatoes clear across the table.

He laughed as she took a napkin to wipe the spittle from the countertop. "No, Pumpkin," he said softly. "This is the key to our future."

As he handed the coin to her, he retold the story of the Sauk leader, Black Hawk and his "British Band."

She had never been called "Pumpkin" by him before. She had

been called many things by him, but never anything remotely as personal other than her name.

She played with the coin, popping it in the air from her palm. It was quite heavy.

She asked, "This is real silver?"

He nodded, "And there's more of it out here. But we have to find it. I may need your help," he alluded.

"More?" she asked intrigued. "Where? When?"

A smile curled on his face as he cut the conversation to one short statement, "I'll explain more to you later."

He stood out the booth and walked toward a stout gentleman with slick black hair, pencil mustache, and a pinstripe suit. The doctor introduced him as one of the proprietors of the resort, Mr. Seth Holland.

"And this must be the birthday girl," the girthy man cajoled. With a toothy smile, he said, "You must be my guest tonight for dinner, please?"

The doctor waved for Molica to tuck the coin away as the two men shook hands.

"We couldn't impose," Gillette countered. "Plus, I have to get this one back home right away."

Surprised, the swarthy gentleman asked, "Oh, you are not staying the night? I had a suite prepared for you, too."

"Well, if you insist," Gillette said. "We accept your offer."

The gentleman reached for Molica's hand and planted a gentle kiss upon it. She was taken aback by the gesture. She was beginning to receive many offers from her male counterparts at school, but they were mere boys. Mr. Holland was a gentleman. Whatever that meant.

They rushed to the hotel suite which really was a surprise to her as she found out her grandfather had brought travel bags for a night's stay. When she inquired how he knew they would be there for the night, he said, "One must be prepared."

Inside a garment bag was a strapless dress that she had never seen before along with a pair of pumps that were exactly like ones for which she had begged but was told by her mother they were too expensive. She also found a makeup kit that she initially balked at as she rarely found a need for anything including foundation.

Her grandfather talked to her briefly explaining about Mr. Holland and how that very hotel was part of a bigger plan to find the treasure of Black Hawk.

Much of it went too fast for her as they made their way to the hotel lobby later that evening to dine at the resort's seafood restaurant.

Mr. Holland had already arrived waiting for the both of them at a booth in the back of the dimly lit restaurant.

Her grandfather offered a toast on her behalf, a birthday gesture.

Holland had champagne delivered. Molica had never had a sip of liquor, but her grandfather gave his approval for this special occasion.

Mr. Holland sat next to her and asked how she like the wine, telling her he chose it specifically for her as the rosy reminded him of her. Molica smiled at him as she got giggly from the bubbles. She really didn't remember much except that the man's breath was extremely hot like a sewer.

Her grandfather had gotten serious for a moment with Mr. Holland as a large frosted layer cake was brought out with one huge candle stuck in the center. Her name was inscribed on the vanilla frosting with no actual birthday written. Holland apologized, citing he didn't know exactly how old she was.

Her grandfather laughed, stating, "You know women, it's always a secret."

The two men laughed heartily at her expense. She, too, soon joined in agreeing with the old man.

"How old do I look?" she said innocently teasing the gentleman as he poured her another glass while the server cut the cake into slices.

Another toast was made in her honor and the three clinked glasses.

A plate of cake was placed before her when Holland opined to her grandfather, "Maybe some addendums could be made to the terms of the contract."

As she took the fork into the flower decoration on the cake, she remembered her grandfather's face was screwed up as he reprimanded Holland, "Have I not kept my end of the bargain with a down payment as promised?"

The old man turned in her direction and said solemnly as she shoved the utensil into her mouth, "Happy birthday, Pumpkin." A sweetness jumped out onto her tongue. It was wonderful, but clearly masking something like cream and sugar would cloak castor oil in a cup of coffee.

It was also the last thing she remembered of that evening.

SHE WOKE in their hotel room late the next morning. She sat up immediately finding the door to the bedroom closed. Her dress adorned a hanger dangling from a hook on the back of the door.

She had lost her virginity with a boy on the basketball team a year earlier, but she knew something wasn't right no matter how cleaned up she may have been.

She made it to the door, noticing crisscross markings on her right wrist. There was a reddish tint to her skin on both wrists.

She opened the door and found the old man packing a briefcase.

"Hey, there, sleepy head," he crowed. "I thought you were going to sleep all day."

He closed the briefcase and gave her a smile that absolutely ruined her.

Next to the case was a slice of unfinished cake which he immediately tossed away in an iron receptacle.

"Hurry up and get dressed," he ordered. "We've got a treasure to collect."

While never confirmed by the old man, she believed a deal was brokered between the two men where she was the bargaining chip or at least a down payment.

They never discussed the events of that weekend, but he bought her a Cherry red Miata the following year for her Sweet Sixteen birthday.

He was on his way to acquiring his second resort less than a year after the events with Mr. Holland.

She never inquired how he even came up with the capital to purchase the first property, let alone move forward on another.

Yet, he always seemed more obsessed with that elusive treasure.

She would find him staring at the coin, begging it to talk to him, tell him where Black Hawk had hidden the rest of the loot he allegedly shanghaied.

She had little faith in the story he was told as a little boy. Just a carny story to keep him amused, she believed.

LAMONT & DAPHNE

⚜

They were heading toward the 94 highway. Molica sat in front with Danny driving, Roni and Lamont were huddled up in the backseat.

The tilt of the steering wheel column seemed awkwardly out of range for Danny, as Molica perceived he either didn't drive often or he had just received his license. She leaned more in the latter option.

They made small talk with no real destination. Molica thought it was just a good way to feel Danny out before she figured how to use him. She felt out of place, careful not to initiate contact with him and have him use it later against her.

"Do y'all believe in ghosts?" she heard the words sail from her sister's lips. Molica turned abruptly and gazed at Roni as the wind whipped her hair all over her face. She kept pulling it back with her hands, but no sooner did she have it in place strands would sweep from the other side.

"What?" Lamont asked with the goofiest of laughs. "Ghosts? Why, no. That would mean I believe in an afterlife."

Molica took notice of that immediately, trying to shift where her bubble brained baby-sister was going.

"You don't believe in an afterlife?" Molica asked.

"Do you go to church?" Roni got out before Molica could stop her.

"Nope," he said plainly and flat. "Don't believe in Heaven or Hell, either."

"Wow, that's deep," Danny said. "What's up with that?"

Molica watched Lamont looked toward the window. With a shrug, he commented, "With all that's gone on in the world, especially my bigger brother losing his legs in the war, and the horrible way my daddy died..."

"How'd your daddy die?" Roni asked.

"He was decapitated in a car crash," Danny said.

Molica stared in horror as she saw a stream of tears fall down Lamont's face. He screwed his lips up as if a bitterness from the image of his father's death came over him.

Roni pulled him onto her shoulder and calmly said, "Jesus loves you. Don't you ever forget that."

Molica suddenly lost focus on the play. The two sisters were both drawn to Lamont's sensitivity. Molica later realized, maybe too drawn by the genuineness of it.

The rest of the ride was pretty quiet.

Lamont was under Roni's spell at that point and Roni was on a mission.

'LaMonica' had to remind 'Daphne' what their objective was. Roni wasn't so sure she was up for the task countering that Danny was the target.

Their grandfather wanted them to stop lollygagging and get the set up over with.

"Good Lord," he blustered, "how hard is it to get a horny teenage boy to try to jump your bones?"

Molica attempted to make plans with Danny later that evening after dinner. He asked her the time and place. As he left her, she noticed him walking gingerly.

She innocently asked if he was all right, praying nothing hindered the plan she had to put together.

He waved off the momentary injury promising to be available for a night in the hotel's jacuzzi – just the two of them.

She suggested she may be able to help him with his throbbing knee and she could take care of anything else that might be throbbing.

She immediately knew she had gone over the line, but he perked up ready to meet her later. He almost slipped down the lobby to the elevator bank.

Once again, the old man wasn't interested in the particulars, just her getting the job done.

The one-piece that she threw on was mighty snug. Her sister looked fantastic in a hot pink two-piece string bikini, but Molica was concerned that her very own natural curvy backside – or as she called it, her black side - might dissuade Danny.

She joked that maybe they should trade places and she take Lamont. He was as harmless as a wet puppy. Probably just drool all over her.

The good doctor was not amused.

"Get it done, now!" Gillette said.

They met in the hotel lobby.

Danny and Lamont had baggy swimming shorts. Danny also had a muscle tee to flex the wrestling outline he bragged about earlier during their drive. Lamont dressed like his mother still picked out his clothes.

Roni grabbed Lamont's hand. They made an incredibly cute couple. Molica wasn't sure who was going to be more devastated when this was over – Roni or Lamont.

Danny's knee was swollen. Fluid sloshed around with the slightest of movement. He grimaced more than he smiled and was too embarrassed to recall the events of why he jumped into the shallow end of the resort's outside pool. He only detailed how slippery the surface was when he landed. Molica realized the resort had not properly mixed their cleaning solutions based off similar problems her grandfather experienced at the first resort when he, too slipped on the bottom floor.

Roni asked, "Does it hurt? It looks awfully painful."

Danny had iced it up in hopes to have flexibility when they caught up with the girls. However, the remedy caused inflammation and tightness in the joint, he relayed.

Molica reminded him, she had the perfect solution for his problem.

She promised Roni and Lamont they would meet them poolside later. At that time, her grandfather had rented out the picnic area for a family outing next to the pool to oversee the setup.

She was going to do this alone if at all.

"I'm taking you to the sauna," she informed Danny. "We'll catch them later."

She escorted him through the lobby to a backway which connected to a separate tower.

Danny was confused by the position. The walk was killing him, and he had no idea where he was. Even though he had been at the indoor jacuzzi numerous times.

She assured him they were taking a shortcut.

It had happened earlier when they went for the drive, she observed Danny had no memory for directions. He got turned very easily and frustrated immediately. He would lose his composure and could be very sardonic to hide his loss of control. They had merely driven a quarter of a mile off, but she could swear he had taken a ramp to another state.

They made it to the third tower and found the sauna. The timing was perfect. They had the entire place to themselves.

She teetered on the thought of witnesses. She was extremely uncomfortable with the role of seductress.

She helped him into the small pool as the jets created a whirl of bubbles. He winced as he took the steps and fell onto her. His hand 'accidentally' fell unto her chest. It lingered before he apologized like he actually had home training, but she saw he was aroused.

He positioned himself against the back of the hot tub as the jets' bubbles swirled around him. She went to adjust the temperature and noticed he glistened in the heated pool. She was impressed at how tone he actually was. He was not buffed, but sinewy.

Not bad for a seventeen-year-old, she acknowledged.

"What are you doing later?" he asked bashfully.

She crept to the edge and leaned over, close enough, but not touching him. She whispered, in his ear, "What would you like to do?"

Without any provocation, he kissed her softly on her cheek. Passionate, not exactly, more like thankful.

She alluringly climbed into the water and stood in front of him. They gazed into each other's eyes as Danny switched positions.

A stream of bubbles from the jets encircled him and she figured out he had the propulsion massaging his tender knee.

She moved next to him as he seemed at peace, removed from the pain.

She couldn't take him down for a peck on the cheek, could she?

Her grandfather would be livid, but she couldn't do it. He was a kid and she wasn't going to let something so innocent take that away from him.

Unlike what her grandfather would do.

They talked for almost an hour, more like he talked as she listened.

Turned out he wasn't so much a jock like she imagined he thought of himself. He was a film geek who wanted to just work a soundboard and mix audio for film.

It was very disheartening to hear the rationale on his aspirations to be behind the scenes of Hollywood magic. The veneer of the extrovert was protecting the little, shy introvert who just wanted to be a part of the process.

He needed a big sister. Big brothers only forced bravado. Big sisters cut through the bullshit and shielded baby brothers. He had plenty of time to get laid. He needed a sister to lean on.

She jumped out the pool.

"We have to check on Daphne and Lamont," she reminded him never once breaking character.

"I hope your sister can swim," he said. "Lamont can't swim a lick. I have been trying to teach him all week so he could impress your sister."

If only she had known sooner. Lamont died that night.

WHEN SHE ROLLED over the next morning, the sun shone right on her face. She squinted as the rays poked in.

She concealed her vision with a hand seeing a blurry blob standing feet away from her staring out the window.

"How long you been up?" groggily she asked as she moved toward her sister to stand beside her.

It had been a long night even after the picnic crowd had dissipated.

Her grandfather had given a police report and promised to deliver Roni to give any information they deemed necessary. With no details to contribute, there was no need for Molica to be interviewed. Danny had already given a statement earlier.

They both watched as Danny and his father placed luggage in the trunk of the Catalina, pulling bags from a hotel luggage rack.

To Molica, neither of the Alexanders appeared to be talking to one another, but the elder did give direction pointing from one bag to another for Danny to hand him.

Her heart ached. She wanted to run to Danny to let him know it wasn't his fault, no matter what he felt in his heart, his cousin's passing wasn't on him.

She felt remorse, wanted to hold him earlier as she watched him breakdown. She told herself if his two uncles hadn't been there, she would have consoled him. After all, she was the one who delayed him.

Maybe, if they had left five minutes sooner, Lamont would still be alive. Maybe, ten minutes sooner. Maybe.

But they weren't there sooner, and Lamont was dead.

Her mother was ordered to get them away from the scene immediately by their grandfather.

Roni was devastated. She sobbed uncontrollably throughout the night. She kept talking about how the spirit wouldn't let her in the water to save Lamont. Molica kept trying to extract what she meant, but she only said, "There was something evil in the water keeping me out the water."

Molica believed the stress her grandfather had placed himself under chasing the ghost of Black Hawk and his phantom treasure had finally hit Roni.

Throughout their stay, she mentioned fingerprints on the walls of their hotel room.

"Can't you see them, Mo? Right there in the bathroom, on the door."

The old man's disease had begun to spread like a virus. Molica had insulated herself within the confines of her studies two thousand miles west and never realized the vise-like grip his 'Rasputin – Mad czar' rhetoric had on her family.

Her mother was no better, but she just ignored her pleas to come home to help. Now she stood resolute on how right she actually was.

A knock came at the door. The knob turned before they ever had a chance to respond and Gillette entered poking his head inside.

"Good," he beamed, "you're up. Get dressed. I got something to show you."

"It was an accident," he said for the thousandth time, trying his best to pound that into their heads.

Roni was completely puffy faced from crying most of the night. She nodded off for no more than an hour's worth of sleep.

Molica was no worse for wear as she spent most of the night trying to convey the same sentiment. But someone was at fault.

He stood looking as if he were disgusted with them both.

Molica didn't care as they sat at the small oval table in the suite. Roni's head rested on her shoulder as she continued to sob.

Chad and their mother were in the other half of the suite, moving around like packrats.

She couldn't understand why they were so busy.

"He was a horrible swimmer," he said. "We were just trying to help him."

"He couldn't swim at all," Molica divulged as tears welled up falling rapidly onto her cheeks. "He was trying to impress Roni."

Roni's head shot up from her sister's arm. Molica knew she had betrayed her with that comment.

"You're saying it's my fault?" she stammered in horror.

"Not at all," Molica said defensively trying to quell what anxiety she already felt. "Danny tried to teach him to swim all week. It was his first time on his own. That's all I'm saying."

"Exactly," her grandfather said. "It was brash of the young man, but it was an accident, darlin'."

Roni got up and immediately ran to the bedroom, slamming the door behind her as she caterwauled all the way.

It was just the two of them now.

He tossed the coin onto the table. It looked different from before, as if it had aged considerably.

"I don't have time for this," Molica said as she began to rise.

She barely noticed him tussling with his hand in his jeans pocket.

When she finally pushed her chair in to walk away, he tossed another coin on the table. A matching coin.

She stopped. Her eyes widened as they met his which burst with an explosion of joy that registered on his face.

"This is the place," he announced proudly. "I knew it all along. This proves it."

She lifted the first coin.

"Where'd this come from?" she asked with impunity.

"Your friend was choking on this coin. I pulled it from his throat."

A flood of information rushed at her.

"What does this mean?" she followed up.

Picking up the other coin, he rejoiced, "This is the place Black Hawk hid his loot."

RONI

*H*er grandfather got the winning bid.
She got the fuck out of there.

She spent her last year in school in seclusion. Apart from the internship with a brokerage house, she kept to herself; 1980 was a very hard year.

Veronica, her mother, and Chad moved onto the lodge's area in the third tower taking over most of the seventh floor.

She and Roni talked often, but she heard nothing but pain in her little sister's voice.

To help with the 'remodeling' of the resort, her grandfather brought in her cousins, two pieces of shit who had believed his story about Black Hawk's stolen loot.

She missed many phone calls as her graduation loomed.

But one call had her rush back when Roni said she saw Lamont.

She'd complained about the nightmares she'd had. How she'd wake up and see him standing in her doorway.

She called her mother to discuss Roni's well-being. Her mother said, "Well you know Roni. She's just so sensitive like that. She'll move on soon enough like I did with your father."

But Roni wasn't moving on. She was going backward. She constantly replayed the moment Lamont help up the coin. Showing her what he'd found.

She said when Chad and their grandfather jumped in to "save" him, that's when she first saw the ghosts. Holding her back from the water. She tried to tell Lamont to swim, but he hit his head and the demons wouldn't let her in the water.

Molica recalled asking, "Didn't you say ghosts at first?"

To which Roni said, "I said something evil. Ghosts, demons, what's the difference?"

"So, when you see Lamont, which is he?" she countered.

Her sister hung up. She couldn't reach her after that.

She reached the "compound" – her sister's term – and had to get clearance from the front desk, employees who had never met her and had no clue who she was.

Her cousin, Shane, was called down to handle a situation with some frantic customer.

Shane, all smiles in a Brooks Brothers three-piece suit vouched for her.

As they entered the elevator to the central office, he confided how off Roni was. She'd been seeing "doctors" off and on until Gillette himself decided to administer all meds from that point on as he was still practicing medicine.

When she finally saw Roni, she was a completely different person. Upbeat, but not so much in a sunshiny way she had always been. Very direct, suddenly, but withdrawn.

They finally had some alone time.

"What's up?" she asked Roni.

"I'll be graduating soon," she said. "Can you believe it?"

She had forgotten, so focused on her own closing date, that she never even acknowledged her sister was two weeks away from a commencement ceremony.

"I'm so sorry," she apologized profusely. "I forgot. Can you still get me a ticket? I promise I will be there."

"Absolutely," Roni guaranteed. "One's been waiting for you."

"Good. I wouldn't miss this for the world," she said with much relief. "Did you go to prom?"

Her sister looked despondent. "He said he'd take me, but he never showed up."

"Oh, Sweetie," Molica grabbed her hands as tears flowed from Roni's eyes. "I'm so sorry."

"He said he'd make it up to me," Roni said, "I don't think he would lie."

"Who's this guy? You never mentioned a boyfriend."

Roni leaned in to share a secret. "He's the cutest guy. I met him here. You will love him. His name is Lamont."

Molica met with her mother who was busy with an exercise routine in a room in the second tower, adjacent to the spa.

She expressed a desire to have Roni spend the summer with her. Her mother refused the offer. It would be the summer rush and they needed all hands available. There was a hope to draw Molica back after she graduated.

She laughed at the idea, thanked her mother for the thought, but she wouldn't be coming back. She asked her mother to reconsider her offer to take Roni back when she visited for the graduation.

Her mother said how much she'd changed. Molica realized it wasn't a compliment.

"Oh, mommy," she said. "I wish you'd both come back with me. We can have a good life in Phoenix."

Her mother turned away from her with a parting wish that Molica never return to the premises. She was no longer welcomed.

She vowed to surrender to her mother's request.

She talked to Roni off and on during the summer. No one attended her graduation. She regretted missing Roni's explaining how she got bogged down training for a new job. Roni's silence on the other end of the line shredded her to her very soul.

She couldn't reach Roni after the Fourth of July. Days past and she finally relented and called her mother. She, too, did not return calls until the first week of August. Only then did she inform Molica that Roni was dead.

On the holiday weekend of the Fourth, Roni had decided to take a horse ride just before a fireworks show. When the show began, a series of explosions had spooked the horse, throwing Roni off its back, and stomping on her skull.

She was dead instantly.

She'd been buried weeks ago.

Then her mother hung up. No good-bye just click.

MO

While working on her series 7 certification to be a broker, she worked for the small company's telemarketing division selling life insurance, primarily term policies.

Beyond studying for her exam, she found no reason to return to her apartment working double shifts making calls outside the state.

She failed the first time she took the certification exam. She barely read the letter in its entirety. She wasn't pissed, nor disgusted. She had settled for indifferent. Her boyfriend at the time tried to encourage her to take a break, then hit the books again – hard. He was certain she could succeed next time.

She really didn't care; she went back to the pit to take phone calls.

She was on a second shift months later, counting down the minutes before they showed her the door for the afternoon. She racked up more hours that week than management allowed their hourly employees to take. If she were management, they'd have no qualms how long she stayed, she'd be salaried.

"One more call, Mo," Steve, her floor manager quietly told her, "then I gotta pull you."

She nodded, preparing for the dial tone.

As Steve walked by her cubicle, he said, "See you later tonight, sugar."

Without missing a beat, she looked at the call back log and began, "Good evening. I am looking for Carol Alexander."

She didn't close the deal on that call. Carol had informed her that her husband handled such things as life insurance. But before that, she said the correct spelling of her name, and the names of her spouse and a college attending son, both named Danny.

Her heart stopped.

After the call she tore the page out of the logs. She pocketed the sheet, telling Steve she had to go to the bathroom.

"Better luck next time," he coached her. He had crystal brown eyes and dark hair with a tinge of blonde in it. He was born with that tall swimmer's body and he loved her.

"Yeah," she took in before she could seal herself in a stall.

She sat down as her head pounded. She didn't ask herself any unnecessary questions. She knew the answers.

She wasn't looking for them. They just appeared. Happenstance. A database full of names and numbers. Thousands, no tens of thousands printed on reams of paper, and that name just came up on her call roster.

What was she going to do with the information she added? What could she do? Call for Danny to see how he was doing? *Hi, how are you. Sorry I haven't had a chance to call sooner.*

The form itself had nothing more than a serial number on it. Techs in the backroom could apply it and extract more information on the customer, but she had no number. The battery of questions she was prompted to ask, plus some liberties she took as part of her call technique as Mrs. Alexander said her background data, she could find Danny if she wanted, if she needed, if she so desired. .

She inserted the key inside the hole. There was a little play before it finally surrendered and turned. She had numerous conversations with the old man about the magnetic key strips becoming less effective. Too many patrons had similar problems.

It was on a list of things to address.

But first…

When he came to her last winter, he made an offer she considered without much debate.

Her mother needed her. Or so he said.

He needed her. He was straight forward once she touched down and made it to the resort.

Her first request, *no demand*, was to demolish the horse barn. He got rid of the horses but kept the barn. He converted it for different purposes that she could live with.

The resort had been shuttered for the winter for "renovations."

He still believed the loot was somewhere near the pool area and had moved it at least four times. More like repositioned it, then reformatted it.

Still no treasure, but he knew better.

That fall of '81, she oversaw the installation of the pool's filtration system. Curtis worked for the operating company managing the pool work.

"I'm afraid I have some news about the filtering system," he told her.

There was corrosion in the piping that connected to the reservoir. She asked to be taken to the site. There she discovered the true nature of the blockage.

Curtis showed her the cracks due to the age of the piping and where deterioration had finally caved the entire line down.

It was what she accidently discovered yards down poking through the line that she couldn't believe.

No more than five degrading burlap bags had cracked through with tree roots that matured their way into the line. In the bags were silverware, papers so yellowed whatever was printed on them had faded away, and one full satchel of silver.

She thanked Curtis profusely, elated the old man's nightmare was over. Curtis told her their problem was deeper rooted. The blockage still loomed on the property and to her surprise meant more bags had seeped through.

Proof was delivered within days before Halloween.

She retrieved a coin. It was identical to the one her grandfather had recovered from Lamont.

In his search on the property for the treasure, he dislodged it but never discovered it, thus rerouting the piping problem.

She stopped the pool excavation, promising to continue the job in the spring.

She would explain her reasoning – once she came up with one – to the old man in the morning.

She carted the materials through a back entrance of the hotel, stopped twice by employees who said to help. She waved them off, thanking them immensely.

When she got to the room, she knew she had to find a place to bury the goods. The only temporary spot was the mini safe they had recently installed in the rooms.

She tried to remember the keypad combination as her fingers rested on a small smidge of red clay. She inspected her fingers, but they were clean save for a small trace of black soot from the bags.

She had seen a pattern of similar prints recently but thought nothing of it.

The cleaning crew may have accidently left some residue. She would check into it when she had the room serviced.

She punched the code once she recalled it being Veronica's birth date and sealed the bag's contents inside. She retrieved just one coin for herself.

After all this time, the old man was right.

She had booked her ticket to arrive at Phoenix Sky Harbor the day before Thanksgiving, weeks in advance.

She knew when she saw him everything would be alright. She was losing her mind with the old man's incessant badgering about the treasure.

Now that she'd seen it for herself, she had to punish him.

For all the pain and suffering her family had endured, she concocted a plan that would address his desires.

Bringing Danny Alexander back to the premises to extract the ghost of his cousin Lamont was a stroke of sheer lunacy. She believed the old man should have been put away, but with Chad practically his right hand she saw no other way than to give him what he wanted while she retrieved the remaining portion of the treasure and left for good.

Two evenings before she left, she'd gotten the urge to pee. She dragged herself to the suite's master bathroom and relieved herself in the dark.

She stood in front of the faucet washing her hands when she saw the green eyes of her sister's staring at her from behind. She screamed, then turned to face her.

She stood before her, a finger drawn to her blistered lips to shush her, dressed in a prom gown of white chiffon and makeup of mortician gaudy. Exactly as they buried her.

Molica was ready to pass out as she heard her sister moan, "Must move."

She awakened a wet mess in her bed as her alarm blared an intermittent beeping. She turned to shut the clock off as she realized it had turned on almost seventeen minutes prior.

Her Arizona State shorts and jersey clung to her as she sat on the edge of the bed in a cold sweat.

She needed to get out of that hotel immediately, she told herself.

She thought about her sister and believed she saw her in her sleep. It felt real, but there was no way she actually saw her.

"*Must move.*"

She bounced off the mattress and checked on the room's safe. She concerned herself with opening it to check on the contents.

"*Must move.*"

She decided to shower, then she would follow her sister's instructions. If that's what they were.

She shuffled toward the bathroom, quickly hitting the light switch before entering. Standing in the doorway she glanced to make sure nothing was in there to jump out at her.

As she settled down, she broke the threshold and walked to the shower curtain. She pulled it back reaching for the faucet's knob seeing the red clay footprints circling toward the drain.

She stepped back finding identical prints in front of the porcelain tub as well.

MS. PHILLIPS

Steve waited outside baggage claim as the automatic doors slid open with arriving guests greeted by loved ones, or at least rides waiting as she walked out with her carry-on bag in tow.

He reached inside the car to honk his horn, then waved when Molica's head followed the sound.

She wasn't the same girl who left him six months prior. She sat in the front seat distant. Even the embrace they shared felt miles away.

He turned onto the Ten Highway toward her destination of the Crowne Plaza less than a mile from the airport.

He asked her a million times if she was hungry, but she shook that off.

Once she checked in, he carried her bag to the room. He still didn't understand why she just didn't stay with him for the weekend.

He had barely placed the bag down in the room when he turned to find her directly in front of him. Her fingers laced behind his head and she drew her lips to his.

She mashed hard with reckless passion that she showed no sign of earlier.

He welcomed it as he wrapped his arms around her. She pushed him back onto the bed and sat on his torso straddling him. Their eyes finally meeting.

"Hello, Ms. Phillips," he said softly.

She said nothing as she searched for his belt buckle and unfastened it.

She lay there cradled in his arms, exhausted as she exorcised the demons within her. She heard his voice so many times after she left during late night calls or afternoon check-ins. She needed the sanctity of his deep sleepy voice which earned him a spot as floor manager within four months of pitching life insurance. His primary success was stay-at-home wives with access to hubby's info.

He brought her in after her disastrous visit back at the resort. They were initially just two former classmates, but once they began working together, they became a force that became a movement.

Her eye was always on getting back to the brokerage firm, but she understood the construct of reading data from the consumer logs.

She had briefly shaken off Steve's idea of setting up their own shop. He had acquired the trust of the bosses and access to the mailing lists they had compiled or acquired throughout the years.

She closed her eyes to join him in sleep. She had put a hurting on him, but he was resilient. "Built Ford Tough," he'd liken himself to. She worked out just enough kinks to finally escape washing out the tub basin of the red clay foot stains two weeks prior.

She'd hit him with her plan after she showed him the treasure of Chief Black Hawk.

But first, sleep.

She'd remembered a nickname.

Lamont had called him by it and Danny explained how he had two families; one that called him by that name, and one that called him 'Lefty' to distinguish between him and another friend who shared the same nickname amongst their families.

The whole family thing was boring to her. More male machismo, but Veronica was fascinated.

The Illinois printout she requested was going to take a while to go through. She needed to vet out the list before she was back in Wisconsin.

She was asked numerous times who she was looking for. She was sure she would find it once she had an opportunity to study the call list which Steve had furnished along with notes from each call that the inside service reps had made.

It was the notes that were crucial to her search, not just the names, numbers, and addresses of those they called, but the information they gathered while trying to close the pitch.

Those notes belonged to the company and were worth their trade no matter who extracted it.

Steve brought her a warm plate of turkey leg, dressing, mashed potatoes, cranberry sauce, veggies, and a slice of pumpkin pie from his family's gathering. She knew she had deflated him when she didn't go there for Thanksgiving dinner, but she was still working the list. She didn't even bother watching television since the debacle of Luke and Laura marry on the U.S. soap opera *General Hospital* a week earlier; becoming the highest-rated hour in daytime television history in 1981.

He asked her to take a break after watching her merely scrape at the plate. She was only at the H-level on the list and she had not made a connection.

He couldn't help because she couldn't describe what or who she was looking for.

She eventually came to bed for a moment of horseplay. Afterwards, he told her some family anecdotes from the holiday gathering. She couldn't keep any of the members straight even the few she had met earlier the year before. Until he recalled his nephew, EJ, then a bell struck.

"Why do they call him EJ again?" she asked as she labored in his arms fighting fatigue that had come to blanket her.

"His father's name is Ernie, he's a junior."

He may as well have hit her with a baseball bat. She sat up

instantly. Sleep be damned. She knew what she was looking for in the notes, but now she had to remember Danny's nickname.

She was furious with herself.

She flew back to the lamp desk against the wall and decided to work backwards from the list.

She promised she'd wake Steve in time for him to shower in the morning. They were going Christmas shopping.

By 6 a.m. that Friday morning, she knew exactly who she was looking for.

Due to the holiday season, she knew she'd never reach the party until Monday at the earliest. She resigned herself with that belief that she had found the person that could lure Danny or "DJ" back to the lodge – his very own buddy – Darnell Wilkins, also known by his immediate family as "DJ", but known to his friends if memory served her correct, as 'Tank.'

She didn't bother to let anyone know when she would be back. She just showed up in time to relieve the graveyard shift at the desk.

She determined it was best to call at eight or eight-thirty that morning to make contact. She had exactly one hour and twenty-two minutes before she would make her first attempt.

She needed to make sure she was covered at the desk when she made her rounds.

She would hit the third tower back to her suite, then make the call.

Joseph was early as he always had been, bless him.

He smiled and nearly illuminated the entire lobby as he welcomed her back.

She gave him the traditional snow globe from the airport as a gift and he thanked her as if she had given him keys to a new car.

It didn't take long for him to get her up to speed on what was happening at the resort. She shared about having Thanksgiving dinner with her boyfriend's family. Especially the story about Ernie, Jr. or 'EJ.'

Guardedly, he asked if Steve had proposed. She felt that twinge of jealousy in him and was utterly grateful she had an admirer. She had become a total bitch at times, and she knew it.

"No," she said. Not even thinking about it.

The reaction on his face was priceless. No one could anticipate when she bolted with the goods. She and Steve and two passports to some tropical area forever.

She grabbed the clipboard at seven-fifty-two to begin making her rounds. She took hold of a walkie-talkie and bid Joseph adieu. She'd be back within the hour.

The brochure read:

Situated on more than one-hundred-acres of lush woodlands and surrounded by three scenic lakes, you'll have plenty of opportunities for outdoor enjoyment, including hiking, fishing, boating, and one of the lushest golf courses you'll ever find. Get involved in some of our many planned activities.

We look forward to seeing you.

She sat at the suite's desk with all the paperwork laid out.

She had culled enough information over the weekend to have an idea the location of the transportation company's main office.

Her fingers were sweaty as were the palms of her hands. She took a deep breath, lifted the receiver, and dialed.

At noon, she knocked on his door. He smiled, surprised to see her.

"I heard you were back," he beamed at her. "How was your trip?"

She closed the door behind her as she walked in preparing to sell him the plan of how to capture Danny Alexander and rid himself of the ghosts that haunted him from finding his treasure.

Alone for the first time in the last year with the man who took her innocence from her.

The plan had come together as she had laid out. A hiccup or two, but nothing she couldn't overcome.

She had realized that if she were to survive him, she had to engage him. Even though she wanted nothing to do with her grandfather.

It was when he had her come to the barn that she realized how far along he actually was. She hadn't been in the barn since she asked for its destruction. His concession of releasing the horses was not really accepting to her, by then she had masterminded her escape.

She dusted off the remains of the snow as she entered through the back of the field house. The motor of the chipper grinding hard as she caught Chad by surprise.

"What are you doing in here?" he asked startled by her presence.

She bumped into a Gun Metal Gray Corvette she'd never seen as she suddenly tried to escape the premises when she caught sight of the blood streaking down the whirring blade.

"Looking for the old man," she said cautiously as she tried to suppress the urge to retch right there.

Her eyes on the remains of the gym shoes told her all she needed to know.

"Not here," he said as he turned to finish his work. "Wait up. I'll walk back with you."

She was already gone.

"Don't regret the past, just learn from it."

Too late, she thought. She was swimming in regret. What exactly did she miss regarding her grandfather's mission?

What did she learn? School was in session at that very moment, but she needed a quick recess.

There was no handbook on the education she had enrolled in when she came back to the hotel. She chose to withdraw while she could still collect half her tuition.

She found herself racing back to the lodge trying to maintain her balance as her rubber soled shoes slipped in the snowy terrain.

She entered the chain-link fenced pool area forlorn that she may have to abandon the plan to recover the blockage in the filtration trap, certain that somewhere within the quarter mile of tubing lay the remainder of the stolen treasure.

She headed inside and knew she had to get to her room and make plans for their getaway.

She had taken Steve to the storage unit only three miles away.

She was elated when he came in for the holidays. She tucked him away with a room in the first tower, but he spent many nights in hers.

She could see the elevator bank and pressed the up button wishing they had updated the cam system for the crane. It was old and in desperate need for refurbishing. It was as slow as the customers constantly complained.

The door finally opened, and she rushed to enter.

She heard a voice call out.

"Hey, hold up."

She hadn't heard that voice in years.

She turned and saw him as he did a limp trot in her direction.

Danny was shortening the distance between the two of them and her heart nearly jumped out her chest.

She couldn't press the elevator close button fast or hard enough. She realized she had a master key to speed it up, but she froze when she saw his face as he approached her.

What would she say to him after all these years? How could she explain all that had happened?

"LaMonica," she heard him shout out.

She closed her eyes as she fought for air. She was beginning to hyperventilate. She was certain she was going to have a coronary attack right there. Tears streaked down her face as she accepted he had her.

The door closed and he stood there watching her.

She tried to address how to contact Steve to prepare for a move. She reached a hall phone as she got off the elevator and dialed his room. She couldn't wait for an answer as she heard the echo of the fire escape clamber as footsteps were bouncing through the walls.

She tried to reach the office. If she made an appearance it would give her time to double back to her suite and call her beau from there. Better yet, just to have him leave, go straight to the storage unit, and meet her at the airport. With only three days left before 1983, they were going to start a new life somewhere tropical.

That would absolutely work, thus that was the plan.

Joseph caught her off guard with the call regarding the phone service. She could easily reset the phone banks as she headed out.

She pushed the key into the suite's door taking mental notes of what she would leave behind.

She prepared a letter that she would drop off on the way to the airport depicting the good doctor's duplicitous ways, making sure she gave an honorable mention of Chad's role, plus members of her grandfather's board who took the innocence of underage girls as down payments for stake in their properties.

She entered the darkness and reached for the light switch. The sound of running water surprised her as she called out, "Steve?"

She heard the spigot shut off as she walked toward the bathroom, "Hey," she said only to see her grandfather standing in the doorway.

"Hey, to you, too," he cracked.

"What are you doing here?" she hissed disgusted by the sight of him.

A smile spread across his face as she noticed the floor covered in water. "I came looking for you. Only to discover a stranger in your room."

She took a step back away from the door, "I don't understand."

"I didn't either," he said. "When I asked who he was, he…" the good doctor chuckled as he paused searching for the right words, "attacked me."

Molica pushed through into the bathroom as the old man stood there. She stared at the figure behind her grandfather.

On his blue jeaned knees and hiking boots, Steve lay with his head resting inside the water filled bathtub. Next to his right knee, a syringe floated on the over-flowing tide of water.

"He had one of these on him," the doctor cited as he raised a silver coin in front of her. "Any idea where he may have gotten it?"

AFTER INITIATION

There was a loud crack as the echo of a bowling ball tackling a row of pins bounced through the arena.

Someone yipped as a small congregation said congratulations to the victor.

Clinton and Wynton sat at a small round table contributing to the cheers softly as their pasty faces sat in reflective modes.

"How do you feel?" Wynton dryly asked his compadre.

Smacking his lips to moisten them, he nodded while replying, "I feel fine."

"I feel like I ate some dog shit," Wynton said.

Clinton moved from a slouch to sit up straight. He rubbed his stomach which stretched out his Triton College sweatshirt.

"I don't know about you, but I'm hungry," Clinton glanced around locking his eye on a small concession stand.

Wynton smiled and perked up, "Me, too."

The gang was finishing another round as Clinton moved from the table. He turned to the diminutive Wynton asked, "What you want?"

As Wynton's hands dropped to his pockets, Clinton shook him off.

"I got it," he said as he used the table to steady himself.

He sauntered toward the booth before Wynton could answer.

Marshall entered the facility through a side door with two black garment bags in hand.

Motioning to the group bowling, he stood over Wynton and patted him on his back. Not a smart move, but Wynton was able to hold whatever else was in his belly down.

"What up, brother? You okay?" Marshall asked Wynton.

Wynton made a half check as he tried to rotate his body.

"Oh, just hanging out as usual," he said.

Carter began to walk over and also patted Wynton down the center of his back.

Wynton's eyes closed as he tried his best to maintain.

Marshall looked around, scouting, "Where's Clint?" he asked.

Wynton turned and pointed to the open window of the bar.

Marshall and Carter were taken aback as Clint strolled back with two beers in his hands.

"You still able to drink?" Carter asked.

Clinton nodded, smiling sheepishly as he handed the Budweiser bottle to Wynton.

"Got some food coming, too," he said.

"Damn!" Marshall shouted.

"I'm a growing boy," Clint said.

"I see," was Carter's retort.

Baron and Larry approached the table and helped surround the new recruits. Marshall handed Baron one of the clothing garment bags and began, "Nearly one year ago, Danny and Nick – both who are not with us at this time – introduced us to the both of you brothers."

Clinton swigged on his beer as Wynton pressed his perspiring bottle to his forehead, both a little fogged to completely appreciate the impromptu presentation.

Baron unzipped his bag. A brown leather sleeve slipped out.

"No!" Wynton exclaimed.

Clinton turned around immediately and beamed.

Marshall said, "It is an honor to welcome both of you into the "Family"."

As Baron completed unzipping his bag, Marshall tussled to open the garment bag he was holding.

"Ta Da," Baron sang as he held before the small gathering a brown leather bomber jacket.

"Wynton," he said, "I believe this is for you. Welcome to the Family."

Wynton tried to gather himself as his emotions overcame him. He grabbed at the jacket impulsively and drew it to himself as Baron embraced him.

Marshall brought out a larger, but similar styled jacket with the word "Family" stenciled on the upper left breast.

Clinton retrieved his jacket and also accepted a warm brotherly hug from both Carter and Marshall. Larry stood from a distance and watched, still a little suspect of the two new members.

Wynton excitedly unzipped the jacket and carefully slipped his arms inside to try it on.

"Turn around," Clinton ordered.

As Wynton made the gesture, Clinton smiled at the embroidered lettering of his name on the back. Wynton continued modelling it, impressed by the relaxed fit of the jacket.

Clinton's also fit, but a little snugger in the chest as he fastened the jacket's buttons at the bottom.

The two beamed with satisfaction at each other and wrapped their arms banding together.

A bowling patron in a club shirt circled by admiringly.

"Y'all some fraternity?" he asked as another short sleeve bowling shirted team member joined him.

"Y'all go to school 'round here?" the other asked.

Marshall shook his head, "No, we're just a group of brothers that have been knowing each other since grade school."

"Oh, so y'all 'family?'" the first bowler asked.

"Kinda," Baron said. "We have been through a lot together. A lot of trials and tribulations since we were kids."

"Huh," the first bowler accepted as he moved closer to feel Clinton's jacket.

"So, y'all don't go to school 'round here or nothin'?" the second bowler asked as he, too, copped a feel of Wynton's jacket.

Larry cautiously said, "Naw, we up here from outside Chicago. Just staying up the road for a visit."

Curious, the second bowler quizzed, "Where up the road?"

Baron said, "Dodgers Lake Resort."

The two men looked at each other.

"Where?" they simultaneously asked.

"Dodgers Lake Resort," Larry said. "Y'all hear of it?"

The first bowler answered, "You don't want no parts of that place, son."

THE DRESS

Sitting up in the guest room's queen bed, Danny pressed a towel covering a block of ice from the hotel's bucket on his forehead.

Trudy, sat on the edge next to him, with the red dress hiked up, as she attempted to apply pressure.

"Let me look again," she softly said, as she tried to nurse him back to health.

Danny slapped her hand away petulantly.

"What the fuck's wrong with you?" he asked.

Taking no heed to his push back, she gently took the towel from his hands.

"I thought you were trying to break in," she said. "You could have been an intruder. It's not like you said 'me' when I called your name."

She looked him in his eyes sympathetically. "I had to protect myself, right?"

"Was that you calling my name?" he asked sheepishly. "I thought…" he paused. "Never mind."

"Next time say something," she implored.

She pulled back to get a better look at his forehead. She grimaced at the knot she placed on him. It was red, glowing, and growing by the second. She placed the ice back on his dome.

"Keep it there for a little while," she ordered.

"Yes, ma'am," he said. "What did you hit me with?"

Securing the towel back on his forehead as a priority, she reached over him to the paddle as it lay in the bed next to him.

"Shit," he crowed, "You nearly took me out with that thing."

"If you were an intruder, that would have been the goal." She applied harder pressure on the block of ice. "Is that what you think?" she asked. "I can't take care of myself? You don't know me very well. I'm not my sister."

"That's for damn sure," Danny returned wincing at the way it came out.

She released the block and it immediately fell bluntly into Danny's lap. He tensed up from the impact.

"What's that mean?" she asked as she applied pressure to the bump. "I want to know."

"Nothing," he said placing the ice back on his noggin.

"You still think I'm like your little sister or something," she placed her fingers under his chin.

"I didn't say you were," he said softly. "You crazy like her, though, that's for sure."

For the first time, he caught a glimpse of her in RaShonda's dress.

"When you change into that?" he asked.

"Oh, you mean this?" she asked nervously, having forgotten she had tried the dress on earlier. "What do you think?"

His eyes never got beyond her cleavage bursting out of the sides of the halter-top one piece.

"It's all right," he calmly said, "I guess. You brought that for Ricky?"

She punched him in the arm getting his attention. His eyes met hers.

"Why, you suddenly jealous?" she returned.

"Of Ricky?" he laughed. "Hell, naw!"

She caught his eyes rolling downward to catch another glimpse of her curvy body pouring out of the tight dress.

"It's RaShonda's for your information," she quickly moved from the bed in her bare feet. Feeling a sense of awkwardness, her steps pounded into the carpet as she moved back into the living room.

"I was trying it on, that's all," Trudy said. "Waiting for my clothes to dry after you messed them up."

She walked back in with the shopping bags and plopped them back on the bed.

"Whatchu get?" she asked. "I'm hungry."

Danny stiffly sat up on the bed. Trudy's curves, hugging her body, made it difficult for him to concentrate.

"You look very good in it," Danny said. "I just thought it was yours. That's all."

Somewhat pleased with the response, she stepped back to give him a better view.

"Really?" Trudy asked as she sauntered away from him.

He thought to himself, she had no idea as she rummaged through the bags just jiggling in front of him.

ANTICIPATION

Fred Sanford was dressed in a seer-sucker suit with a bow tie on their TV. Clearly a product of the mid-seventies, the light blue ensemble brightened the character's face, almost highlighting him out of the picture. Every wrinkle and hairline was pronounced by the dark colors Bubba, Esther, Donna, and Lamont wore in contrast.

Trudy's laughter filled the room as she laid on the bed next to Danny with her head nuzzled up on Danny's hip as her upper torso curled onto a down pillow.

Danny sat with the pillow arching his back as his head cradled the cushioned headboard. He draped his arm over Trudy's shoulder, protectively more than romantic.

The side drawer next to Danny held the ice bucket and towel wrapped ice block that diminished in the last hour since it was applied to administered medical aid to the swollen bump in Danny's forehead. Two brandy snifters sat nestled between the white bucket and a telephone.

The twenty-inch television sat atop the chest of drawers, cabinet combination surrounded by a set of glasses and a second ice bucket separate from the larger one used earlier for the festivities the night before.

She giggled like a little girl as she clearly experienced the delivery of Redd Foxx for the first time. Material like this when originally broadcast had been taboo in her household. The television primarily only serviced to present news programming, PBS Broadcast, and family-oriented viewing.

Danny felt the softness of her ripple as bursts of laughter that imploded in her body. She was a wonder.

The throbbing of his brain had subsided quite a bit, replaced by blood rushing to the nether region.

Her position between pillow and him was unbearable. The words pursed on his lips, but he couldn't really ask her.

"How old are you again?" he finally pushed out.

She suddenly turned serious as her eyes narrowed, aggravated by the prodding, the implication.

"Why do you want to know?" she said.

She began to uncurl but applied pressure where he least wanted her to.

He groaned lightly, as she moved up and placed a leg between his. If she moved just a centimeter, it was all over for him. He wasn't going to jail labelled "short eyes" because this girl had no idea she was traipsing into the field of womanhood.

"You've never seen Sanford and Son before?" he quickly said.

"I told you, no," she scolded. She swiveled upward applying more pressure onto his lower extremities. She was totally clueless as to the effect she was having on him.

She inched herself up and glanced at his bruised forehead. Her fingers lightly traced the protruding bump, then pushed the center softly as if she were checking the readiness of a Bundt cake.

"Eighteen, born October ninth, nineteen sixty-four," she said.

His eyes fell deep into the crevasse of the low-cut dress. He could smell her, the fragrances she had mixed, light and airy, but extremely womanly. Very much like his work-wife, Juanita.

She poked her finger hard into that center and all the pain came back immediately.

"Ow, damn, girl," he croaked in agony. "What the hell is wrong with you?"

He nearly bucked her off as he rolled over until he was on top of her.

"Get off me," she said through clenched teeth.

He laid there on top of her, looking into her dark brown eyes. She returned the stare but for different reasons before turning her head away.

Whipping her head back, she kneed him simultaneously and he rolled over and off the bed crashing to the floor.

"Told you to get off me," Trudy said with a growl.

He rose up ever so slowly, with pain in his upper and lower areas.

He began to hobble to the other side of the bed to retrieve the towel wrapped ice block. Mostly melted away, he pushed the soggy cloth to his forehead as a torrent of water cascaded down his face.

In frustration, he threw the towel and ice onto the tabletop of the side drawer and marched into the guest bathroom.

Trudy jumped out the bed behind him. She leaned into the doorway and watched him stare at the contusion that was still swelling.

"I'm sorry," she docilely said. "You all right?"

He stood there with a glower look on his face.

She had mixed emotions. She was terrified at the moment. She truly did not want anything to happen to him. She wanted to explain she had no intentions of hurting him, it was just a reflex.

It began less than two years ago when she began to go through changes, physical as well as emotional.

She really hadn't noticed it all that much but wondered why boys were getting nowhere with her sister, but suddenly became interested in her.

Overnight, she began to gain notice of boys who once would

swarm her house trying to get the attention of Regina. Suddenly, their focus had become her.

More "hey, baby," "what up, girl," and "what's them digits?" exploded at her like a water balloon bursting on impact.

Regina laughed and told her those boys were just rebounding. Couldn't have her, so they go for Trudy. Making it sound like she was sloppy seconds.

She was mortified. But why then when Regina had them knocking on their door since she was thirteen and Trudy was eleven. Regina had developed and become a woman as soon as she became a teenager. Her teeth were straight, she had the "good hair" of the family, she got straight A's in school while doing none of the work. And womanhood met her at the corner of thirteen, walking her a few blocks – a few good blocks.

Trudy, named after her maternal grandmother, Gertrude – well start with that name and go from there. The biggest blessing, she received was the nickname, "Trudy." What a disaster, every time someone discovered her birth name; she died. "Gertrude," "Hey Gertie," "Flirty Gertie," "Dirty Gertie," "Birdy Gertie." From preschool to her junior year of high school, she just looked like a Gertrude. Butterfly glasses, natty hair, a waddle to her walk (bow-legged), and buck teeth that caused kids to tease her. "Bucky Beaver, two-by-two, let us do our dance for you." She went home devastated, crying for years. But her grandmother, who also endured the same agony gave her the gift of a name, "Trudy," until she was ready to carry the mantle of the name "Gertrude."

With the exception of two "boys," most came after her with a fervor of trying out for some semi-league football after bombing out with the pros. In this case, that would be her sister, Regina Nia Hardaway.

The first boy to take an interest in Trudy herself was Ricky Williams. It wasn't that he was smooth or a player (although he seriously thought he was). He had no known history with her sister, and he clearly had intentions when he suggested this current trip. He actually was as unbearable to her as the other boys she had to push off her.

But here she was.

That second "boy" stood in front of her staring at a potato sized lump on his noggin that she was going to have a hard time getting over. It wasn't that Danny was different. She had known him a long time.

Much had changed from the days when he was a sweaty, overweight gangly kid. When he hit high school, he just changed, physically more than emotionally, but she had noticed him. Oddly, he never went after her sister like most of the neighborhood boys. No, he...

"What happened between you and Darlene?" she asked.

Danny's eyes slowly picked her up in the reflection. The agitation rolled from his eyes onto her.

"What?" he said.

Darlene had been her best friend even though she was one year older. They were inseparable like sisters when they met at Irving Elementary. They walked to and from school together, they hung out at Darlene's house most of the time on the weekends.

Darlene was also, smart, funny, and cute. Trudy often believed she hung with her to make her feel good about herself when no one wanted to be bothered. Regina claimed it was to attract the boys she tossed off knowing they wouldn't talk to Trudy.

That hurt.

By the time Trudy hit eighth grade however, things began to change. Darlene started to wear makeup and the application was flawless. Trudy's skin was breaking out all over the place and jokes were abound about connecting dots on her face, while Darlene looked like a Johnson Product cover ad.

And the boys flocked like vultures on a soon to be dead carcass.

One of those vultures was Danny Alexander. Danny had been visiting his old grade school and immediately asked Darlene to escort him to his high school homecoming. After that date, they were one.

They broke up during the summer before Danny's senior year which Trudy never got a real understanding about. Darlene just kept going on about how Danny had changed. Something was wrong with him and he kept pushing her away. She still believed they would get back together, going as far as talking about future children they would have.

The summer after he graduated from high school, they reconnected. They spent most of the summer together even as Danny tolled at a summer job to have walking around money for his big move out the state to Ohio.

Darlene would go on about him for ages. She even made the dreadful decision to see him his first year at Xavier University. She took a Greyhound bus to surprise him for a three-day visit, but she was back within thirty-six hours.

Danny was with another girl on campus. He made no attempt to hide the relationship telling Darlene she had no right to spy on him.

She was devastated.

When Danny came home for Christmas vacation to patch things up, Darlene took him to hell and back. But mostly, she hid from him at Trudy's. Trudy supported her friend through thick and thin, thus becoming a mortal enemy of his.

When Danny wound up continuing his secondary education in Chicago, they rekindled their relationship sharing an off and on thing until Danny got the radio internship.

First, the two went to concerts and various radio events for free as Danny covered them for the station, but something changed between them and Trudy began to see a lot of Darlene…until she didn't.

"Darlene," she said. "What happened between you two?"

She could tell he wished he could burn a hole right through her.

He bolted out the bathroom, knocking straight into her, spinning her around.

"Why don't you ask her?" he pouted as he grabbed the ice bucket off the chest of drawers and headed for the living room of the suite.

"Where you going, Slow Poke?" she asked innocently.

That name again.

"Where's it look like?" he asked. "To get some ice."

She ran behind him to the door and reached for the bucket.

"I can go," she bargained. "Don't want you to pass out in the hallway."

Offended, Danny opened the door. "It's okay. You'll get lost."

He tried to slam the door behind him, but the spring slowed it down. He grabbed the knob to no avail and gave it one more tug, dropping the bucket.

He snarled in anger.

SLOW POKE

Wynton tightly gripped the steering wheel as the side door to the van slammed shut.

"Everybody in?" he asked as his co-pilot, Clinton slammed his door.

"Let's go!" Clint yelled.

The bowling alley parking lot was packed with snow covered cars that Saturday night.

Baron leaned in his chair and grabbed the back of the plush leather driver's seat.

"You sure you know how to get back?" he asked.

Wynton let out a low growl of a belch that was complemented by Clinton's higher pitched rumble.

Both appeared in the throes of another retching session. Clinton wiped his lips with the sleeve of his bomber jacket. He lifted his head upward, then turned to Wynton.

"You good, baby?" he asked.

Wynton shut his eyes, then raised his head. He gave a slow nod as he said, "Yeah. Where we going?"

"Just drive," Clint said. "I know the way."

The tires squealed upon the snow fallen blacktop as Wynton punched all the gears into drive.

The four held on tightly to their seats in the back as Wynton took off.

The fervor which fueled them was ignited the minute the men in the bowling alley inquired about their lodgings.

The guys listened intently to the tale that was shared with them. Initially, they just thought it was some drunkard's story to set off some frat boys.

Maybe it was their youth, but the story was too close to what had happened to Danny years prior.

He might be right, they realized. The resort may have been the place where Danny's cousin died. More important, he may have been murdered.

Clint pointed at the stoplight, "Turn left here," he said.

Wynton floored the van as the light changed from green to yellow. As he turned, the caravan skidded on two wheels.

Marshall and Baron gripped their seats and shut their eyes. Larry slid out of his seat onto the shag carpeted floor, while Carter balled himself up. Each releasing some semblance of a yell.

Clint grabbed the grip above his door and continued to navigate as all four wheels touched the ground, fishtailed close to the curb, then straightened out.

Wynton maintained his grip on the steering wheel with no intention of letting go.

"Keep straight?" Wynton asked.

Clint, ever sure of his piloting skills, nodded, "Yep, until I tell you otherwise."

Wynton wiped his brow and pressed forward, as the van roared its way to the rescue.

Finally making it to the ice machine was a bigger chore than Danny had imagined. His sense of direction was for shit. What surely should have taken no more than two turns down the hall, wound up sending him to the second floor and a full corridor over.

Even though he could hear the churning of the cube maker, he was stunned to find nothing more than two vending machines on his floor.

If it weren't for the leaking ceiling, he would never have guessed to take the fire exit up.

Once there, much to his chagrin, he found the big metal box empty as he opened the pod door. Nothing more than a pool of glassy water sitting in a pocket was available.

"Fuck me," he groaned out loud.

The box began to whirr, and a cranking sound soon emitted as Danny began to walk away. He returned immediately when the tinkling noise of ice falling on the metal shelving began.

Pulling on the handle of the box again, he was dismayed to see a handful of cubes sitting in the puddle. He snatched them with the chained scooper and plopped them in the bucket.

Pathetic, was all he could elicit as he heard the machine sputter. It was like watching a rabbit take a dump as another small load popped out.

Quickly, he shoveled that in and placed the top back on the ice container a lot more grateful.

He headed for the stairwell accepting defeat, willing to give the trinkets of ice cubes to Trudy, then head outside and compact some snowballs for his forehead. There would be enough out there to take care of his needs.

As he hit the exit door, the machine made a wailing cry. He quickly opened the door and escaped to the other side. He pushed the door closed with all his might nearly dropping the bucket. Before the door could completely shut, he heard the cascading sound of a solid hitting the inside of the metal sheeting.

Slowly he opened the door and emerged back onto the second-floor level. He glanced down the hallway to inspect its tenancy.

The floor appeared to be under construction, striking Danny as odd. How could there be a grand opening when the resort was still unfinished. Possibly the first floor would be open to the shareholder residents, but this floor – at least this wing – was not open for business.

More clanging surrounded him, causing him to jump. He entered the small cubby hole and lifted the lid once more. The engine whizzed as it spewed more ice chips. Suddenly, the box was a quarter full.

Danny took the bucket and placed it inside to spoon more pellets of ice. He began to forklift the ice as a flurry of chips fell onto his arm nearly encasing it like a splint.

He was shocked at how cold the frozen pieces were and attempted to wriggle his arm free along with the buried bucket.

The machine hummed louder as he strained to get his arm out. Another avalanche of ice tumbled out and his shoulder was caught. A force slammed him against the box and the door shut on his pectoral muscle.

"Aw, shit!" he said. "Unbelievable."

The ice began to solidify quickly into one large piece at the base of the bicep. His hand began to go numb as he tugged to break free. He finally grabbed the metal scooper and used it as a pick to chisel his way out.

He used his free hand to crack the ice as his trapped arm lost its feeling. The scooper made headway and he could see the sleeve of his sweater. He twisted his arm and finally broke free with the bucket intact filled with large chunks of ice.

He pulled back as the lid slammed shut, cutting the chain on the scooper, trapping his salvation inside the box.

He moved toward the exit door and opened it.

"Danny," he heard come from the corridor, but no one was there.

He skipped through the door certain it was the effects of the bump on his head.

Why was that girl here again?

This was turning into one hell of a birthday.

He shuffled down the stairwell as quickly as he could until he reached the first floor's door.

He switched hands to carry the bucket, relieved to see only a small blistering around puffy red fingers on the other hand. He wriggled them wildly to assure he still had feeling and control in them.

He careened into a wall as he flung himself through the hallway. The walls were a lot older than the rest of the hotel. It felt to him like wood paneling had been repurposed and rebuilt for use over hundreds of years.

Odd, but he didn't recognize the hallway at all. As if he had not ventured the corridor before.

He reached the end and turned right. Certain their suite was close to the end of the hall, he looked at the numbers of the rooms.

Knowing he was looking for 1048, he realized the numbers were edging past his series. He stopped at room 1077.

"Damn," he reflected. "I must be going the wrong way."

He approached another door to his left that read 1079. Across from it, 1078.

"Fuck," he blurted out.

He turned around to head to the other end of the corridor. His fingers tingled as he shook them furiously, as the sensation was a warmness from a slight frozen induced slumber shades from frostbite. He wiggled them again just before switching the bucket to tuck it under his right arm and chest.

He didn't bother to look at the numbers on the doors until he crossed to the other side of the hallway. He marched toward the middle of the aisle before he reconnected with the numbers. Room 1122.

"What the fuck?" he thought.

He turned and looked at the area already ventured.

He pondered whether it was worth the journey back or to forge ahead and continue to the corner.

As the ice froze to his ribs, he pulled the bucket by his thumb and placed it on the carpet.

His head was pounding again. He grabbed a handful of ice and compressed it to his forehead. His palm immediately went raw, cold as he applied pressure to his dome. The cool relief ended as he experienced a different type of brain freeze. He tossed the ice back into the bucket and chose to walk down the new corridor to see where the turn took him.

Oddly, the numbers suddenly made sense as he hit room 1064. His heart leapt as he continued down the path. He approached the corner and looked back at the other end.

A figure stood at the corner. He squinted but couldn't make out the body.

"Danny," called the voice.

Slowly, the figure moved down the hallway. He turned the corner and picked up the pace a bit. The voice sounded familiar to Danny, but there was a tinge of excitement that took over as he reached into his pocket for the key.

It wasn't in the left pocket of his jeans.

He switched the bucket to the other side and searched the right pocket to no avail.

"Danny, help me," the voice called out slightly familiar to him.

He reached room 1054 and relief was overwhelming him. He cocked his head as he was nearing the middle of the row to make out the figure just turning into the aisle.

"You hear me calling you," came from the hall.

He turned around; sure, it was Ricky. "What, nigga, what?" he shouted, but no one was there. Blood was surely rushing to his head.

Room 1048, finally.

He tapped his pockets again. The bulge in his left from house and car keys. The bulkiness in his right from change at the tollbooth.

He decided to knock. Then was no answer. He knocked again.

"Trudy, open up," he said. "It's me."

Nothing. Then...

"Me, who?" came from inside the suite.

"Ha ha," he said. "Let me in. I got ice for your Pepsi."

"I wanted Diet Coke," she said. "Come back with Diet Coke and I'll let you in."

He banged his head on the door in frustration. Big mistake.

"Open this door!" he said. "Right now!"

He was tired of this silly bitch right now. Ricky could take her home with him, immediately. They deserved each other.

"Now what, nigga?" Danny heard from the other side of the hallway.

His clothes were bloodied and partially torn but standing in the corner was none other than Ricky Williams.

Danny still had problems seeing clearly but was 99.9% sure that was him.

"Nigga, go home, and take this bitch with you," Danny said.

He turned toward the figure as it convulsed and shook, revving itself up.

Danny placed his hand inside the ice bucket gripping it tightly to weaponize it.

The figure Danny believed was Ricky raised its head and made a ghastly howl as it percolated. It began to march toward Danny, leaving him no choice but to prepare to knuckle up. It had been awhile, but in Danny's mind, it was time for closure.

The figure slowly ascended on Danny, as the top bolt to the door unlatched. Trudy opened the door and stared at Danny as he positioned himself toward the hallway.

"Who you talking to?" she asked.

She peaked her head out the doorway. Her eyes widened to see this incarnation of Ricky coming their way with eyes ablaze.

No time to think, she snatched Danny by his collar and pulled him in tossing him as far into the room as she could as he still gripped the bucket of ice.

She placed her weight on the door and tried to shut it closed when the gnarled right hand of Ricky crypt through. His swipe going through Trudy left a chalky shine on her shoulder.

She shrieked as the red clay smeared down her sleeve. Danny picked himself up and rushed to the door to add heft to her struggle.

The door vibrated heavily from within the frame as they were able to seal the lock. Their bodies leaned on the door as it tremored profusely from an energy source they had never encountered before, as if platelets were shifting from below.

As immense and quick as it had started, it ceased.

Side to side they pressed against the door too tense to rest but catching a breath from the respite.

Danny lowered his head, with his hands on his knees.

"Thank you," he said as he felt her nearly slump onto him.

Trudy went limp before she tensed up. Before Danny could sense the cause, she released a scream that was ear shattering.

He asked why the shouting, when his eyes followed her pointing finger. He squinted at the plate glass of the sliding door not fully making out what the problem was.

With the drapes fully open since RaShonda had originally drawn them, there was a faint shadow waving as if the wind had taken hold of a defenseless tree and shook it senseless.

A vibration caused the screen door to shake.

"Shit," Danny said to himself.

"What is that?" Trudy asked.

The light fell upon the window illuminating a pale face of a brown-skin male with matted dirty hair.

Danny blinked and took his weight off the door and slowly moved toward whatever it was standing outside the door.

"Where are you going?" Trudy shouted.

His feet dragged across the living room floor watching as the image waved for him to come closer.

"No," Danny murmured.

Still with her back flat against the door, wiping the powdery chalk off her, she called out to Danny, "What are you doing? Are you nuts?"

"It can't be," Danny said to himself.

Drawn toward the door, Danny's heart plundered with each step. He was beyond curiosity with his eyes straining to make sense of what he believed stood before him.

"You fool, where are you going?" Trudy pressed.

Danny suddenly stopped with roughly a quarter of the way left before he reached the door. He turned to Trudy, searching for words, pointing to the double pane glass doors.

"It's him," he panted. "It's him."

"Who?" she asked frantically as she stepped away from the door.

The image stood in front of the glass partition as a light bounced from the window frame. Trudy's eyes fell upon two gray pools where eyes once were and froze. Fear enveloped her, gripping so tightly it wouldn't release her.

"Lamont," Danny said as a tear fell down his cheek.

The window rattled as Lamont motioned for the door to be opened. His mouth agape, then closed, but neither Danny nor Trudy could hear him. Still he pointed to the door handle and gave it a tug.

Danny moved forward while Trudy, filled with uncertainty, moved back.

"Where are you going, Danny?" she moaned. "What are you doing?"

"I'm letting Lamont in," he said as if offended by her rudeness.

"Why?" she shrieked.

Ignoring her, he approached the sliding door. As another tear fell, he placed his hand on the door handle watching as this grayish figure continued to say something to him. Danny pulled the door, but as it was still latched, didn't budge.

There was an urgency in Lamont's face. It too reached for the handle of the door with little effect.

Trudy was lost in madness as she realized this was the cousin Danny had discussed dying not too long ago. If that be the case, Lamont being dead and all, then how was he standing there in front of them?

Barely setting her back on the door frame, the door trembled furiously. She screamed and bolted from the door as it started to become unhinged.

She leapt forward in a frenzy to halt Danny from this ludicrous act of engaging this demon.

Before she got to the sliding door, Danny slipped the bolt upward opening the door.

She stopped less than a foot behind Danny as a large gust of wind entered the room.

With Danny out of reach, she screamed, as she watched him walk onto the snow into the arms of the figure appearing to be Lamont.

It grabbed Danny by the collar of his shirt and pulled him toward it and gave a banshee cry of, "Must move!"

The door frame splintered as Ricky emerged from the other side.

Danny turned and stretched his hand out for Trudy's, grabbing her and pulling her out the suite in her flip flops.

The snow encased her toes immediately frosting them. She wriggled them and ran, soon outdistancing Danny as she overtook him. Not sure where they were headed as they followed Lamont's floating apparition, Trudy huffed as she hit stride with Danny lagging behind her.

"C'mon, Slow Poke, run!" Trudy yelled.

BUCK BUCK

Springfield Street was the quickest route back to the resort, however Wynton accidentally changed routes and landed on Spring Street heading north when he should have been headed west.

The unfamiliarity captured Clint's attention by the fourth intersection, but he didn't act impulsively believing he could put the markers together in his head soon enough to get them back on track.

Clinton wondered where they were as they began to follow a camper from a four-lane highway to a two-lane thoroughfare.

Wynton's eyes were as wide as saucers as he was still fighting to keep down the dog food chili he half ate. His brow was furrowed and sweat still dripped from his forehead as beads lined up and dropped like dew on a windowsill.

"Aren't we on Springfield Street?" Wynton volleyed.

Baron grabbed the back of Clint's chair to pull himself forward. He was able to get a better view of the road and the inebriated driver.

"What's wrong?" Baron asked.

Clint, with heat at full tilt, was completely dry and clear eyed, said bluntly, "We are going the wrong way. We're supposed to be on Springfield Street, not Spring Street"

Wynton took his eyes off the road and stared directly at Clint as he blathered, "I thought you were navigating. You didn't tell me we were on the wrong street."

Baron's eyes widened as he stared ahead noticing the brake lights illuminating ahead.

"Brake, brake," he shouted at Wynton.

Wynton and Clint both turned forward to catch sight of their encroachment on the camper directly in front of them.

Wynton mashed the brake as Clint grabbed the dashboard and mock braked as well. All three had faces of seeing life flashing before them as the tires of the van tried to grab traction on the snow fallen pavement.

The headlights of an eighteen-wheeler directly behind them shot through as if it were attached to the rear of the van. The carrier began to jackknife as Carter turned to watch through the van's port window.

The van fishtailed as the tires sputtered unable to catch any pavement. Wynton released the steering wheel which spun wildly until Clint snatched it with his left hand.

Straightening the wheel out until Wynton finally regained composure and added his hands back at ten and two, Clint held tightly allowing the van to run slightly off the road into a small mound of snow. The van narrowly missed the camper edging next to it as the eighteen-wheeler was also trying to re-angle itself without hitting the van.

Baron released his grip on the two seats and pushed himself back into his chair with his eyes on Marshall who never once moved from his bucket seat accepting this was his final ride.

The sound of flatulence whistled in the cabin for nearly ten seconds catching the passengers by surprise. Particularly, the person emitting the sounds and smells of fear. Larry gripped the small table set with his head laying on the tabletop. His arms trembled uncontrollably as he watched the cab behind them slide off the road.

"You all right?" Carter laughed as he smashed Larry's muscle-tensed back with his free hand as the other squeezed tightly onto the back handrail.

His eyes bulged out, darting wildly.

Marshall shouted out amidst the laughter, "You didn't shit on yourself, did you?"

Massive group laughter broke out heartily at Larry's expense. Even he smiled sheepishly as he was from the embarrassment.

Baron leaned forward in his seat again, turning toward Wynton and asked, "Where'd you learn to drive?"

Clint shot back, "Why do you think I'm always the one up here next to him and not y'all?"

This driving excursion was the least of the escapades Clint and Wynton had experienced together.

But nothing was more important to the two of them, nor the four sitting behind them choking on the intestinal gases in emission that Larry had released.

Without hesitation, they all reached for door handles to escape the stench that permeated the air of the van's enclosed heat stuffy cabin.

With the motor running, Wynton threw the shift into park as he jumped out the van for safety, followed by Clint on the opposite side. Baron and Marshall jumped from the swinging side door as Carter pushed open the back door with the fake tire attachment, as Larry choked and laughed rolling out behind him.

The freshly falling snow was still accumulating as they found themselves make light tracks that were buried as soon as they were made.

Another burst of laughter came from the young men as they gathered themselves with first a look from behind at the truck's cabin skewed over an embankment.

"Damn," Larry tossed out, "that shit is messed up."

Behind the truck's open doors were boxes of eggs strewn over the single lane and onto the snow-covered island where the cabin now sits.

The driver of the eighteen-wheeler jumped out of his cab ready to bum rush Wynton only to check himself once he caught sight of the other five men in their bomber jackets.

He proceeded cautiously as he slowly approached.

Larry and Carter were on his rear as Wynton reached out his hand to shake for an apology.

"What the fuck, man?" slipped from the driver's mouth.

He edged closer to Wynton as he acknowledged, if he couldn't keep his head, he'd have to address the two behind him.

"Can't you drive in the snow?" he said hoping he could build up enough nerve to take all three men on. At 6'2" and roughly 240 pounds, he believed he was solid enough to get some licks in.

Wynton, with extended hand, said, "I'm so sorry. It couldn't be helped."

The presence of Clint, Baron, and Marshall became apparent as they came from the front of the van.

"What's wrong?" Clint asked as he ran to his partner's aid.

Wynton innocently appealed, "I was about to explain there is a camper stuck in front of us."

Never acknowledging Wynton's gesture, the trucker moved forward to see the camper sitting in the lane.

The driver of the camper had his window rolled down as a knit capped driver stuck his head out the window.

The truck driver feeling his oats walked toward the camper jacked and ready to take a swing at the unsuspecting driver's noggin. Realizing he had a party of six following behind him, he felt an urge to get a punch out of his system. He banged on the side of the camper to get the driver's attention as he made his presence known.

The driver's head swiveled back as his left arm waved out the window.

"Can you believe this?" the camper driver asked incredulously.

Revved up and ready to throw a blow, the truck driver caught sight of a sphere spinning sideways in front of the recreational vehicle.

Jumping out the RV, the driver, with a slight lead on the truck driver and the entourage of six, followed behind.

As he walked, the RV driver turned to the others slightly alarmed, "It's the craziest shit I have ever seen," he proclaimed. "It just happened, next thing, I'm on top of this."

The truck driver stopped at the camper's front bumper, muttering, "Holy shit."

The two men disappeared from sight as Carter and Larry finally caught up, only to stop dead in their tracks.

Carter turned and waved for the remaining four to hurry up.

As Clint, Baron, Marshall, and Wynton finally made it to the front of the camper, their eyes widened at the sight of a Yugo turned on its side perched up by the carcass of a deer trapped underneath still waggling its head as a reflex for stretching of muscles still able to react from its impact of the car.

Wynton turned to Clint, citing, "That's muscle memory."

TRUDY AND SLOW POKE

She was outdistancing him by a yard, even in flip-flops. She lifted her legs and kicked high, as RaShonda's dress wrapped around her thighs like it was part of her skin. The snow drenched them both sticking to the exposed skin.

Winded, Danny turned to look behind him having already lost the vision of Lamont in front of him.

"Head for the lodge!" he yelled to Trudy who was bee-lining in that direction.

The lodge would only be a quarter of a mile away. He could see the building even in the haze of the snowfall.

Behind him was nothing. Whatever was following them was no longer giving chase.

Danny began to slow down. His insides burned. His chest felt like it would burst. He had no idea what fuel beyond sheer terror was propelling Trudy to continue pushing, but Danny was truly exhausted.

His head throbbed maddeningly. He needed to rest, but if that thing was still behind him, he needed to keep pushing.

His ribcage was caving in on him while he took in snow like a vacuum. He choked on the flakes that rested on his tongue and fell face down to a soft padded area where the picnic grounds began.

Trudy turned and doubled back toward Danny as he lifted his head to reveal himself wearing a mask made of snow. The feathery flakes dripped from his face as he pushed himself up.

Trudy stopped and grabbed him by the elbow as he hunched on all fours. He wheezed in an asthmatic fashion as she tried to dead lift him to no avail.

"Damn, you heavy," she commented. "Stop playing. We got to make it to the lodge."

Danny shook his head furiously.

"Not...playing," he spit out. "Go...on...I'm right...behind...you."

Trudy stood there before him torn. She couldn't leave him. The knot on his forehead grew bigger.

Danny removed the last portion of snow on his face and pushed her on.

Her feet in the flip flops were redder than the nail polish she wore on her manicured toes.

"Go," he said. "I'll be behind you."

"You better, Slow Poke," she said watching him slowly rise.

"Go!" he said.

She hesitated, then she was off again.

Danny, with his hands on his knees, lifted his head as he was able to regulate his breathing. His shirt and pants were soaked.

He took a couple of steps and trotted slowly. He turned his head left and saw the old horse barn.

The whirring noise no longer coming from it, but the stable doors were wide open.

Snowflakes fell into his eyes and he shut them quickly from the burning sensation they created.

Tearing up as he opened them, revealed the shape of a car sitting inside the barn.

Danny veered off the path toward the lodge, hoping that Trudy would continue onward to safety.

The stable's wooden doors had blown open and swung wildly in the snowstorm. Danny approached with the hope of catching his breath, then continue toward the lodge.

As he moved closer, he was drawn by the Gun Metal Gray exterior chassis that was immediately unmistakable to him.

He entered the stable taking measured steps toward the car. His mind racing as he recognized the custom painted pinstripe.

Even though the windows were raised, the T-tops had been removed. He searched inside the silver interior.

He walked around the car's body and found himself at the driver's door. He checked out the true spoke wheels as he opened the door. He lifted his leg and sat in the leather bucket seat.

As he climbed in, he reached for the glove compartment. It was empty as he rummaged his hand in the box. He stretched a bit as his fingers hit the back panel. His fingers crawled and drew back when he heard the tinkle of two little keys. He snatched them quickly and jumped out the car.

Fumbling with the keys, he moved to the rear of the car. He examined both keys, then chose one. Once he was certain, he placed it into the trunk's key port. The trunk door swung open. Danny's heart was heavy. Unsure what he'd find, he held his breath as the door slid upward.

In 1968, Danny's parents had prepared the house for guests on a Sunday afternoon. Danny's aunts and uncles all arrived with streamers, balloons, and a huge banner that they hung in the entrance of the living room.

Danny was allowed to miss church that day to run errands with his father. They wound up at Zayre on First and Roosevelt.

It wasn't often that Danny went shopping with his father. It was extremely rare at that time. Danny did his best to not pick up anything except what his father directed him to get. Even then, he would call out to his father before he laid a finger on the item. They spent more time in the checkout line than they did shopping. His father was a no-nonsense shopper. Get in, get it, get out.

When they returned, the house was bustling with noise as family members arrived at one o'clock bringing plates of food to add to the festivities.

Danny scratched his head for a while, not sure what holiday they were celebrating. Memorial Day had passed, and it was too soon for the Fourth of July.

His uncle Cameron brought in a sheet cake which he was given strict orders to not come near.

Even his grandmother was there. She never left her house except to go Christmas shopping which she only did once a year, buying underwear and socks for everyone.

At two that afternoon, a white Continental with suicide doors pulled curbside in front of the house. Danny's aunt, Martha and her latest husband, Roy exited the car.

Uncle Roy, a detective with the Chicago police opened the left passenger door to allow Randee out. Upon seeing him, Danny nearly bolted out the door only to be pulled back by his grandmother.

"Not yet," she said in his ear.

It had been a very long time since he'd seen his cousin whom he loved like a brother. His heart leapt with joy as he watched Randee slowly crawl out the back seat, grabbing each leg one at a time and plant them onto the curb.

Randee grabbed the roof of the car and after retrieving a pair of crutches hobbled toward the house with his mother chasing behind him.

Danny knew Randee had gone overseas to fight in the war. He was a Marine. The greatest fighting unit the United States had ever produced.

Danny first thought his cousin must have slipped on some ice, but it wasn't winter.

As Randee took one stair at a time with Uncle Roy and his father helping him up the concrete steps, Danny pondered if Randee had broken his leg goofing off like Danny had done a couple years back when he was playing baseball.

When Randee got into the house a roar of surprise caught him off guard. It was a rare time that Danny saw tears run down his cheeks.

Long before Danny met Lamont, Randee's baby brother, and preceding meeting two of his very own brothers, there was a bond between the two of them that was extremely brotherly. So much so, that Danny tore out of his grandmother's arms to finally welcome his cousin home.

Danny opened his arms wide ready to wrap Randee in them to let him know how much he missed him the eighteen months he was gone only to be stopped short as his father grabbed his collar nearly choking him on his own t-shirt.

"Give him some space, son," his father laughed. "He's going to be here awhile."

It was a celebration with family members, neighbors, and family friends joking, cajoling, drinking, and eating. Carousing for the world to see what love and joy a people could have for each other and with each other.

Randee asked Danny to make him a plate, to have ready when he returned in fifteen minutes. Danny immediately hit the kitchen, grabbed a paper plate that had to be doubled due to the weight of spaghetti, and fried chicken with coleslaw, a smattering of ribs. Everything that Danny saw, he placed on the plate.

Unaware of the time it took to actually put the plate together. Danny folded a napkin on top and hunted for Randee.

The house was a 1,100 square foot single story with a basement. Danny followed the noise to the sublevel to hand deliver the plate, but Randee was not amongst the crowd.

He scampered back up the main floor and checked the bathroom, but it was empty.

With no sign of Randee in the living room, nor Danny's room, the only place left to venture was his parents' bedroom.

It struck Danny as odd, that the wooden door was shut. For all the years his family had been in that house, the door was never closed. Not when his parents dressed, prayed, or wrapped his

Christmas presents. His parents were the most open couple he had ever known throughout his short life.

But now, the door was closed.

Danny reached for the brass doorknob and jerked it only to find it was locked. This was really an oddity.

Danny knocked and his Aunt Martha's voice came from the other side asking, "Who is it?"

Danny wondered if she was dressing in there and respectfully apologized.

"It's all right, baby," was her response.

"Have you seen Randee?" he asked. "I put a plate together for him and can't find him."

His response came in the form of the door unlocking. There was a dragging swoosh of the door's bottom against the newly laid carpet and his aunt stood in front of the partial opening blocking Danny's view.

"Why don't you put it in the oven, baby?" she cooed. "He'll be out shortly."

Danny was more than happy to comply and turned around to return to the kitchen.

Aunt Martha began to struggle with the friction of the door and the carpet when Danny heard, "What'd you get me?" come from the room.

Danny was barely on his way when he pushed the door open to answer. His eyes opened in horror as he saw only the bloody stumps where Randee's legs once were.

Randee lay flat on his back as Danny's mother and Aunt Marie, his father's youngest sister worked on cleaning his joints. The smell of rubbing alcohol permeated the room. Red streaked gauze lay on the carpet next to a pair of wooden prosthetic legs.

Danny was mortified at the destruction that had wrought his beloved cousin. He was hurt, crushed, and devastated.

If this could happen to his cousin, then Superman could be

defeated, Batman could be killed, and Wonder Woman could be tamed by her own lasso.

There was no hero greater to Danny aside from his parents than Randee. The enemy has decimated his cousin.

"You go take care of his plate, like a good boy, okay?" his aunt Marie shooed him off.

His eyes fixated on the triage being performed.

"I'm okay, big guy," Randee assured him. "Make sure it's nice and hot for me. I'll be out in five minutes, ya hear?"

Danny turned to head back to the kitchen with big tears streaking down his face.

Randee didn't lie to him. He was all right. And got better as the years went along.

Later, Randee got married two times, had four children between two wives and three more from two flings.

He started two businesses that were short lived, but Randee thrived.

He had a penchant for fast cars for the fast life he was living. The past five years he had traded in sleek racing cars that he taught Danny to drive before receiving his driver's license. This car that Danny was entering being the latest.

He had also changed his legs throughout the years switching from wooden versions to newer, lighter, metallic models which he placed the most expensive alligator shoes on.

Danny was staring at the prosthetic titanium legs with a pair of Florsheim shoes still attached.

"I've got one more question, then you need to go."

Randee lowers his head so Danny can see his eyes slowly roll toward him behind his sunglasses.

"Do you think someone killed him?"

Danny turns away, ready to bolt from the car as a flood of emotions converge upon him.

Randee grabs him by his left wrist, his eyes still trained on the youth.

Danny reluctantly turns toward him and realizes he is not in control. Emotions will speak for him. Not his head, nor his heart, but this entanglement like a ball of string ready to unspool. A knot emerges inside reminding him of seeing his mother's hand raising to God, then collapsing under a swarm of comforting arms.

"Yes!"

"What are you doing?" came from behind Danny.

He spun around to see Trudy limping towards him.

"I told you to go to the lodge," he said. Crestfallen, he shut the trunk immediately.

He was reeling. *How could Randee's car be here? Why were his legs in the trunk?*

"I was heading there, when I turned around and didn't see you," she said. "I thought, now where is Slow Poke?"

"I was tired!" he said.

As she approached him, she looked down and began to scream as she stood next to a wood chipper.

Danny jumped.

"What's wrong?"

She excitedly pointed downward unable to answer.

Danny edged closer to gain a view at what her hand pointed toward.

Smeared in blood was the yellow sweater that Ricky wore. Danny grabbed Trudy's hand and pulled her tightly to him as she sobbed uncontrollably.

It didn't take him long to assess where Ricky had gone. Plasma the color of chocolate was splattered on the blades of the wood chipper.

He, too, closed his eyes and silently asked God for forgiveness realizing Ricky could be alive if he hadn't argued with him.

She squeezed him tightly and in a muzzled cry, said, "I want to go home."

He slowly walked her out the barn's opening. "Me, too. Let's get to the lodge."

His leg throbbed as their hips bumped.

A dog's bark turned their attention toward the time share.

"Get 'em, boy," they both heard. Danny was struck that he believed he knew the voice.

From a distance, they could see a mist of air rising. Then they the dog panting.

Danny knew immediately it was the devil dog.

"To the lodge," he shouted at Trudy as he shoved her forward. "Run!"

YUGO I GO

Charlie pumped his shotgun and lowered the barrels. Everyone agreed. This was the most humane method to handle this situation.

The young adult buck raised its head. Its eyes pleading for mercy as it struggled to get back on its feet, trapped beneath the Yugo. Minus the engine, it probably weighed as much as the car. It wound up in the position solely because it didn't meet the car head on. There would have been a decisively different outcome had they gone head to head.

It, however, made the simple mistake of crossing the road from one side of the forest preserve to the other in a perilous search for food that snowy evening.

Taking its time, it began to cross the median, first the single lane road heading west before stepping onto the island. Its hooves lost their footing as they stretched into the eastbound side. A beam of lights caught its view and it was never able to react fast enough to bound toward the few shrubberies it was in pursuit of. The Yugo hit its midsection pushing it upward.

The brakes on the car never got the traction they needed as the driver pumped immediately but was still too late.

The collision lasted less than two seconds, but within that time, the buck's hind legs landed on the hood of the car with such a force, it tipped the mini car onto two wheels before careening it over on its side. The front legs of the buck trapped under the car with its back legs kicking the front plate in.

Marshall had briefly tried to talk to the couple trapped inside the car. He only got a response from the driver. Blood spilled from the passenger's forehead flowing onto the window.

Percy, the truck driver, was trying to dispatch some patrol unit on his CB radio. The storm made it somewhat impossible to get a clear frequency, but he was certain he had finally gotten through and a response of a unit being en route he could finally communicate.

As he got out his cab, he saw a row of headlights bouncing across the single lane. Horns incessantly honked out of frustration on this cold, wintry evening. People got out of their cars to assess the situation and inched forward only for updates on how long they would be stuck.

The sound of the shotgun racking up then the explosion of the gun going off alarmed many of those who sat in the log jam. The timorous boom echoing as it reverberated off the sides of the road dividers sent many to cover in their cars.

The worse however, was far from over, as the hardest part was just beginning.

The trick was always removing the couple from the car which Baron and Marshall had thought would be an easy task. Even with the help of Larry's brute strength, they could not manage the door of the driver.

The Yugo driver had found himself engorged by his very own seat belt and no one asked him to remove the safety feature once they discovered his predicament. His female companion was another matter. She was unresponsive to any of the call outs as she lay there resting her head on the window bleeding out. Wearing a knitted skull cap, her blond hair was strewn over her face. There was a mixture of strawberry where her very own plasma leaked at the base of her right temple and sat on the cracked passenger's window forming a small puddle that had grown within the last five minutes.

The initial plan was to remove the car and the deer off the road. Given the entanglement, the deer had to go first.

Clint, Wynton, and Carter foolishly attempted to tangle with the buck, but even in dire pain it fought them off with its antlers as its eyes ever wide furiously looked for its attackers. It moved its head up and back, slamming it down as it tried to defend itself.

It was Percy who conceded that the deer had to be put out of its misery. Charlie, the driver of the love van volunteered, as he had the weapon much to the surprise of all those standing around.

They watched as the parka wearing long haired, groovy guy moved to his flowered decaled vehicle and emerged with a shotgun.

Charlie was clearly not just for love, peace, and happiness.

Baron's glasses fogged up, as the rest tried to figure out what to do with the carcass of the deer.

"Anybody got a hacksaw?" Carter asked.

Realizing all eyes were on him, Percy shook his head as he said, "Why would I have a saw?"

There was still a mangled mess entangled with the Yugo. Only the head had been torn clean off from the blast.

"Any ideas?" Clint quizzed.

Larry stood next to Charlie marveling at the work he had created with the shotgun. He reached for it as Charlie stood gazing at his handy work.

"Can I touch it?" Larry asked.

The man moved back, stepping away from the odd request.

"No," he said.

Larry, offended, walked away heading for the van.

"Where you going?" Baron asked.

Larry shrugged his shoulders, "What else can we do?"

Wynton walked around the small lime green car. The hideous color was nearly neon. He outstretched his hands and rocked the car.

Clint, Marshall, and Baron looked on as flakes continued to fall on them.

Wynton proceed to walk to the other side of the median. He glanced upward to look at the highway signs. Then he trotted back nearly slipping before a car headed in the opposite direction.

His friends jumped momentarily at the sight of him losing his footing from the white Keds he wore.

He came back and joked, "Watch out for that last step. It's a lulu."

A private joke between the two as Clint slapped at Wynton's extended hand.

Marshall asked, "What was that for?"

"Honeymooners," Wynton said. Before he could continue, Baron and Marshall stared at each other.

"No," Baron interrupted. "What'd you run over there for?"

"I wanted to see how far the next exit was. Thought maybe we could find someone to get help," Wynton said.

"And?" Clint asked.

Wynton raised his eyebrows, "And?"

Marshall was exacerbated, "How far?"

"Oh," Wynton chuckled. "Six miles."

Percy said, "There should be help on the way soon. A trucker friend of mine called for assistance."

"How long should that be?" Baron asked.

Clint looked at his "family," and said, "We may not have thirty minutes."

Baron and Marshall nodded in agreement, pointing at the Yugo, then Baron asked, "What do you suggest we do?"

Clint clapped his hands, replying, "Let's move this bitch."

THE CHASE

Run hard. Be strong. Don't quit. This was the first mantra Trudy learned when she joined the track team.

Lift, kick, drop, dig was another. She was lifting and kicking as hard as she could at that moment. She'd drop one leg and dig in one side, then start the process on the other side.

As she approached her senior year, she had gotten complacent during the winter practice.

Coach had the team coming in at 5:30 in the morning. She was beginning to cherish the extra half hour sleep she had during the time off. She was out of bed by 5:45 in the shower at six immediately after her father washed out the tub from his bath. She'd catch a ride with him to school as he headed for the Eisenhower Expressway. They'd share buttered raisin toast which they noshed on during the brief ride. She was daddy's little girl.

When coach started the winter practices with two-a-days, first in the morning two-mile runs, then immediately after school for two and a half hours, she was in zombie land. She lacked the discipline to go to bed at a reasonable hour. Who goes to bed at 9:00 P.M.?

Starters, that's who.

She just had a natural talent and speed. She'd spent three years on the varsity team and never really felt like she belonged until this winter season, but she still hated the ungodly hours. Going to the campus before the sun came up and going home long after it had set for the day.

Some days she just stared out the classroom windows longing for the day to end.

Lift, kick, drop, dig.

She earned a starter's spot on the 4x40 relay. She was positioned as the second leg the first month of practice, but she was too fast for her hand off and constantly wound up making up for time lost once she received the baton. When coach made her the first leg, she gave a tremendous boast to the team's time, but her friends told her there was no real glory because the remaining leg would lose the momentum she put forth.

She was named captain of the team, one of four the prior Spring. The pressure was overwhelming, but it afforded her the opportunity to be the final leg. She closed things out with ease.

Her confidence was at an all-time high.

Boys dug athletic girls. They loved the competitive spirit that lived inside of them, but they couldn't stand losing to them. Boys hated losing to them. However, when Trudy ran, she was a goddess and she demanded nothing less of those who wanted to spend time with her.

Unlike her sister, Regina who was born with the gifts and attributes of a woman to be desired. She was a girl with all the gifts which made her mother her greatest ally, but her father's fiercest sentry. He loathed having to watch all the boys who vied for her attention usually chasing all of them away. Their mother was her protector, mostly from their father. Thus, he wound up aligning himself with Trudy, almost seeing her as the son he never had.

But track was changing that, and he soon lost his second daughter.

He had a few boys he'd let around his girls. Young men he really warmed to. Kevin was a year ahead of Reg and had gotten an academic scholarship to Boston College. Shannon joined the Navy. Markus, still trying to find himself was at the community college, but he did come around. After he received his Associates, he enrolled in Lewis University with an eye on accounting.

Danny, however, daddy couldn't stand. Hated him when he showed up at the doorstep at eleven years of age. He was constantly ringing their doorbell to get Reg outside. He was obnoxious, rude, fat, and smelly.

When he got to high school, he lost a ton of weight and didn't smell anywhere near like a walking ass, but he still had a confidence streak that Trudy's father liked to knock down a peg or two.

He never had a shot with Reg. Even when he started driving sports cars his cousin would loan him.

Her father pranked Danny and took one of the cars for a long spin around the block. Didn't come back for hours. They were all nervous, but daddy was actually parked two blocks south watching a baseball game with a neighbor tucking the car in an alley garage.

Danny lost his mind. But her father had almost messed up. Failing to call home to let his family in on the joke, the girls' mother became sympathetic with Danny. That sympathy opened the door for him and Reg to talk as she tried to calm him down.

They shared a kiss that afternoon. A very long kiss that Trudy witnessed firsthand by accident.

Regina even made dinner for him. Nothing special, just a can of SpaghettiOs, actually with Oscar Meyer hot dogs cut into little pieces and mixed in. Her specialty. She didn't do that for anyone, but family, and rarely even for them.

Regina opened up her repertoire for Danny. She got out of canned food and started really experimenting. First through cakes and pies. Danny had to back off during wrestling season. He couldn't afford to carry the weight and he had a tremendous sweet tooth. If it was a confection, Danny had to have it.

The night she told him she was seeing Steven Gamble, she made him a triple chocolate layered cake. He was licking the Dutch chocolate frosting off his fingers when she dropped the boom on him. He smashed that cake before Trudy could get one slice.

Trudy was livid.

So blindly in love was he with Regina, he spent the next two years torturing Trudy simply for being her sister.

"What up, Hamhock?" he would tease.

The first time he laid that line on her was her freshmen year. She had joined the track team just a month prior when the team had to share the field with the varsity football team for one hour a day during the teams' spring workout sessions.

Ever the clown, Danny picked on her the moment he spotted her. She was forever this little sister type to him as long as he held a torch for Regina.

But she settled that score immediately – almost.

It was the third week of practice for the football team. Danny found himself having to run a few laps for a missed tackle as she and a few girls were practicing wind sprints.

She stretched in the middle of the field as Danny rounded the outer track. He was barely making it with a trot, but still had the audacity to yell out to her as the two other members were outpacing him.

"Hamhock, where them beans?"

Initially, she was going to just flip him the bird, but as her teammates said to his comment with little titters, she called him out.

"You run more than just that mouth, Slow Poke?"

He stopped in his tracks as his teammates called him out on her remark.

"You gon' take that?"

"Short stack called you out."

"You let a girl challenge you?"

Danny, winded, had no choice but to respond, "You think you can beat me in a race, Hamhock?"

Trudy stood straight up and carried her 5'4" frame to the chain link fence that separated them.

"You want to go a full lap, Slow Poke?"

Already self-conscious about her size and the weight distribution of her body still carrying what her grandmother joyfully called "baby fat," she felt compelled to show Danny and all his friends exactly what this Hamhock could do.

Baron, Marshall, Carter, and Larry rested against the fence as the two of them lined up.

With a lane separating them, they focused on the gravel path. Trudy had on the school's blue with white trim shorts with the matching school t-shirt. Danny kept the practice pants and scuffed up black cleats on with just a sweaty white tee on.

Baron moved to the other side of the fence to get the race going.

"You good?" he asked Danny who just nodded his head perpetrating some locked in fortitude of focus.

Confident as she was in her ability, Trudy was extremely nervous. She had no idea what skill set Danny had, but she knew she would be devastated if he beat her.

Baron asked about her well-being and she said without hesitation, "Let's get this chump of the track."

Much to his surprise, his friends began to cheer Trudy on. Baron started the backward count starting at three-two-one...

"Go," Baron shouted.

Scores of teammates gathered to watch this main event as if it were a televised match between two bitter rivals.

Trudy started right away kicking her leg out, lifting it nearly to the middle of her stomach. She had a natural gait that her coaches found so hard to replicate. Her heft always left them confused. She had not developed on the top and her lower half was monstrously toned even though it was thicker than the average mile runner.

Danny was slow out the gate, watching Trudy advance him nearly one yard by the time he started.

Trudy pushed hard, but the grace with which she ran put to rest who was going to be the better runner that day.

Danny was winded before he even got halfway around the track. Only his pride stopped him from quitting in front of his boys.

Trudy only had a quarter of a mile left as she caught sight of how far she was outdistancing him on her final turn. She laughed to herself, but knew until she was whizzing past Baron, she could ill afford to wave the victor's flag.

Baron stood in front of her now, less than ten steps away. This victory was going to be sweet.

She lifted, kicked, but on her drop her right heel didn't dig properly. Her knee buckled as she pulled her hamstring. The tightness came as a surprise and she winced as she collapsed to the sharp gravel stones, shredding the skin off her exposed thighs.

She grimaced in pain, rolling around as Baron ran to her to help her up.

Danny trotted by her breathing so hard he wheezed to the end. He collapsed to his knees and crouched down to get air in his passageway.

A bevy of teammates surrounded her to lift her off the track, as tears striped her cheeks in humiliation.

Danny slowly ambled over, placed his hands on his knees, and gloated, "Not so fast now, hah?"

This tore her apart.

They never had a rematch.

This chase was the closest thing they had ever had to that day and while it had been weeks since Trudy had trained, she saw nothing that was going to stop her this time.

"Get to the lodge!" Danny yelled as she sprinted toward the entrance to the spa hutch.

The snarl of the dog giving chase, Trudy could also hear behind her in the distance.

Her insides were on fire as she finally hit the camp grounds. She had long ditched the flip flops and now found herself digging onto snow and hard frozen patches of dirt.

She ran past the barbeque pit and landed onto the marble slab of the swimming pool. She glanced at the Olympic-sized pool that glistened with a sheet of frozen ice as its covering.

The soles of her feet were numb and felt like they could crack every time they hit the cold concrete, but the marble was somewhat slippery as the snow fell upon it.

Nearly slipping on the edge of the pool, she caught her balance still afraid to look behind her. Praying that Danny was close to her as she prepared to reach for the door to the spa.

Her fingertips were also without feeling as she wrapped her hand around the knob. She sobbed uncontrollably at the elation of reaching the building. Once inside, Danny could navigate them to the front desk.

The door had barely shut behind her when she heard the rottweiler growl, then yelp loudly.

She stopped as exhaustion attacked her insides. She cramped from her ribcage and the tightening was unbearable.

Where was Danny, she thought.

As she approached the pool, she saw the dog struggling to stay afloat surrounded by broken ice as it snapped its jaws downward.

But she saw no sign of Danny.

The mutt cried out, seeming to paddle then dunking under the water.

This happened three times before she saw Danny's head. Frantically, she began to search for something to distract the dog so she could rescue Danny. The deck was empty as they both disappeared beneath the ice.

She heard the door open and a tall graying man pushed through. She backed up careful not to fall into the pool.

"I believe you dropped your slippers, Cinderella," came a gravelly voice from behind her.

Arms encircled her with the left hand dangling her flip flops.

I GO YUGO

They had spread out around the Yugo still sorting out the best way to attack the little car.

The most logical was to tip it back over onto all four tires. The problem was the car would still be immobile with the single lane now backed up easily to the length of three miles.

Between the six friends was a combined weight tipping nearly thirteen hundred pounds to lift the nearly eighteen-hundred of the Fiat mini-car barely released in the U.S. at that point.

Percy, boo-hooed about having a bad back and a touch of lumbago. Touched all right, Clint thought.

Charlie was so slight, the most they could do was thank him for addressing the deer and keeping the driver alert while they tried to figure out the best way to move the car so they could continue on.

They had removed their bomber jackets and placed them in the van. The evening chill wasn't that alarming considering they all hailed from the "windy city," where the "hawk" reigned supreme especially during the winter.

Mostly attired in jerseys and jeans with variations of boots, high tops, they sloshed back to the car with the intention of Clint and Larry getting under the passenger's side to hoist the car as Carter, Marshall, and Wynton anchored from the sides to take hold of the bumper with Baron monitoring the driver's side hopefully with an assist from Carter and Marshall who would be closest to him.

The trapped couple's name was Warshowski – Mike and Frieda – and they were expected their first child in a month or so. Mike had suggested a quick trip to visit family and they had stayed way too late. Frieda was out cold. The plan was to turn the car over and get help to aid them immediately.

"What about Danny and Trudy at the hotel?" Clint asked.

Charlie volunteered to take the couple to a nearby hospital but as bad off as Frieda was, Mike wasn't in any shape for amateurs to carry off. *Did anybody know of one nearby?*

Wynton had a suggestion on how to temporarily treat Mike. His entrails were spilling out to the side as the seatbelt had ripped right through him.

Wynton searched his van for items that would suffice as a tourniquet to hold the man's guts in place until help arrived. Hopefully, he could alleviate any shock the driver clearly was suffering.

"On my count of three," Marshall coached. "Clint and Larry, you two just raise the car up enough so the rest of us can get our body weight under."

"On three," they all said as they placed their gloved hands atop Marshall's for a break.

Percy and Charlie remained on the side of the road to not interfere as the six surrounded the car.

Larry slid his thick gloved hands under the passenger's side close to the rear. As a former IHSA linebacker, he got into a stance with his knees bent and his butt in the air.

Clint knelt down as well. Both were roughly two hundred and fifteen pounds apiece and solidly built.

"One," Marshall began the count.

Larry turned to Clint and grunted, "You ready?"

With eyes closed tight, Clint was locked into concentration, as he strained to answer, "Yup!" not to exert himself too much.

"Two," Marshall said as if quarterbacking the final play to a big championship game.

Carter and Baron ducked down under the car on opposite sides with their fingers ready to mount the grill.

Wynton's role was to place pressure by leaning face forward on the driver's side as Larry and Clint lifted. Along with Marshall, the two would balance the car until Baron and his younger brother could slide to lend support.

"Three!" Marshall said.

Larry and Clint ducked down as their hands slid down like massive cranes straining immediately to hoist the car. They grunted and groaned, but as Baron and Carter added their contributions, the chassis began to rise.

The car groaned as Larry and Clint struggled to upright the vehicle. Snot flew from Larry's nostrils like fire from a dragon's snout. He tried to wipe his nose on his sleeves but felt his grip shift every time he moved. He had to reposition himself to match Clint who was sweating amidst the rivulets of snow beads that descended upon his forehead.

Shattered glass fell onto their shoes while they shuffled their feet for better traction. The car rose, as Baron and Carter stretched out their arms to grab the sides of the car. Pivoting against each other, one on the right leg, the other on the left, they added the necessary muscle to pull the little bug up. Carter's footing a little too awkward as he had to side step the carcass of the deer.

"Keep it coming," Marshall said as he and Wynton prepared to brace themselves against the car.

The driver whispered a prayer for his pregnant wife ignoring the situation he himself was in.

"Please be gentle," he said softly.

More than a quarter of the way up, Baron moved himself closer to Larry, allowing the mountain of a man to shift to the center of the passenger's side. Larry's hand slipped and he nearly pushed inside the car around the broken window. A sliver of glass caught his wrist as blood trickled down his sleeve.

"Shit," he passed as he was more irritated at the destination of his sweater with a stream of snot nearly touching his lips.

Baron lifted his elbow toward Larry, offering the forearm of his pleated shirt. Larry leaned over and ever so gently swiped his nose over it streaking onto the shirt.

"Thanks, brother," he granted.

"Da nada," Baron groaned in return.

The car was nearly three-quarters upward as Wynton and Marshall placed their hands on the top of the driver's window.

"Steady now," Marshall said. "We're almost there."

Carter was now on their side buckling the hood. His Isotoner gloves gripped hard at the base of the car and outside the front plate of glass. He spit and watched as blood from his bitten tongue hawked out a rosy red logic.

Clint yelled out as they were nearly at one hundred percent. His eyes met those tear-streaked pupils of the expectant mother who thanked him and the others for their mission of mercy.

Marshall, Wynton, and Carter braced themselves as the car rocked toward them. Their feet separated to control the shift of weight and the left tires crept closer to the pavement.

Upon touching down on all fours, the car teetered as Marshall warned, "Not so fast, let it down gently."

The chassis rocked back and forth as the impaled driver moaned, writhing in agony.

Percy and Charlie grabbed the remains of the deer and moved it off the road onto the side embankment.

The six men leaned forward on the car, exhausted by the effort.

Larry leaned over, embracing Clint, patting him heartily on the back. Wynton received an embrace from Carter and Marshall simultaneously.

"Good job, everybody," Baron congratulated.

Still, they were unable to move the car for fear of injury to the patrons inside.

"What are we going to do now?" Clint asked.

High beam lights ahead flashed upon them as an engine roared yards down barreling toward them on the opposite side of the road. A white dust cloud encircling the bright yellow lights of the snowplow streaming through.

Larry tapped Clint on his shoulder.

"What do you know about those?" he pointed at the Snowcat plow.

Charlie and Percy, close by, looked on with disbelief.

ON THE ICE

Shards of ice surrounded them as the dog's weight plunged them deeper into the depths of the pool.

Fiercely, the hound kept nipping at Danny's forearm as it was blocked from its true target – Danny's neck.

The volume of water and the icy frigidness made the attack feel more like a scratch as the devil beast's teeth made contact, but it continuously released before completing its bite.

Danny had miscalculated its whereabouts and its proximity as he attempted to reach the spa after seeing Trudy, shoeless, but safely inside.

He was clearing the wire fence, hitting the concrete slab as his footing slipped.

He could hear the dog gaining on him, when his right knee buckled beneath him. Still, he could ill conceive missing a step.

He saw Trudy turn around, but with the little breath he had left, yelled for her to continue on. He was sure he could defeat the dog.

Once inside the barn, Danny and Trudy had to decide on how to report the finding of Randee's car and Ricky's sweater.

But those prosthetic legs sealed everything for Danny, and he knew what he least wanted to know or believe – that something sinister was afoot at the resort.

The dog made a second attempt to sink its jowls into Danny's arm when a string of bubbles escaped its mouth. The pooch's eyes widened suddenly with the dog kicking wildly to free itself.

The dog began to paddle back to the surface for air. Its extremities were stiffening from the few seconds it spent in the water slowing it from reaching air.

It barely had its snout break surface when it submerged into the water from behind. It kicked and snapped at the cold water refusing to have to surrender back to the deep face down. Its front paws paddling quickly before it resigned itself to the fact it was in a fight. The final yelp it released bounced into the air.

And its master picked up his pace.

"King!" Gillette called out.

Danny could barely grip its paw let alone maintain it. Hypothermia was in its initial stages of progression in his body. Everything slowed it down.

His chest pounded as he struggled to breathe during the last forty-five seconds.

The cold water also did no good for the headache which had been raging between Danny's temples.

The mutt's attack on him as he tried to get his footing on the pool's slab was the most humiliating moment as it leapt onto him.

They both landed on top of the ice with the dog flashing its incisors at Danny, snapping viciously at his face. It grabbed hold of his arm and shook it like it was a rag doll.

Danny screamed in pain and kicked the dog in the nether region. It barely winced as it jawed its way on his arm like it was a turkey leg.

With nearly twenty pounds over Danny, it sat on him like he was a raft. Danny tried to roll it over. His foot kept slipping on the icy surface. The vicious canine maintained its balance even when Danny heard the first crack.

His back immediately became wet from the water that broke through.

"No," he thought aloud while he tried to pound the dog in the face. That attempt only made the vise-like grip it had dig deeper into his flesh. He was certain it had severed a vain as he felt the mix of the hound's saliva with his very own blood.

He pushed again and the dog was riding him as if on a surfboard, but never releasing its bite.

The dog pushed its paw on Danny's chest and Danny could feel the ice begin to split under him. Water converged and wrapped itself to his chest. Danny's body immersed itself in the cold water as the dog clamped harder to not lose its bone.

It released immediately when the water entered its muzzle as it tried to snuff liquid out.

Again, it attacked Danny while they both crashed into the water. Danny's weight took his body downward as the dog fought for buoyancy. It shivered and sneezed incessantly, as each expulsion of air lost its control. It tried to paddle out the water while it circled using its hind legs that kicked onto Danny's torso.

Suddenly, it had nothing to sustain it. But it saw land and using its front paws swam toward it.

Paddling a few strokes, the dog felt the grip on its hind legs, turned and nipped at the frigid water. Helpless, it tried to lap up the chlorine liquid before it was completely pulled down.

Once its head was engulfed by the water, it angrily bore down on Danny. With teeth chomping away, it attempted to gnaw on Danny's face, but Danny circled behind it still holding onto its paw. It flexed its body as one would see a dog try to chase its own tail.

The more it fought; the deeper Danny plunged taking it down with him. The dog released a flurry of attacks, to no avail. Finally, it opened its jowls and accepted an intake of water. Its lungs attacked and the hound puffed up in the chest as asphyxiation seized it. Its body convulsed, jerking, and twisting uncontrollably until it released a stream of excrement.

Danny let it go and it slung upward. By the time its head emerged from the icy pond, it had passed. Its eyes glazed over while fixed on its owner, before it eventually drifted downward into the depths of the pool.

Danny tugged at it one more time, pushing the dog's body to the bottom as his own body seized up. Cramps took over and he accepted it was time to take that last breath and let the water enter his body.

He closed his eyes to say a prayer, a genuine prayer to God Almighty. It had been years since he even thought about talking to God, but he had two last requests: for God to keep Trudy safe, and to take away all the pain his mother had suffered since Lamont's death.

It was a quick prayer that he hoped God would listen to and answer in all his omnipotence.

Danny opened his eyes as from the murky depths of the last fathom a figure emerged that embraced him.

He was too weak to scream when its hands took hold of his face. He surrendered as Lamont dove him to the lower depths of the pool.

LAMONT

As Danny was seized with contractions, he watched the Rottweiler drift toward the next fathom. His heart pounded harder and echoed in his eardrums. He no longer had the will to hold his breath and mentally he had to accept how vicious the cold water would be as it entered him and expanded his lungs to near implosion.

It had been a long time since he had said a prayer and he found it incredibly hypocritical that now – now – he found himself throwing in a quick call to the Lord Almighty.

Unbelievable!

But he did. While he didn't really know what lie on the other side, his prayer started with the safety and protection of Trudy. That she made it to the front desk of the lodge and the cavalry came in to save her.

That his mother found peace of mind from the unrest that haunted her the past four years. He also prayed that his father's heart softened and forgave his mother for making such a ridiculous claim that opened the floodgates to such a young life cut short before his journey could ever start.

He thanked God for giving him the treasure trove of friendships that so many clamored to experience just once, but he had exponentially.

He, then embraced the end when he opened his eyes. In horror, he discovered a set of gray eyes staring at him. A pair of pale calloused hands immediately clutched his face and he tried to scream. Taking in a flood of water, never allowing his gaze to leave this embodiment of Lamont.

As his decaying hands held him, Danny convulsed. The expansion of his lungs taking in water as he felt tightness constrict his chest bringing him to darkness like an electrical blackout followed instantly by a flash of light that hung above him.

He feels a surge of energy as he swims to the light. A shimmering hanging above him that becomes a pair of green eyes sparkling like a set of emeralds. Beneath those eyes, a smile ascends upon him while a set of arms sit themselves upon his shoulders.

A giggle, innocent and girlish yet filled with womanhood brimming to get out bounces into his ears.

"You were down there a long time," the voice says. "Find anything you like?"

He pinches his nostrils to get the water drained from his nasal passage.

She leans in and pecks him on the lips.

There is a swelling in his heart unlike anything he has ever felt before. He rises in the water, his legs kicking, and he places his arms around her waist as he returns the kiss.

She pulls away. Her eyes dart to her right at a picnic taking place. A tall, slender man with short blond hair, trimmed beard disconnected to mutton chops stands over a barbeque pit slathering sauce on a rack of ribs.

She kicks her feet to reposition herself in the water to not be in sight of this man. She gives a tighter hug, bouncing against his chest. Her torso leaving an impression onto his. Her eyes wander over his shoulder once again as the loud bark of a Rottweiler chained to a fence that separates the pool from the picnic area reverberates onto the water.

"Tired?" she playfully asks.

He shakes his head.

"You sure?" she asks. "I don't want you to push yourself."

"I'm fine," he says.

Her eyes search his. She is looking for something from him. He can look at her eyes forever. He knows this. There is much to look at as far as he is concerned. Daphne is a vision from Heaven, and he thanks God he is with her now strange, he concedes, yes, there is a God!

Her skin is a porcelain white. Smooth, creamy, and flawless. He imagines a goddess that has relinquished her place above Earth to live amongst her human subjects and has chosen him, Lamont Christopher Rhimes as her eternal betrothed.

"Race you to the bottom, then," she challenges. "First one to reach the bottom and back wins."

He knows he can't conceal his excitement.

"Wins what?" he asks.

She rubs against him with her hands stroking the back of his head. She places a very light kiss on his lips again.

"What would you like?"

A billion words jumble in his mouth. His brain is on overload. Dictionary times ten. Noun or verb. Pronoun or personal noun.

What would he like?

He tries to maintain the dogpaddle Danny has taught him.

"Okay," he feebly answers.

She laughs. Her auburn hair is slicked back as it clings to her shoulders. She pushes off him and plunges to the bottom.

Okay, he thinks. He begins the pursuit.

His eyes still have problems adjusting to the chlorine burning as he tries to find her. Her feet wave in mermaid fashion. There is nearly a fathom between them as he gives chase.

She is incredibly fast and as waves of water encircle him, he realizes she has powerful legs. She appears to have been swimming all her life.

He has only six days under his belt thanks to Danny. Their first day at the resort, his cousin took him to the shallow end of the pool and gave him an hour's worth of acclimation with the water.

Mostly, he taught him to get over the fear of the water.

The second day, Danny took him to the depths of five feet, then tricked him to nine. Lamont nearly crapped himself as he plummeted toward the bottom, but Danny bailed him out and coached him well.

The third day, he tried to race Danny. He lost immediately, but his confidence grew.

Now, he is chasing this girl to the lower depths on the sixth day. His eyes ache, but he still pursues with every intention of catching her.

He is beyond a fathom when she grabs him from behind and sneaks a kiss onto his lips. Bubbles float from both their mouths as she sticks her tongue inside to tangle with his.

She releases him and points downward. She starts downward, as he follows, then she jackknifes and begins to ascend.

Damn, he thinks, she's beaten me.

He continues downward. His head is light. He contemplates cheating and not reaching the actual bottom. What's the point? Plus, he wants another kiss.

He continues his descent noticing the pool's lights reflecting off the bottom. His eyes burn so badly, he can't tell what they are reflecting from.

He careens into the wall of the pool as jet streams blow from a vent at the side. He nearly crashes into the bottom as the lights hit his eyes. His fingers probe the pool's floor and he clasped onto small metal. His hand wraps around it as he begins his ascent.

His head is woozy as he begins to fight for air. His lungs expand and he pushes upward, paddling fast and fatiguing himself.

He can see rays of light in the horizon and waves of water as he makes out Daphne's feet wading in the pool.

She is so fast she is out the water.

He emerges from the water and coughs instantly as water and air hit his lungs.

With a free hand, he wipes the water from his face. His eyes are on fire. He opens them and can't quite make out Daphne but is mortified that she has doubled in his vision.

A hand reaches out for him. He swings wildly to grab onto it. It catches him. He hears, "I got you, son."

A gruff, but pleasant man's voice.

The hand pulls him to the edge of the pool.

He wipes his face again rubbing his aching pupils.

"You all right?" the voice asks.

The moonlight reflects off the man's pate. Wearing a Hawaiian print shirt and black shorts, the man offers to pull him out the water.

He can see Daphne standing behind the man on the edge of the pool wrapped in a beach towel covered from her shoulders to her knees. Her reddish curls fall all over her face.

He surrenders his clinched right hand for assistance. As the man squeezes his wrist to pull him in, the coin pops onto the deck.

"Whatchu got there?" the mountainous man asks.

He scrambles to grab the coin, then pushes back into the water.

The man apologizes and smiles, "Where are my manners?" He offers his hand again, "I'm Dr. Gillette. I'm Daphne's grandfather."

Fatigue becomes cramps, but he keeps kicking in the water. His legs are tired, and his gut is seizing up. Every muscle in his torso tenses up.

The man reaches out his hand again.

"C'mon, son, let me help you out the water," the man pleads.

"What's the problem, Gil?" another male voice asks from behind him.

He shifts and can see the man formerly at the barbeque pit has entered from the other side and advances on him.

"I think he's found our treasure, Chad," the old man asserts. "Grab him."

He pushes off and finds himself caught in the middle of the pool as the lanky man's long arms reach out for him.

His eyes move toward Daphne. He begs for help, but she moves back from the deck as the two men continue to claw at him.

He needs to swim to the other side to climb out and run for help. He places the coin inside his mouth as the older gentleman dives in after him.

He panics and dives down as the intruder approaches. He feels the hands collapse onto his shoulders and with a force bulldozes him into the pool's wall.

His head slams into the brick as blood drips into his eye. The coin has lodged itself into his throat, and suddenly he can't breathe.

He waves wildly in the water for air as darkness encroaches upon him. He feels his body being slammed into the wall again and a punch in his back.

The moonlight fades as blood continues to blind him.

Air is depleted and his heart races hard.

He splashes, thrashing around as the men grab him and push his head into the water.

He tries to cry out, but he has nothing left. His eardrums boom at the sound of his beating heart, then muffles until it beats no more.

Danny's eyes reddened as his vision cleared. No longer afraid, he kicked one last time as Lamont placed a silver coin into his palm before disappearing into the lower depth.

SNOWCAT

The two paramedics were gingerly placing the driver into the back of their truck alongside his wife who was beginning to have contractions.

An oxygen mask was placed over their faces as the team prepared the trauma unit to address the hemorrhaging of the driver's innards.

A state trooper closed the double doors of the EMT unit for privacy. He pounded on the door alerting the driver he could move forward.

With an escort of three other state cars to lead the way, the lights began to flash as they slowly shoved out.

Snow continued to lay a blanket upon the stranded drivers as a remaining unit helped to clear the debris from the incident.

Wynton, Marshall, and Carter re-entered the van waiting for the signal to move forward.

Percy climbed back into his cab. His rig had been secured and he was certain he could make up for the lost time stuck on this narrow road.

Charlie had shown his papers for the shotgun and given clearance to leave as well. He hit the ignition and crept slowly as a Triple

A truck towed the Yugo onto the side before craning the car up out of the drivers' way.

Wynton was slipping his arm into his bomber jacket as Marshall buckled into the passenger's bucket seat.

The clicking of Carter's seatbelt was cue for Wynton to turn the key. The engine roared as he grabbed the stick and laughed out "PRNDL."

Marshall turned to the driver and asked, "Do you know where you're going?"

As the van slowly inched forward, Wynton gave a partial nod, "I have a clue."

Carter leaned as far as the belt would allow and said, "Hopefully, they made it there by now."

Wynton pulled up to the trooper waving them on and rolled his window down, "Officer," he said, "we need some assistance."

The Snowcat's beams illuminated the entire road ahead with the potential to blind any on-comers that many had attempted to pass. Fortunately, none did try as the road to the lodge was empty.

Inside, Clint shifted gears as the Trak tires rolled through the un-shoveled back route that led to the time shares.

Baron sat cramped between Clint and Larry sharing space with the stick as Clint's hand bashed against him.

"Sorry," Clint said.

"Damn that," Baron said. "Hurry up, I'm getting a cramp up my ass."

The high beams hit a parking lot of cars yards below them.

Larry rolled the window down and secured himself as he opened the door.

Clint stopped the engine before entering the parking lot as he and Baron followed behind Larry's charge toward the building.

Baron retrieved a key from his jeans pocket as he caught up with Larry who stood at the glass entrance to the lodging.

As they opened the door, Clint lagged behind huffing, "What up?"

Overhead lamps flickered throughout the hallway as the three men ran at full burst toward their suite.

Baron and Larry rounded the corner, immediately sighting their door nearly blown off its hinges.

By the time Clint entered, Baron was coming out the guest room while Larry assessed the damage in the living room.

Baron called out their names, but to no avail.

As Clint brushed away shards of glass, he asked, "So what do you think happened here?"

Snow drifted into the suite from the open balcony doors. Baron stepped to the sliding partition and noticed the footprints.

"I don't really know, but I suspect we may find out if we follow this trail."

Baron stepped out the door and began tracking Danny and Trudy's and a third set of footprints.

Clint was directly behind him as Larry picked up his fraternity paddle.

FINALE

Stepping toward the precipice of the pool, Gillette held Trudy by her shoulders. Shivering uncontrollably, she struggled in his grip.

She watched the water shimmer in the moonlight as it slowly began to refreeze.

The temperature was easily in the single digits as she quickly regretted ever trying on RaShonda's dress. As elegant as it was, the halter tying neckline was cutting into the back of her neck and the intricate crochet laced trim top was clearly too shear for her in this weather as Gillette's eyes barely moved away from her cleavage.

"It's a shame you will soon suffer the fate of your boyfriend and his cousin," he said in her ear as he stroked her bare shoulders. She could tell he was ogling her and felt repulsed by him.

He stroked the front of her pleated chiffon bodice, tracing her outline with his fat pig in the blanket fingers as his index finger circled her barely covered nipple.

"Can't believe he came back to this place after the unfortunate accident involving his cousin. What on Earth brought him back here?" the old man asked.

"You knew Lamont?" she asked as a northeastern wind licked under her dress from behind. Whatever the old coot had planned for her, she truly wished he would get to it or take her inside and finish the job.

She was awash in fear with no valid game plan for escape. She was alone. There was a fire in her that raged against how she ever let the likes of Ricky Williams talk her into coming all the way to Wisconsin, knowing full well what his plans were all along.

"Who was the other young man?" Gillette interrupted her thought.

She closed her eyes as the cold enveloped her, from her flip-flopped pedicured toes to her wet mopped head. She was beyond frigid as this lascivious old man continued to blow in her ear.

"What other young man?" she hesitantly asked.

"The one with the older model black Dodge," Gillette answered.

The bottom fell out as she was sure he was describing Ricky's car. The poor desolate gas guzzler that she had to put ten dollars in to help refill as Ricky claimed the pinging sounds in his ride to be attributed to some bad gas he got from the Aamco station on Seventeenth Avenue.

"You know who I'm talking about, don't you? Good news," he said as he flecked away the teardrop that fell from Trudy's eye, "he made a wonderful meal for King."

He peered into the pool trying to find the cadaver of his beloved rottweiler.

"Pity that was King's only taste of him. He did find your friend quite tasty. Came for seconds, which is rare for King," Gillette said.

Trudy groaned. She couldn't stomach much more.

"Let me go!" she screamed as she tussled with the old man again. His grip was stronger than granite.

"I could find other ways to use you," he permitted. "Would you like that?"

He nuzzled up to her cheek and placed his lips close to her mouth. She didn't know whether to pass out or puke right there. The rancid smell of Bourbon was on his breath mixed with a horrible cheese odor. Tears tumbled down her face as she contemplated whether a long tortuous murder was in store for her or him turning her out for tricks on the stroll. Did Wisconsin have a stroll like Chicago's Rush Street or Madison Street or Roosevelt Avenue? Many times, her mother told her sister that's where she might wind up, "on the stroll," working for some pimp if she didn't stop with her fast ways.

"None of this would be happening if only that association hadn't come up with an offer to buy all this land for their golf club," Gillette said. "Busted our offer by nearly a quarter of a million dollars. And they knew nothing about the silver buried beneath this land by Chief Black Hawk after they came here victorious in the Black Hawk War of 1832. It's our land now."

With his hand he grabbed Trudy by the jaws turning her head in his direction.

"Where a bunch of uppity niggers get that much money to buy a golf course, huh?" Gillette asked.

He squeezed her cheeks tightly. She closed her eyes shut from the mere glimpse of rage she sensed in his eyes.

"The owners at that time had both groups come down to address their decision on a final offer."

His breathing accelerated as his voice growled.

"My son-in-law got a heads up that we were about to lose the bid. That that nigger golf club was about to have their offer tendered."

He stroked her cheek with a light playfulness.

"Don't get me wrong," he said. "I don't have a problem with you blacks – my granddaughter – Molica, did you know her?"

Trudy shook her head, still squirming to free herself from the rugged aged hands of this man as he squeezed her tighter than a vise.

"Anyway, my granddaughter is black," he paused, reflected on that briefly, then went on, "was black. She's dead now."

With his right hand over her shoulder gripping her mandible, he stopped again and pondered.

His eyes drifted to what must have been a remote time, as his mouth opened for a brief moment. The whiskers on his face chafed Trudy as the gray hairs on his chin grazed her skin.

"She liked your Danny," he said. "Very much." He pulled Trudy closer and held her very tight. She had no energy left to exert. She very much wanted this over with.

She was tired of being afraid. She had spent too many of her young years being so only to have to swallow the bitter piss taste of it now.

"Just do it," she said. "Do it."

She thought of all the ways he could do it: shoot her, stab her, choke her, snap her neck, throw her in that freezing water, or just keep breathing on her. She wanted it as quick and as painless as possible. She assumed she would have to feel something, but she knew she didn't want something that would take hours. Pleasurable hours for him as he listened to her beg for her life.

"No, sir. Take me now," she said.

"What?" he asked. "Fool girl. You'd like that wouldn't you?"

He jerked her by the hair and declared, "No, I've got plans for you."

Gillette edged away from the concrete slab dragging Trudy back. She fell back to the ground. He rushed to pick her up as he heard a ping hit the cement.

He looked down to see a silver coin perched on the ledge of the pool.

"What the hell?" he asked.

He quickly bent down to grab it as Danny sprang out the water, snatching Gillette by the collar of his jacket.

Trudy immediately gave a quick boot to the old man's rear as he found himself unbalanced, unable to resist loosening his grip on the coin.

Danny pulled him into the arctic chilled waters plunging them both to the lower depths.

Trudy begged silently for the strength to lift herself up and retrieve Danny as quickly as possible.

Her knees popped as she stood up. She had not ever felt such an ache.

Water washed over ice and quickly remarried itself to a slender sleeve of compound.

"No," she shouted, resolute to not be alone.

Polar vortex be damned, she accepted defiantly, as she plunged into the icy cold water.

The moment his footing left the travertine docking, Gillette found himself submerged nearly a fathom of the twelve-foot-deep pool. His arms exerting energy through the twenty thousand pounds of water as he tried to elevate himself back to the surface before hypothermia completely took over him.

His rapid descent heightened by the weight of Danny riding his back forced him to wave wildly to buck the one hundred eighty pounds of force strapping itself to him.

Reaching behind him, he tried to throw Danny off. Finally, able to turn over he faced the dead eye stare of Danny's.

A tingling surged through his hands as he wrapped his hands around Danny's wrists. They tussled as they both continued to fall deeper to the bottom of the pool.

The old man labored as he fought Danny, surprised by the amount of force the boy was able to apply to him.

Danny's fingers couldn't close however, and he was unable to maintain a grip on the man. He swung and hit Gillette in the face forcing him to take a breath. The elder's eyes opened wide from the shock of his lungs swelling as water entered his system. Danny attempted another blow only to find it countered with a strike to his chest. The impact had more force than he could imagine, and he fell back wafting in the water.

The old man turned to flee at the bottom, scrambling to get away, when he bumped into the bloated stiff body of King. The rottweiler's jaws atrophied into a vicious snarl, but he was dead, nonetheless.

Distress filled him as the burning ache of numbness was disabling him from moving at a rapid speed.

As determined as he was to get to the shallow side of the pool, so was Danny determined to keep him below for as long as he could.

Danny swiped at the man's boot catching only the heel, but as the burly man frantically kicked at him to break free, it also caused the old man precious air he did not have to give.

Danny prepared himself for one more swipe, knowing he could ill afford to not capture him, or the old man could break through the thin ice bed and make his escape.

Danny pushed off and stretched his left arm as far as he could go. His fingers locked on the man's pant leg.

The kicking effort was feeble at best as Danny finally gained on him. Bubbles burst through as Gillette fought to not surrender while Danny was able to climb his back.

The sensation of doom invaded every pore of the old man as he faced the superior strength that Danny possessed.

He was prepared to turn and surrender to Danny with the hope that he would mercifully bring him back to the surface.

Suddenly, he was free. No longer bound by the arms that were encroaching him, he flipped around to see Danny being lifted by the collar. Trudy kicked her feet pulling Danny further away from him.

Danny flailed but was overpowered by the lack of mobility. His eyes fell upon the old man with a nasty scowl on his face.

Gillette returned to the bottom and proceeded to kick off as a hand grabbed his ankle. With a force stronger than before, Gillette couldn't believe Danny had broken away and converged upon him that quickly.

He kicked to free himself and was immediately pulled back. With wild abandon his arms swung to help him escape the confinement of arms that entangled and roped him in.

Closer and closer he got until he was facing the decaying paleness of Lamont Rhimes. He screamed emitting a stream of air bubbles which in turn became the vessel that choked him as Lamont placed a silver coin into his mouth and shut it tight before carrying him off to the second fathom of the pool.

As Danny floated back to the surface, a smile wiped onto his face as the frigid cold overtook him. He became dead weight ascending to the top as Trudy fought the bitterly freezing water.

Her hand surfaced and the chilly wind bit her fingertips. Raw, she took what she hoped were final strokes to the ledge, but she, too, was exhausted. The water temperature was taking its toll on her.

She was cramping like crazy. Every muscle was tense and reacting to the arctic liquid encasing her.

She gasped as she tried to maintain a grip on Danny. Her knuckles spasmed and she released him. She fought her body to grab at him again. She could feel his collar even though her fingers burned while she clamped onto him again.

"Oh, God," she cried out as she looked behind her to ensure she still had him.

His body was listless. She turned to get his head above the waterline. She smacked his cheek despite the intense throbbing in her joints.

"Don't you leave me, dammit!" she screamed.

His body dropped again.

Anxiety had taken control of her as she dove in to retrieve him. Her arms wrapped around his waist and suddenly, she was spent. She had nothing left to bring him back to the surface.

His body leaning against hers pushed them to the wall of the pool. What strength she had left, she used to keep her arms around him even as he began to lower them both.

The horrific thought to let him go shot through her mind. She blocked it out as quickly as possible, but the seed was planted. The only way she was going to reach the surface was to drop him. Let him go and save herself.

She closed her eyes prepared to let fate decide what she should do.

Fingers pinched the base of her neck. The halter top tightened on her torso and she flung back against the wall of the pool with a wicked force. Still she maintained Danny, but he wasn't nearly as heavy.

"Got you," Clint exclaimed as he pulled her by the strap of the dress until he had both of his arms around her waist. He hoisted her up as Baron reached over to assist in reeling in Danny.

Ecstatic, her head was overcome with joy as the leather jackets embraced their dripping wet bodies.

Hysteria overtook Trudy as Clint laid her on the pool's slab. Before Baron struggled too long, he was by his side to draw Danny to safety as well.

Pointing to the cabana, Clint grabbed Trudy and flung her over his shoulder, informing Baron, "I'm taking her inside this hut to warm her up."

"Good idea," Baron said. "I'll get Danny."

As he hustled inside the cabana area, Clint gently placed Trudy onto a wooden bench outside the sauna. He sprinted to the inside of the hotbox and began to heat the room up.

Baron dragged Danny in by his shirt collar through the double wide doors until Clint helped to hoist Danny and bring him into the sauna.

"Go get help," Baron ordered Clint as Larry entered the small spa area carrying his paddle. A swath of blood from his attack on Beecher was smeared on one side.

"Cops are on the way," Larry informed both. "What happened here?"

They all did a quick study of Danny and Trudy.

Trudy rolled over as she still shivered from the exposure of the frigid air. She hacked up water from her lungs and coughed ferociously.

"Danny," she heaved out frantically.

She sat up and dragged herself to Danny's side. She stroked his head, but he was listless.

She bent down and placed her lips near his ear and said, "Danny, can you hear me?"

Nothing.

Baron moved toward them and asked, "Is he breathing?"

Tears rolled down her eyes as Larry draped her with his family jacket.

"I don't think so," she said. She placed her head on his chest to listen for a heartbeat. Then she slammed her fist upon him.

"No," she cried out, "you don't get to go. Not now, you don't."

Danny's fists were balled up tight. His brown skin was pasty.

She shook him, "You hear me? You don't get to leave."

A paramedic followed behind Clint into the small sweat room as Trudy pounded Danny one more time.

"You hear me, Slow Poke?" she shouted hysterically. "I got you this time. I got you."

The paramedic moved closer to take over when Danny hurled out a gasp of water. He rolled over as another rush of liquid exited his mouth.

Trudy laughed intoxicated with a mixture of relief and hysterics. She grabbed his tight-clenched fist as the EMT continued to help remove excess fluids.

Clint grabbed Trudy to break her hold on Danny, allowing the first responder to do his job.

As she pulled back, she opened her hand to find a silver coin in her palm.

EPILOGUE

Closure

It was the beeping that woke him. When he first opened his eyes, natural sunlight shut them tight. That beeping picked up its pace, then it calmed down and smoothed out.

Slowly, he allowed his left eye to take in the rays of sunshine that immediately caused his head to throb.

Though blurred, he could make out a face with flaxen black and red streaked hair cascading downward looking at him. He raised his eye but was at a loss as the face was still foggy.

"Trudy?" he murmured.

"Over here, Slow Poke," he heard from his right side.

Keeping the right eye closed, he shifted his head. Trudy's caramel colored face was streaked with red marks as her skin had peeled from exposure of the icy cold pool water.

He gasped in horror. "What happened to you?" he asked in shock.

"Funny," she said. "That knot on your head must have taken your memory."

"What day is it?" asked the voice from his left.

He jerked his head back allowing his right eye to open. He realized he was looking at Trudy's older sister, Regina.

"Sunday," he said.

"Damn," Regina crowed. "Sounds like your brains are truly scrambled. It's Monday."

Danny shifted in bed. He had no bearings on his location until he sat up.

"Monday?" he asked. "Where the hell am I?"

Regina pursed her lips. She rolled her eyes upward toward her sister and said, "Girl, you better get your man up to speed before the cops come in to 'terrogate him."

Regina turned and started to walk out the hospital room.

"Interrogate me for what?"

Trudy called out, "Gina, where you going?"

Regina opened the door as she said, "First, to tell the nurse this fool is awake. Second, to let mama know we can go home." She stared at her sister, then smiled, "You in so much trouble."

She pushed through the door, then turned around and winked at Trudy.

"See you around, Slow Poke," Regina giggled as the door closed behind her.

She whipped her head back into the room, popping her head inside, "Hurry up, girl. Mama wants to go before traffic picks up."

Trudy shooed her away, "I'll be there."

Regina was gone again.

Danny stared at the tubes attached to his right hand leading to his bandaged arm. The hospital bracelet dangled on his left wrist.

"What happened? How'd I get here?" he asked.

A shockwave came over him as he realized no one would be there for him once Trudy left. He grabbed her wrist weakly, but it startled her.

"Cops want to question you," she said matter of fact.

"For what?" he coughed as he tried to sit up. His mouth was extremely dry. He looked around and saw the water carafe.

Trudy grabbed the remote and punched a button to slide his head up.

She reached for the yellow plastic pitcher and after removing its wrapping, poured a cup of water for him. She placed a curly straw in the cup and brought it to his lips.

He choked on his first sip and he coughed again, this time spitting up water.

Trudy reached for a tissue and dabbed his lips dry.

"Want to try that again?" she asked.

He nodded his head, as the straw poked and parted his lips again. This time was a smoother transition.

He took a breath as she placed the cup down.

"What do you remember?" she asked.

He blinked a couple times as he envisioned the tussling between himself and Gillette.

"Just fighting that old man until you grabbed me," Danny said. "Why?"

She searched his eyes.

"Nothing else?"

"I don't even know how I got here," he gently took her hand. "I just know you saved me."

Trudy shook her head, "Not exactly. Your friends saved us. Good thing they came back for us. We would have drowned or worse."

She stared at him. "What happened when you were down there?" she quizzed.

"Me and the old man fought. He lost. That's it."

"You knew him?" she said.

He was quiet as he tried to figure out what to say when the police asked him that question.

"I'd met him before," he relented.

"Where'd he go?" she asked.

Stunned, he tilted his head and sat straight up.

"I don't follow," he said. "What do you mean, where'd he go? To hell, I presume."

"Then hell must've been in the shallow part of the pool," she said.

"The cops," he said, "must've pulled him out."

She shook her head.

"Uh-uh. No sign of him."

"No shit?" was all Danny could offer. "Did you see him?" he asked reluctantly.

"I'm trying to tell you, no one saw the old man. He disappeared," she said.

"I mean Lamont," Danny said softly. "He was down there, too."

She cocked her head. Her eyes teared up as she believed he may have been under water longer than she thought.

He vaguely remembered the moment Trudy collared him and Gillette partially vanished as he sank deeper into the pool.

Then Trudy pulled him from Lamont's grasp.

Danny could see the viaduct opening as Lamont dragged Gillette into the hole.

"You don't think he'll come after us, do you?" she asked.

"He's not coming back. I promise," Danny said.

The door swung open and a nurse with long blond hair entered.

"Oh," she said. "I see you are awake."

She walked over to the bed and immediately stuck a thermometer in his mouth.

Trudy backed away from the bed.

The nurse smiled, "I'll just take his pulse then I'll give you two a minute."

She pulled the thermometer from his lips, "Ninety-nine-point-five degrees. I think you'll live."

She grabbed his wrist to check his pulse, then asked, "You hungry?"

Danny laughed, "Starving."

She headed for the door and said, "I'll get you a menu."

"Thank you," Trudy said.

"You'd better get going," Danny proposed. "Your sister and mom are waiting for you."

"Yeah," she agreed. "Moms gonna ask me a whole lot of questions. She's furious I came down here with Ricky." She stopped, then provided, "He's dead, you know?"

Danny grabbed her hand and pulled her toward the bed.

"But you are not. This is not your fault. Don't even act like it is."

He pulled her to the side of the bed and kissed her. It took her by surprise. She let it linger, then pulled back.

Bashfully, she giggled, then grabbed him by the back of the head and pressed her lips against him again. She stayed there for a moment, then released him.

She saw the advice her sister had given her when she began to notice boys in his eyes.

"Always leave them wanting more."

"I'll see you soon," Danny nearly stuttered.

"We'll see, Slow Poke," she laughed. Then waved good-bye. She turned to walk toward the door, then paused.

She twirled back around and headed straight toward him. In her hand the silver coin.

"I believe this is yours," she said as she tried to place it in his hand.

He pushed it back into her palm.

"Uh-uh, keep it for me," he said. "I'll be back for it."

The door opened behind her and a tall balding man walked in.

Trudy took the coin and tucked it in her pants' pocket. She leaned down and kissed him gently on the cheek.

"I'll see you again soon," she said and turned to the doctor. "Take good care of him. I think the blood has rushed to that bump on his head."

The doctor laughed and assured Trudy that Danny was in good hands.

Danny watched her walk out knowing he was going to get that coin back.

The End

B. LOVE PUBLICATIONS

Visit bit.ly/readBLP to join our mailing list!

B. Love Publications - where Authors celebrate black men, black women, and black love.

To submit a manuscript for consideration, email your first three chapters to blovepublications@gmail.com with SUBMISSION as the subject.

Let's connect on social media!
Facebook - B. Love Publications
Twitter - @blovepub
Instagram - @blovepublications

CPSIA information can be obtained
at www.ICGtesting.com
Printed in the USA
LVHW021538260220
648290LV00012B/843